PHOENIX RISING

BRYONY PEARCE

To my parents, Mike and Mary McCarthy,
adventurers both. Especially to my mother,
who set off on her next adventure far too soon.

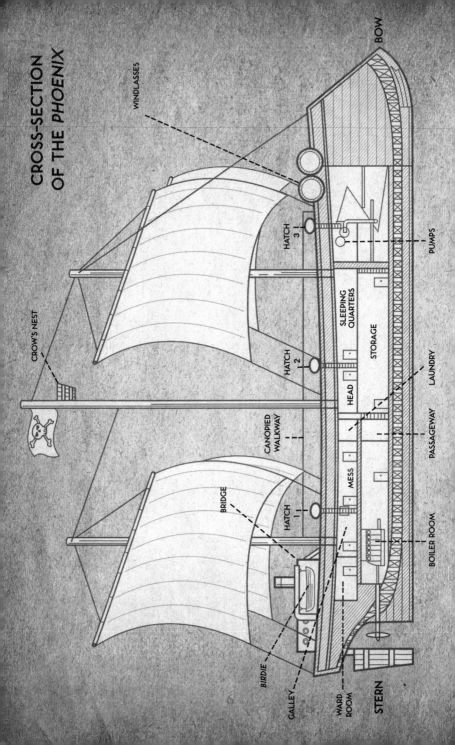

CROSS-SECTION OF THE PHOENIX

BOW

WINDLASSES

HATCH 3

PUMPS

CROW'S NEST

SLEEPING QUARTERS

HATCH 2

STORAGE

HEAD

LAUNDRY

CANOPIED WALKWAY

PASSAGEWAY

BRIDGE

MESS

HATCH 1

BOILER ROOM

BIRDIE

GALLEY

WARD ROOM

STERN

BIRD'S-EYE VIEW OF THE *PHOENIX*

BOW

STEERAGE

WINDLASSES

WINDLASSES

ICE-BREAKER HULL

HOOKS

HOOKS

HATCH 3

SAIL

MAST

MAST

SAIL

STARBOARD

PADDLES

HATCH 2

CROW'S NEST

HATCH 1

CANOPIED WALKWAY

FARADAY'S CAGE

PORT

PADDLE CAGE

SAIL

SAIL

MAST

MAST

WREN

BIRDIE

BRIDGE

STERN

Desecration of nature reserves

Ruin of Alaska

Environmental agencies are horrifi
by the way big oil has dea't
huge gouges i

JACOBSON RESIGNS

Shell boss catapulted for fuel crisis chaos

The president of Shell Oil has resigned under a d

Shell will continue under new management, focusing on a change of direction to accommodate the desperate need for

22nd November 2033

Top ten banks face collapse

'Too Big to Fail'

JP Morgan Chase, once hailed as 'too big to fail', has collapsed in the

Other banks likely to follow closely in their footsteps include BP

4th December 2035

Tensions escalate amid calls for calm

The EU president called for calm last night, but war seems inevitable. "Lack of power means clean water is at a

Countries where overtures of peace have broken down, especially China, India and

Government talks science

Where will our money go?

choice between solar energy, wind farms and nuclear fusion to be made, given limited budget

The UK government is consulting with top

Return of rationing

Only supermarkets will now be allowed to stock food, effectively creating

In a move that has not been seen since the country was at war, the government has reintroduced oklets can

Rolling blackouts worsen

Power outages across Britain will now be the norm. Rolling blackouts leave us with less than two hours

War over North Sea Oil?

Soldiers at Sea

protect the last of our fuel reserves from foreign powers while also dealing with rioting in the inner cities?

Our military for

Martial law

Martial law has now been imposed   riots over food followed by attacks

Farewell address from The Independent

19th May 2038

RIP 1986-2038

In its final address, The Independent newspaper, youngest of all the UK ... sad day for us all ... doors. The questio... impact on free spe...

24th April 2039

Cars back o... the roads

Solar power boost

Finally, cars are back on the roads. The first fully solar-powered ...lances and buses have been

People now asking if this is the ... sign that we are coming out of the worst recession in the...

Country will keep running

The Government has promised enough power for hospitals, water ...tment plants, food distribution

5th No...

Yellowstone Changes – Warning

The US Geological Survey reports that the ground in Wyoming has tilted, lake edges ...changed and the ground is swelling

A rush of anxiety as evacuations of Montana and Wyoming is slowed by fuel-less vehicles blocking the roads out of the state...

29th March 2040

Yellowstone Supervolcano eruption – first pictures

Pictures of the erupting volcano make terrifying viewing. The first explosion at 10 p.m. GMT was caught by self-styled volcano-watchers

Scientists predict debris will reach European skies within hours, blotting out the sun for a period of up to ten years. More details on page 10.

Death of the sun

The cloud of ash moving across Europe has now reached Great Britain. As people across the country took to the streets and rooftops to see their last view of the sun, scientists predicted that it could be de...
before i...

Finally, devolution. Goodbye United Kingdom!

24th May 2040

As Scotland finally followed Northern Ireland out of the United Kingdom, the Scottish parliament moved from Westminster and the borders slammed shut. The English army is now prepared for a battle with our Northern cousins for the last oil reserves. Meanwhile, Wales proved the fragility of its own commitment by raising a wall from Dee to the Severn Estuary. Battalions of the Welsh Guards are now patrolling, to guard against incursions from the North-West of England.

Army interference in English Government grows

30th June 2040

Last night the Prime Minister spoke from Westminster about the worrying increase in military interference in government decisions. As he

Death knell for England

2nd August 2040

Last night's military coup started with the takeover of Parliament but did not end there. As the king was barricaded in Windsor, his own guardsmen turned on him. This reporter watched with tears in his eyes as the king was forced to his knees and executed in front of a silent crowd. We are now a militocracy. This is the last time this news report will ever run, so it remains for me to say simply good luck, England, may God be with us

A new kind of hero for the state of St George

7th November 2070

These are the scientists making strides to keep St George great: Barnaby Ford, Alistair Maddox, Nell Wright and Jacqui Graves. Experts in computing, mathematics, earth sciences, recycling technology, engineering and physics, these scientists are working tirelessly to make the future from Great Britain's junk. Soon we will be using

From the mess the Prime Minister of Great Britain left, these heroes are working to give you, the people of St George, working technology that will see us through the years of hardship ahead. New ways to store energy, defend ourselves, make medicine, keep sea levels from rising, grow food in the darkness, keep warm at

Internal Memo – CONFIDENTIAL
1st June 2075

To: Professor Barnaby Ford
From: Edward Bolton
Subject: Military Defence

Congratulations, your work on junk dams and ultra-efficient energy storage has come to the attention of General Hopewell. Please pass all your notes on the Phoenix project to Alistair Maddox and attend a meeting in the Red Room to discuss the military application of your existing research.

TELEGRAM TRANSCRIPT
22nd September 2076

Increased pirate activity off Irish coast stop Naval attention all haste stop Possible sighting of Phoenix stop Containment and capture highest priority stop Repeat back Report delivery Get answer

PROLOGUE

The ship was empty; silent but for the creak of rigging, the ticking of the boiler and the hiss of the fire as it consumed the fuel Toby had fed it. Every other pirate was visiting the German port where they had docked – trading for supplies, swapping news and taking a day's break from the salt.

Toby glanced at the open porthole, which faced the poisonous sea. Outside, the dam was holding back an ocean of junk. Toby could see it pressing against the wall – a looming mass of old cars, vans, washing machines and prams, the litter of a civilization destroyed by human greed and the vengeance of Mother Nature.

"You won't be able to see anything." Polly glided from her perch and landed on his shoulder. "You may as well clean out the boiler."

Toby turned from the window with a sigh. "Sometimes I dream of land."

"That's natural." The parrot fluffed her feathers. "I've never seen a tree in my life, but sometimes, when my processor shuts down, I see leaves."

Toby sighed again, then went over to the brushes. "I just wish they'd dock so my porthole faced the jetty."

Polly tilted her head until she was looking into his eyes, her beak clacking as she hung almost upside down. "If you were spotted…"

"I know." Toby shook his head. "And I'd probably hate land anyway. Crowded."

"Dirty," Polly agreed.

"Smelly." Toby grinned. "Nothing like the *Phoenix*, then."

Polly leaped from his shoulder and landed on the boiler's control panel. "Let's get this over with. I hate it when you clean the blowers out, the soot sticks to my feathers."

"All right." Toby was halfway up the ladder, his brush over his shoulder, when he stopped. "Did you hear that?" He frowned as he listened for the sound.

"It's just junk knocking against the ship." Polly's plumage bobbed as she shuffled from foot to foot. "Ignore it."

"There isn't any junk here." Toby climbed back down the ladder. "They have a dam."

"It could be anything, Toby. It's not our concern."

"Listen." Toby ran for the porthole and leaned out.

His eyes widened. Beneath him was a tiny raft, barely more than two planks wrapped with cord. On it was a red-haired man, his arms wrapped around the wood and his legs kicking weakly against the tide that tried to drag him back to shore. As Toby watched, the raft knocked against the side of the ship once more.

"Hey, down there!" Toby called and the man lifted his head. A violet bruise ringed his throat and his face was livid with broken blood vessels.

Toby gasped. "Polly, he's been hanged!"

"Help me!" the man croaked.

"We have to get him out of the salt." Toby spun round to Polly. "His skin'll be burning off."

"Stay out of it, Toby."

"And leave him to die? I don't think so." Toby ran for the boiler-room door. "I'm going out."

"No, you're not." Polly flew in front of his face. "The captain would skin me alive."

"Then how do we help him? Just let me throw him a rope."

"What if he's a spy? What if he's been sent to capture you and you help him climb on board the ship?"

"He's not a spy, he's injured, look at him." Toby went to open the boiler-room door. "I'm not just going to let a man die, Polly. I'm going out."

Polly caught Toby's hair and flew backwards, but he

didn't even falter. Toby spun the wheel, opened the door and stepped into the passageway.

The passageways of the *Phoenix* were eerie; dripping with condensation and free of the rowdy men and women that usually filled them. Toby ran to the nearest ladder, shinned up it and hit the next level at a dead run.

Polly followed him, shouting as she went. "The captain will kill you and he'll put me in the fuel compressor! What happens if he's after you? How do I explain that to your father?"

Toby hesitated.

"Last chance, Toby. Turn around and pretend you didn't see anything."

Toby shook his head and opened the door as Polly continued to shriek, "It's too dangerous!"

Sunlight hit Toby like a hammer, making him blink in the fresh air. This close to land, the *Phoenix* was covered in gulls and, as Toby stepped out, they took flight with raucous caws.

Toby allowed himself a look at the dock and saw that it was busy with traders. He caught a glimpse of riotous colours and the scent of cooking reached him. To the right of the pier he spotted a gallows where three men swung, black crows weighing down their shoulders. One of the ropes hung empty and Toby could make out a disturbance in the crowd – Greymen searching for the escaped convict.

Toby shuddered and ran for the port side of the ship. He leaned over the gunwale and looked for the tiny raft. The man wasn't moving.

"What if he's unconscious," Toby wondered aloud.

"Then he'll drown," Polly squawked unsympathetically.

"You're not usually this cruel."

"And you're not usually this stubborn." Polly nudged him with her wing. "I'm programmed to protect you, Toby, not some criminal. You don't know what he's done. He could be a murderer."

Toby uncoiled a rope and tied it to the rail. Then he threw it over the side. It unwound as it fell and the end splashed into the water beside the man's outstretched arm. Toby winced as corrosive salt hissed on his shirt, but the man didn't move.

"I've thrown you a rope," Toby yelled. "Grab hold and I'll pull you up."

"He can't hear you –" Polly ruffled her feathers and looked around anxiously – "but other people might. You tried, now let's go back down."

Toby grabbed the rope and wriggled it until the thick hemp knocked against the raft. He held his breath as the planks wobbled in the waves, then the man looked up slowly. He saw the rope beside him and wrapped it around one arm.

Toby started to pull, his muscles popping beneath his threadbare shirt from the strain. "He's heavy," he groaned.

"Then let him go," Polly snapped.

In answer, Toby braced his legs on the rail and heaved.

After a short while Toby could feel the rope move faster through his hands and realized that the man was trying to help by walking up the side of the ship. Toby renewed his efforts. His shoulders ached now but he distracted himself from the burn by focusing on the pictures the crew had scrawled on the deck and the gunwale. Mostly they were doodles imagining the island they were searching for. Each was a little prayer – a hope that next week, next month or even next year, they would find that island and make it their home.

Eventually the man's hand appeared on the rail and Toby was able to release the rope, grip his wrist and pull him to safety.

The man sagged on to the deck. His legs twitched – he wasn't going anywhere without Toby's help. Toby wrapped the man's arm around his shoulder and dragged him to the hatch. He pushed him down the ladder and winced as the man collapsed at the bottom.

"Sorry."

Toby followed more carefully, slamming the hatch behind them, grateful for the sudden darkness that hid them from the crowd on the jetty. He watched as the man crawled to the wall and propped himself up. Toby sat opposite him in the narrow passageway. Polly placed herself between Toby's knees, glaring at the stranger, her claws glimmering in the dim light.

For a long moment there was silence.

"Thank you." The man hung his head and his bright red hair flopped into his eyes.

"They tried to hang you." Toby tilted his head. "It was a risk, going into the water."

The man nodded. "But you saved me."

"The captain could still throw you back in."

"I hope not." The man pushed his hair back from his face and Toby winced at the sight of his raw throat. "My name's Marcus."

"I'm Toby. This is Polly." He gestured and Polly squawked a warning. Toby's blue eyes crinkled. "You better not mess with her. Welcome to the *Phoenix*."

ONE

One year later

Waves crested and shattered over the broken plane.

The *Phoenix* was carving her way towards it, but her current course would churn the drowning aircraft into her wake along with the rusting engines, plyboard cupboards and thousands of cans that festooned the waves of the poisonous sea.

Toby clung to the crow's nest and leaned out as far as he could, watching Polly as she swooped towards the plane. The surf covered it before she could get there, and Toby held his breath. Would the current suck their prize out of reach? Then the plane's wing peeked through the masses of junk once more and Polly wheeled back towards Toby.

Too excited to wait for her return, he was shouting before the parrot could land. "She's worth salvaging, right? She is, isn't she?"

Polly thumped on to his shoulder and knocked Toby off balance. He scrabbled with his feet for a firmer grip on the bolted jigsaw of car bonnets that made up the crow's nest and grabbed the railing, unwilling to take his eyes from the plane for more than a second. It was still in sight, surrounded now by a flotilla of shopping carts. "I was right, wasn't I?"

"It looks good." Polly ruffled her feathers. "But I wouldn't bet your life on it."

"If I call it wrong, the crew will eat me alive – remember how angry they were with Arnav last time." Toby wrapped his fingers around his binoculars. "But there could be fuel in there, and cargo – there might even be building materials, clothes, D-tabs ... tinned food."

"Or she might have been flying on fumes and carrying suitcases." The parrot's wings jerked up and down in her approximation of a shrug.

Toby stared hard at the wreckage as if he could force an answer. In the cockpit the pilot still gripped the throttle, trying to accelerate from beyond the grave. "What brought her down?"

Polly shuffled. "Hard to tell."

"She might've run out of fuel, then." Toby drummed his fingers on the rail.

"Might've," Polly echoed. Then she squawked, suddenly

agreeable. "More likely she's a casualty of the wars." She cocked her head, her plumage tickling Toby's chin. "There's damage consistent with small tactical munitions."

"She's been in the water a long time – anything could've done that."

"No guarantees at sea, Toby. But the pattern of damage suggests a drone strike. It'll be good salvage – if the hookmen can secure it."

"They've salvaged bigger. Dee's a pro." Toby leaned over to spot the ship's second in command. She was just coming out of the fibreglass bridge, dark curls flying beneath her red scarf as she walked next to Marcus. All the crew wore the red scarf – the closest thing they had to a uniform. Marcus usually wore his around his throat to cover the evidence of his brush with death; Toby also wrapped his around his neck, as added protection from Polly's claws. Others covered their mouths, forearms or even their shins, depending on what jobs they had to do. Rita tied hers around her chest and Big Pad used his as a belt. The splashes of scarlet made Toby think of the sailors as the *Phoenix*'s very own flames.

Despite the additions to her deck – lean-tos made from lorries, sheds made from old fibreglass hulls and walkways under swinging canopies – the *Phoenix* herself was not colourful. She had first sailed way back at the start of the millennium – a cargo ship. She would have seen the leaping dolphins, shoals of fish and basking sharks that were now long gone. She had sailed before the oil crisis, the economic collapse, the riots, the wars and finally the eruption of the supervolcano that had changed the earth forever. But once the seas were clogged with rubbish and turned into floating junkyards, she had been forgotten.

Barnaby Ford, whose talent lay in repurposing cast-offs from the old world, had discovered the *Phoenix* rusting in a dry dock. St George, the militocracy, had paid for the years he spent turning the ship from an oil guzzler into a sail-subsidized paddle steamer. Jobs that would once have taken a couple of hours with a blowtorch required weeks of work. Everything on the ship had been salvaged, including the crew.

Beyond the electrical pylon that housed the crow's nest, four further masts had once been telegraph poles. Ford's supervisor had somehow procured them during the Darkness, when almost all wood had become fuel. This made the masts, for a while, the most valuable items on the ship.

The silver sails had been stolen from a satellite and on each side a great paddle, ripped from a power station's cooling system, turned inside a razor-wire cage.

The *Phoenix* chugged through the water with the force of Niagara Falls.

The *Phoenix*'s hull was taken from an ice-breaker ship, designed so she could carve through the junk in her way. Toby imagined that long ago sailors had cruised to the music of rolling waves, but now the typical sound of the sea was the smash and crunch of debris being shoved aside by vessels with the strength to move it: pirates, desperate traders and Navies. The rest of the world left the salt well alone.

The ship's original engine still existed, but hardly ever ran. The fuel to turn it was as rare as phoenix eggs, yet it was just possible that right here, in this sea-battered plane, Toby had found some. Above him, as if to remind him why he was there, the skull and crossbones snapped, gunshot loud. Toby jumped.

"All right, Bones, we won't let her get away." He had been clutching his elbows, but now he dropped his arms to his side and straightened up.

Polly bobbed on his shoulder. "You're calling it?"

Toby nodded. "I'm making the call. Even if it means we'll be back in the boiler room before the end of the watch."

"Yuck." Polly began cleaning her feathers as if she could feel the soot on them already.

"Knock it off, Pol. It's not so bad. I'm the best engineer

on the ship, who else would you have in there?"

"Anyone!" Polly looked up from under her wing. "Why couldn't you have trained as a cook? I wouldn't mind sitting in the galley all day."

"What, and work with Peel?" Toby shuddered. "Come on, Pol, engineering's in my blood. Besides, you'd be bored in the kitchen." He jigged as he caught the speaking tube from the hook. "Captain, course adjustment. Two degrees port."

The query he received in return was garbled and grainy, but Toby understood the jumble of sounds perfectly.

"It's a plane," he replied. "We can see at least one wing, the cockpit and –" he hesitated to increase the drama – "what looks like intact fuel tanks." He lowered his voice. "Polly thinks it's good."

Toby pictured the activity now overtaking the control room and gripped the mast with one hand as the *Phoenix* began to turn. He swayed as she smashed through the junk in their way. Then he released his hold, snagged a dangling rope and wrapped it around his thighs. When it was secure, Toby ducked beneath the Jolly Roger and perched like a diver ready to springboard backwards. Then he stopped.

"What's the matter?" Polly nudged him with her beak.

"Nothing. I just want to enjoy the air for a second."

Toby inhaled a deep breath and turned his face to the sun.

Although it had been years since the sky cleared, the sensation of warmth on his cheeks still gave Toby tremors – a mixture of excitement and fear that it could all be taken away again. When he was small the sky had been a dusty parasol between the earth and the sun – the result of the eruption that had wiped out half of America. The older pirates suffered the effects of the sunless decades: osteoporosis, curvature of the bones and endless aches and pains. Raised in a twilight world, they still had to cover their eyes on bright days or risk being blinded. Toby was younger and had been far less affected, but even he struggled when the sun was at its brightest. Much of the *Phoenix*'s deck was shaded to shelter the pirates from the glare.

As if she heard his thoughts, Polly stretched a wing over Toby's face. "Watch your eyes."

"I'm fine, there're sight savers." Toby pointed to the sprawling clouds that slid lazily towards distant shores that were finally turning green with new vegetation.

"Look! Bad weather to come," Polly squawked, drawing his attention to a line of grey on the horizon.

Toby inhaled a deep breath of clean air and jumped out of the crow's nest.

"Maybe," he called. "But not yet."

As he abseiled towards the scrubbed deck, he got a face

full of stinging spray and quickly wiped it off. A body length above the crew's heads, he brought himself to a stop and kicked off from the pylon, swinging outwards with a cry. "Salvage mission!"

Polly launched from his shoulder and flew beside him, his crimson and indigo shadow.

As Toby spun over the crew, legs cycling, yelling his alert, the captain appeared from the control room. The crew immediately turned and looked to their leader, who pumped a fist.

"Move it, we have salvage!"

Bringing the *Phoenix* to a stop was no simple task. Barnaby Ford had built her to forge through the junk-filled sea. If she lost momentum there was a chance she'd be trapped in near-solid waste, unable to move.

After half a dozen missions had left her wallowing as easy prey for the various Navies who sought control of Captain Ford and the *Phoenix*, he had dry-docked her once more and devised a system for salvaging junk that did not involve weighing anchor at all.

Each crew member now had specific duties during a salvage mission – back-breaking tasks, which meant that if a mission was called unnecessarily they could get pretty resentful. The last mistake had old Arnav eating alone for a week.

Swinging to a stop Toby muttered under his breath, "It's good."

Polly fluttered back on to his shoulder and nuzzled his ear. "I'd have called it myself if I wasn't a parrot."

Toby smiled. "I'd like to see their faces if you did. Even after all this time, they still think you're an ordinary bird."

Toby dropped to the deck with a thud that vibrated through his ankle bones. He tossed the rope away and made for the sternward hatch that would lead him down past the galley towards the boiler room.

"Divert power to the pumps, Toby," the captain yelled, as though Toby hadn't done the job dozens of times. "Slow this old girl down."

Toby waved acknowledgement of the order and ducked beneath a swinging canopy made of plastic chair backs. He spared a look upwards. Arnav was already shinnying towards the crow's nest, his crooked toes confident on the rigging despite his age, his bow legs and the twisting of his weakened wrists.

Coming towards him down the passageway, Big Pad was leading twelve of the strongest pirates. "All right, lad. Reckon you've spotted real treasure this time?" He jogged past Toby, already wrapping his hands with hessian in preparation for turning the winding gear that would open the hull. Each of the four windlasses required three men to operate them.

Most of the other crewmen were heading in the same direction, towards the bow, and now Toby had to fight against the tide.

"I reckon you called salvage 'cause yer bored." Crocker barged Toby with his shoulder. "No thought for those of us gotta do the actual work."

"Be silent, Crocker." Amit slid in front of Toby. "Ignore him, Toby, he has a gaand main keera."

"A bug up his—" Amit's teeth glinted as Ajay, his twin, translated. "Get to the wreck room, Crocker, we have a pump to prime."

"Let Toby through, you fools. You can't do your jobs till he does his." Dee was perching on top of the deck housing, sunlight shining on the dozen rings dangling from her right ear. Dee waved, then jumped down and started to herd her team of seven towards the hooks that would be used to grab and steer the salvage.

The crew parted in the passageway, forming a human tunnel towards the boiler-room hatch. Toby ran, ignoring the gob of phlegm that Crocker hocked after him.

When he arrived at the hatch, Toby took a last breath of fresh air, spun the wheel, pulled the door open and jumped inside. He shot one hand out to catch the top of the ladder, his feet curved for the rungs and with barely a jolt he was climbing downwards.

"I wish you wouldn't do that," Polly muttered.

Toby grinned. He was one floor nearer to the boiler room and on the same level as the captain's ward room and the galley. He hopped from the ladder and looked along the passageway, checking it was empty before he ran full tilt.

The passage was empty – the whole crew, fifty in total, were on salvage duty. Feet echoing in the hollow silence, Toby raced towards the second ladder, slipped the arches of his feet around the outside and slid down.

On his shoulder Polly spread her wings and slowed him enough that his toes touched down almost gently. She nipped his ear and flew down the passageway ahead of him. Toby sprinted after her.

TWO

The heat inside the boiler room hit Toby the moment he entered. Air from the huge forced-draught fans hammered at his face and he groped for the goggles that hung by the door.

Back on his shoulder, Polly hunched and muttered crossly as superheated steam whistled through the supply pipes and soot billowed out, settling on everything in sight. The boiler room was filled with the remains of old kitchens, desks, chairs – anything remotely flammable that Simeon, Theo and the others dragged from the salt to feed the combustion chamber – and it was all black.

It still amazed Toby that valuable combustibles had once been considered worthless. They had been tossed into the vast, floating rubbish dumps that broke apart when the supervolcano eruption triggered a chain of tsunamis and polluted the whole sea. Not that anyone cared about the sea, when the sun had vanished.

"It's not that bad, Polly, stop whining." Toby tightened his goggles and focused on the boiler that had been repurposed by Captain Ford to run on burning junk.

"What's that supposed to mean?" Polly squawked, outraged.

Toby responded to Polly's scandalized sputter with a smile but, as he checked the feed water level, it vanished. "Look at the water level, Pol. The gauge glass is only half full." Toby cocked his head as he listened to the chug of the boiler drum. "What do you think Harry was doing down here while it was my turn up in the crow's nest? Having a kip, probably."

"He's got a lazy streak. I'll mention it to the captain next time I'm uploading his log." Polly hopped from Toby's shoulder to her perch above the attemperator.

The main job of the boiler was to make high-pressure steam that could then be used to power the paddles, heat the oven, operate the pumps and cutters in the wreck room and warm the ship. The steam from the boiler travelled through the coils of a superheater, which dried it out. The attemperator was used to make sure the dry steam remained at the right temperature and Polly preferred to roost above it, where she was sheltered from the fans.

Below Polly the attemperator was quietly ticking.

"You hear that, Pol?"

"Can't hear anything above the banging and clanking – infernal racket." Still she tilted her head.

The attemperator's sound was a sour note in the boiler's usual melody. Toby ran his eye over the gauges. Everything seemed all right. Pulling his spanner from his tool belt, Toby tightened two bolts and listened again. The ticking had quietened.

"That's better." Polly nodded. "Good ears."

Toby tucked his screwdriver under his arm as Polly pointed a claw towards the control panel.

"You'd better divert the power from the turbines—"

"To the pumps, I know." Like a pianist Toby ran his fingers over the control board.

He could feel the *Phoenix* ploughing forward, getting closer to the plane. If he didn't stop her turbines, the paddles would keep turning at full speed and they would batter through the salvage like a wrecking ball. Toby shuddered at the thought and began to flick switches.

Once the wings that formed the ribs of the hull were winched open and the sea was churning into the *Phoenix*, the pumps would need power to get the water out of the wreck room again and stop the ship from sinking.

Toby's shoulders strained as he pulled the lever.

"Done."

He leaned his forehead against the soot-blackened wall

and felt the paddles grow sluggish, only moving now with their own slowing momentum. As the *Phoenix* started to rise and fall in time with the flotsam on the sea, Toby allowed the relative quiet to seep into his bones. For a moment, even Polly was still. Then he pressed his fingers against the hull as if he could see through it.

"Were we in time?"

Polly's claws clicked on the pipework. "We'd hear if not. The captain would call down." She indicated the comms tube.

Toby nodded. Each silenced paddle told the crew that the pumps would be operational when the hull opened; it was their signal to start working. Sure enough, above the whistle of the steam racing to the turbines, the sounds of the salvage mission drifted through the vents. Toby could hear the banging of Uma's drum as she kept time, making Big Pad's team turn the windlasses beyond screaming muscles, bleeding palms and torn calluses. He felt the tortured grinding as the hull spread open. Then the shouts of the hookmen rang out as they fought to catch the plane.

Toby turned, eyes right, as burnt-orange seawater rose above the level of his small porthole: the *Phoenix* was getting heavier as the wreck room filled. He pressed his hands against the hull, feeling for the irregular hum as

Amit and Ajay pumped madly to fight the incoming tidal wave.

Polly glided from her roost. "We'd better move it, if you want to see the salvage come in."

Toby burst from the hatch and on to the gangway.

Amidships was empty and the *Phoenix* felt full of ghosts, so Toby sped towards the action at the bow. The *Phoenix* bucked beneath him, fighting incoming water, but Toby's feet remained fixed to the gangway, his toes secure.

He vaulted on to the rail surrounding the bridge for the best possible view. The captain waved him off as he strained to see past the steerage, so Toby swung from the rail and ducked below the mast.

"Dee, can I help the hookmen?"

"Not now, Tobes." Dee's long curls had escaped from her scarf. She ground her teeth as she used her hook to manoeuvre the plane towards the *Phoenix*'s open hull.

"You can help here, my boy." In front of the hookmen, Uma's team slumped over the windlasses. Job done for the moment, they had to regain their strength for when the hull needed closing again. Uma handed Toby a packet of two-year-old beef jerky. "Hand this out and don't let that parrot get hold of any."

"She doesn't eat meat."

Polly ruffled her feathers and glared at Uma as she walked between the men, distributing cups of filtered water and patting shoulders with a motherly air. The ship's doctor looked like a cuddly matron, but a club dangled at her waist and beneath her soft exterior she was all muscle and old scars, as hardened as any of the pirates on board.

Toby followed her, pressing jerky into work-scarred hands. All the time he strained to see the plane, but it was out of his line of sight.

"All right, lad? Come to see your salvage?" Big Pad smiled tiredly around a mouthful of beef. "Can't hardly see you, though." He gestured to his face and Toby rubbed his cheeks, thinking Paddy was talking about the soot that covered him. Only then did he realize that he was still wearing his goggles. He pushed them on to his head, pulling his hair back from his face as he did so.

"Better." Big Pad stretched his shoulders with a crack. "It's going to be good salvage today, lad, I can feel it. Don't much like the look of that weather though."

"What weather?" Toby hopped to grab some rigging and leaned out. In front of him the hookmen were guiding the plane smoothly towards the open hull. The sky ahead was as blue as Polly's wing feathers. He turned to ask what Big Pad meant and blinked. The grey line Polly had pointed out earlier was now a thick band across the heavens. The Irishman was right; there was going to be a storm.

Toby's mind raced as he measured the distance. "It's a while off yet. I'll have the paddles running ages before the front reaches us."

Big Pad nodded. "You'll see us right, lad."

Toby was about to vault back on to the deck when he spotted waves breaking over something vast; a shadow that was moving with the current towards his plane.

"There's something under the water. Something big." Toby pointed. "There."

Polly stretched her wings for balance as she leaned to look. Then her eyes widened. "Big rig! Big rig!" she cried.

"Ashes," Toby breathed. She was right – the submerged cab had been knocked aside by the opening hull. Now it was being pulled towards the trapped plane, on course to hit Toby's salvage. If the hookmen didn't let the plane go, they might be dragged overboard when it hit.

His eyes flicked to the straining team. "Dee, there's a rig down there – it's going to take out the plane. Let it go or we'll lose it altogether! We can pick it up again once the lorry's gone past."

"Are you sure?" Paddy bounded to his feet.

Toby pointed as a breaker surged and the submerged lorry rose to the surface. Rust and a few remaining streaks of green paint made it look as if the sea bed was rising up to defy them. Now the rig was free of the pull of the open hull, it was speeding towards the plane.

Paddy gasped, then spun towards the hookmen. "Dee! Listen to Toby, release the plane."

"Hooks off," Dee shouted.

Her men groaned, but released the salvage without demanding an explanation.

Toby held his breath as the plane bobbed free and began to move away from the *Phoenix*. It was no longer trapped, but it was still in the path of the oncoming lorry.

Dee leaned over the side, tracking the rig, and she and Toby yelled in unison as it drove into the plane like a sledgehammer. The plane screamed with a sound of metallic distress and Toby's grip tightened on the rigging as one wing sheared off altogether. Surf covered the wing and the current took it swiftly out of sight along with the big rig, which had done its damage and was now sinking back to the seabed.

"Damn it." Dee's hair flew across her face and her red scarf blew from her head.

It fluttered out across the junk that clogged the sea and as Toby traced its path, his eyes widened. In defiance of the current, the plane was now heading back towards the *Phoenix*.

"Dee, get away from there!" He swung down from his perch, grabbed Dee around her waist and dragged her from the railing just as the plane slammed straight into the hull in the gap between the paddle cage and the bilges. The noise was like a bomb going off.

The pirates were knocked from their feet.

"Ashes, Dee, you nearly went overboard." Still shuddering from the impact, Toby tried to jump to his feet, but Dee pulled him into a tight embrace.

"Thank you," she gasped.

Toby felt her trembling and the fact that she had almost died hit him in a wave. Without Dee, the *Phoenix* would be a totally different ship. She'd been there right from the beginning and was at the centre of all he knew. Dee was the one who had persuaded the captain to let him work in the boiler room. He tightened his arms around her.

"It's OK – I'm fine."

Toby nodded. He could feel the crew's eyes on them. He jumped to his feet and offered Dee his hand, but she shook her head and pushed herself to her knees.

Marcus ran to her side. "That was close."

Dee waved him away. "I'm fine, thanks to Toby. Where's the plane? Is it still worth bringing in?"

"Worth bringing in? Of course it's worth bringing in."

Around Toby, other crew members who had been knocked down were getting back on their feet. Captain Ford stood above them. His fists were planted on his hips. His cheeks, as far as they could be seen above his grey-speckled beard, were flushed scarlet and his eyes, the same blue as Toby's, flashed. A brass compass swung from a leather strap around his neck.

The deck shuddered as he jumped to land beside them, boots crashing into the gangway.

"We're not losing this salvage now. Bloody well done for spotting that rig, son." Barnaby slapped Toby on the back.

He caught his father's scent of sun-baked leather and the fish oil that he used to clean his tools.

"Hookmen, back to your places." He leaned over the gunwale to judge the placement of the plane. "Toby, we need to reverse if we want to catch that plane. Get some power back to those paddles."

"Aye, Captain."

Toby ran for the hatch. If there was a chance the plane could be salvaged, he wasn't going to miss it. He raced ahead, skidding dangerously on the spray-slickened metal. Polly flew after him, gulls called overhead, and the storm drew closer.

THREE

Toby hit the boiler-room door like a tornado, already pulling his goggles over his eyes. As soon as his heart stopped pounding, his ears caught a strange sound.

"Something's changed." Toby pulled his screwdriver from his tool belt and stalked around the boiler.

The captain's voice echoed from the speaking tube. "Why aren't we reversing?"

Toby hesitated, his eyes narrowed. Over the whine of the turbines, he made out a gentle hissing, like a trapped snake.

"Toby, what is it?" asked Polly.

He spun back to the boiler and tapped the water-level gauge. "Water's adequate and operational pressure is fine. When did I test the feed water for impurities?"

"Twenty-six hours ago." Polly's claws clicked on the floor as she followed him. "You injected the chemicals, it should still be balanced."

Toby scrubbed furiously at the salt drying on his cheeks.

"I can't see anything wrong. Can you?"

Polly flew to her roost. "Nothing appears out of order."

"Something's not right; I can hear it hissing. Ashes, we haven't got time for this."

"Toby, we're going to lose the salvage." The captain's tone was urgent.

"We're not losing that plane, not after everything." Shoving his worries to the back of his mind, Toby closed his ears to the distressing sound and reached for the lever that would send the paddles into reverse.

Polly bobbed up and down. "If you say there's something wrong with the boiler, then there's something wrong with it."

"It'll have to wait." Toby closed his hand around the warm metal and moved the lever one notch. Immediately he heard the whistle of four-hundred-degree steam rushing along delivery lines that were usually only opened when manoeuvring the *Phoenix* into dock.

He licked his lips. He hadn't pinned down the source of the hissing, but the boiler seemed to be running with no problems. The *Phoenix* bumped in the water as the paddles came back online and then, torturously slowly, she began to reverse.

Toby fidgeted as he timed her, thirty seconds … forty.

Then the captain's voice came back over the speaker.

"That's enough, now."

Immediately Toby slammed the lever back into position, returned the paddles to null and diverted all power back to the pump room.

The *Phoenix* was once again in position to salvage the plane. Toby paced around the boiler room, listening. The hissing had quieted.

Polly hopped on to his shoulder. "Go and see your plane come in. If there is a problem, you can work on it later."

Toby hesitated, torn. Then he nodded. "You're right, it can wait." He gave the attemperator a tap and dragged the goggles off his head. "But I'll be back."

Toby anchored himself into a rope at the prow, never tired of the sight of the *Phoenix* closing up and shutting out the hungry sea. He could hear the bellows of the men driving the windlasses over the water's roar as the doors got closer to sealing. Finally the sea pushed against the pressure of the determined *Phoenix* one last time and lost.

The clang as the doors locked rang out over the waves and Toby placed his palms on deck. Beneath him he could feel the pumps hammering as the last of the water rushed from the outlets.

For a moment the *Phoenix* was quiet as she bobbed in

the water alongside the junk. Then the hatch in the prow cracked and the pirates from the pump room began to file on to the deck. Soon the pirates were all around Toby, rowdy with adrenaline. The captain jumped from the bridge.

"I'm going to check on Dobbs and his team in the wreck room. Raise the rigging, get those sails up. Then everyone have a rest." He glanced at his son. "You too, Toby. If the furnace has enough fuel, you can leave the boiler room for a bit."

Instinctively Toby looked behind him, tracking the storm.

Barnaby followed his gaze. "We have a few hours yet and the sails will give us some headway. Have some time with the crew, I'll tell you when we need to get the paddles moving." He pulled his glasses from his pocket and put them on. "I'm going to check on that plane."

Toby opened his mouth.

"No, you cannot come, Toby. The salvage team don't need you underfoot." Barnaby smiled to soften his words. "I know it's 'your' salvage, son. I'll tell you if it's any good." He addressed the rest of the crew. "Sails up."

"Perudo?" Dee appeared at Toby's shoulder.

Toby's legs moved in a restless jiggle as he considered. He should go and work out what was wrong with the boiler, but his captain had told him to take some time out. Besides, he wanted to be on deck when the verdict on the salvage was delivered.

His eyes went behind Dee to where Uma waited with Marcus and Rahul. If he went below, he'd be missing a good game. Finally Toby nodded and Dee led the group to a quiet spot among coils of rope and out of the wind.

"Lay your bets, pirates." She settled herself comfortably.

"*I'll* bet the boy has never kissed a girl in his life." The voice that came from behind Toby's back sounded like the rust of old hinges and ended with a low, satisfied snigger.

"Crocker." Dee acknowledged the pirate, and Toby clenched his fists.

"I've got some bets to lay if you'll 'ave me play." Crocker wormed his way into the gap between Toby and Uma before anyone could object. His bow legs curved into the space and forced Toby to edge away to avoid pressing against him. Despite himself, Toby glanced sideways.

Crocker patted his hooked nose. "Doncha worry, *boy*, it'll 'appen one day." Then he sniggered again. "Oh, wait, there aren't any girls on board, are there? An' you aren't allowed off ship, are you? So maybe it won't 'appen after all. Might as well cut 'em off." He gave a snort that sprayed over the box of dice.

"Say that again, you—"

"What have you got to bet?" snapped Dee, silencing Toby. She wiped the box with the sleeve of her windcheater.

"I got information," Crocker grinned. "I know where the captain's been taking us this last week."

"If the captain's been taking us somewhere and hasn't shared it with the rest of the crew, then he has a good reason. You shouldn't be spreading rumours."

Marcus tucked his long red hair under the clashing scarlet scarf wrapped around his throat. "How would *you* know, anyway?" he sneered.

"I know because I delivered him his mornin' brew and saw the map he's usin'. You recall that garbled information we traded the spare sextant for at the last port? Well, he's worked it all out and plotted a course. We're on our way to something that'll make this salvage look petty."

"It won't be petty." Toby ground his teeth. "And he'll tell us when he's ready."

Crocker shrugged but his leg muscles tensed against Toby's. The pirate wasn't as relaxed as he seemed. "Well, then, how about some of the spicy sausage we robbed off that farmer in Almeria? Chorizo, they called it. I got some of that off of Peel. And three pickled eggs left from Scilly."

"All right," Dee nodded. "You're in. Marcus?"

Marcus scratched his head. "Got some free time on rotation tomorrow, I can offer that."

"Works for me. Rahul?"

"Vitamin tabs." He patted the top pocket of his windcheater. "Ds. Half a pack."

Uma leaned back. "I'll do an extra laundry duty."

Dee scratched a note with her penknife on the side of the bridge as the sails creaked and groaned overhead. "I've been making a short sword from a propeller I pulled on hook duty a few weeks ago," she said finally.

"A sword?" Toby sat up. "Serious? No way food and free time is worth a sword."

Uma and Marcus agreed, while Crocker rubbed his hands together. "Could do with a sword, me."

"Up your offer, then," Toby snapped.

Dee shook her head. "I'm happy to bet. I don't reckon I'll lose and then I'll have a sword, all that food *and* some free time to eat it."

"Yeah, but..."

"What's *your* bet, boy?" Crocker leaned closer, his sour smoke-and-garlic breath told Toby that the chorizo was smaller than it had been.

Toby frowned, trying to think of something he could offer that was worth the same as a whole sword. "I-I'm not sure." His feet tapped on the deck. "My tool belt. I've got that."

"Your tool belt?" Uma frowned as she spoke to him for the first time. "You need that."

"Not my tools." Toby shook his head. "Just the belt."

"Not much use then, is it?" Crocker smirked.

"Well…" Toby paused. "I've been working on some clockwork. I've got a little engine that goes—"

Crocker guffawed. "A toy! What're we going to do with a toy? There ain't no kids on this ship, in case you 'aven't noticed, Toby. You're the only one who wants to play with toys."

"It's not a toy, it's a prototype."

Dee and Uma glowered, but it was Rahul who spoke. Scratching his bad leg he tilted his head thoughtfully. "I would like a toy, Toby. It's a good bet."

"Pah," Crocker spat. "What'll you do with a clockwork engine? Trade it in the next port?"

"Could do," Rahul nodded sagely. "See, so it is a good bet for all of us." But he wasn't looking at Crocker when he spoke. Toby followed his gaze to a rowdy card game run by Oats on the prow.

"You and Nisha?" he gasped. "You're together?"

Rahul blushed. "So, you see – a clockwork engine would not be so bad."

Quiet dropped over the group. Finally Dee slapped the box of dice into Rahul's hand. It rattled like bones. "We'll miss you, Rahul: both you and Nish."

"Yes, we wish that we could be together *and* remain on

board. It will still be some time before we have to leave – weeks yet before she even starts to show. We'll take our time and find somewhere to settle next time we are sailing in the waters off Bangladesh State."

"Nish isn't wanted any more? Has she been pardoned?" Dee frowned.

"That was the news we received in the port before last – why Nisha has been so happy. A regime change. The Minister had to escape with his family in the night. They were caught heading into Bhutanabad and hanged. No more hiding for Nisha, she can go home."

"And you?" Toby swallowed. "What about you?"

"They won't be looking for me in Bangladesh State, especially with such big changes to consider. We will blend in, hide away and raise our children in sight of the sea."

Uma put her arm around him. "I'll congratulate Nisha later."

Rahul showed bright white teeth. "Not yet, Uma, wait till she shows. She's superstitious."

Marcus laughed. "We're pirates, Rahul, we're all superstitious."

"Enough of this." Crocker's hand banged on the deck in the centre of the ring. "Toby's bet stands. Are we playing or not?"

Rahul shook the dice into his hand and divvied them out, three to each of the six players.

"Toby starts, he's the youngest," Uma said. Then, as Polly squawked, she looked up sharply, understanding that she hadn't thought her words through.

Toby tensed, sensing Crocker's mirth. "Fine," he gritted, looking at the dice hidden between his knees. "Four sixes."

"Five sixes," Crocker replied.

"Six twos." Marcus rubbed his forehead and Dee grinned at him.

She leaned back, as she gave her response. "Six threes."

"Six sixes." Rahul rubbed his hands.

"Seven … threes." Uma licked her lips. "Back to you, Toby."

Toby ground his teeth. Were there likely to be seven threes showing among the group? He calculated swiftly. Eighteen dice and ones were wild. Crocker seemed to like sixes, the others had bet twos and threes. So were there likely to be more than seven threes and ones together showing in eighteen dice? His brain said no, that Uma had made a mistake. But she might have a handful of threes; it was possible. If she did, then among fifteen dice she only had to find four ones and threes. And Dee had also bet threes. Toby pressed his lips together and his feet jiggled wildly. If he didn't challenge, he had to up the bet. But that meant he thought there was more of another number. Did he?

"Seven … fives."

On Toby's shoulder, Polly stiffened. "Polly want a cracker," she muttered.

"Nah." Crocker rubbed his hands on his greasy trousers. "No chance. Dudo."

"You sure, Crocker?" Dee raised an eyebrow. "Eighteen dice out."

"I can count. I'm challenging." Crocker licked his lips. "Dudo."

"Fine. Show your dice."

Crocker moved his legs to reveal his. Two sixes, one three. No fives. That left fifteen dice and seven fives still to find.

Marcus held his dice on his thigh. He lifted one hand. A one, a two and a four. That left twelve dice and six fives to find.

Dee's dice showed two threes and a six.

Nine dice, six fives to go. Toby turned his eyes to Rahul, pressing his nails into his hand. Rahul moved his foot to show two ones and a six.

Toby nodded. Six dice. Four fives remaining.

Uma grinned and opened her palm: two threes and a one.

Three dice left; Toby's own. Three fives left to count. Crocker was already grinning, his chest swelling. He reached out a hand to Toby. "Come on, *boy*, hand over a die."

Toby met Crocker's eyes then, without looking at his own dice, he opened his knees.

"A one and two fives, Crocker. That makes seven."

Crocker's lip curled. "You little…"

"You challenged and lost, Crocker. Throw in a die." Dee's voice was low and calm, but they all knew she was the captain's second for several excellent reasons, not least her ability to out-think and outfight most of the pirates on the ship.

"Fine." Crocker threw a die so hard it bounced off Uma's shoe and landed beneath Rahul's. "There's still a long way to go. My start."

They shook again and looked to Crocker. He glowered directly at Toby. "Three threes."

They went round again, until the betting reached Toby with Uma's bet of five fives.

Marcus had bet fives, too. Toby glanced at his hand. Twos and threes. He shook his head. "Dudo."

"Show your hand." Dee turned hers up and Toby's heart sank. Marcus and Dee both had fives and ones.

With a sheepish grin Toby tossed a die. Now he and

Crocker both had two dice and the others remained with three.

Round and round they went, until Polly flew off to sit on the gunwale and Marcus threw in his last die with a groan. "It looks as if I'll be working my free time tomorrow."

Rahul was next to go out. He dropped his vitamins on to the deck next to his last die. A shout from the card game propelled him to his feet. "I'm going to see how Nisha is doing." He limped over to the prow.

Crocker grinned evilly. "Last *man* standing, eh."

"Stop it, Crocker." Uma shook her dice with an angry flourish.

"Right though, aren't I? I'm playing with women and boys now. Maybe you should just give me all the winnings. Save us some time." He reached for Rahul's abandoned vitamins.

Uma's club materialized above the packet. "Touch them, Crocker, and I'll break your fingers."

"Humourless cow." He curled a lip again. "Only joking, wasn't I?"

"Maybe you should stop talking, Crocker." Toby glared at him. "You're the one losing. Down to one dice, aren't you?"

"So's Dee," he snapped.

"Yes, but Uma and I have two."

"We'll see who wins, *boy*." He pulled his hand back.

Toby's eyes narrowed. "Stop calling me that."

"It's what you are, isn't it? We've all seen you grow up. Except you 'aven't grown up much, 'ave you, *boy*."

"That's enough, Crocker," Dee warned.

Uma sat silently.

"We all think it. He's never been off ship. Never been in a fight. A pirate what's never been in a fight! He's a *child*."

Toby launched himself sideways at Crocker. Immediately Polly's shriek rang in his ears and Uma blocked him from behind. "You can't fight Crocker, Toby. He plays dirty. Look at him, distracting you from the game, trying to make you bet bad. He's after winning. No less."

Crocker laughed like sewage gurgling down a drain. "Yes, Toby, let Mumsy protect you from the big bad *man*."

Polly landed between Crocker and Toby, hissing through her beak. Crocker aimed a kick in her direction. "Filthy bloody bird."

As Toby struggled, Dee got to her feet.

"That's enough, both of you. Without Toby, Marcus would've been hanged or drowned in the salt. You're nothing but trouble today, Crocker. It's time you left."

Crocker smiled a narrow, self-satisfied smile. "No can do, Dee. A bet's been bet and accepted. The game has to be played out. That's your own rules, ain't it?"

Dee stood for a long moment, fuming. Uma's arm tightened around Toby. His whole body felt like a combustion chamber ready to burst. But he didn't dare take his rage out on Uma. He sagged, and Dee sat, dragging him to her side. Polly scuttled to press her body against his thigh, glaring with her yellow eyes at Crocker.

"We play," Dee murmured. "But quickly."

Uma bet first. "Two threes."

"Two fours," Toby ground out.

"Two fives." Crocker grinned and rubbed his remaining die between his fingers.

"Three threes." Dee licked her lips.

Uma hissed. "Only six dice left." She looked at Toby. "Four threes."

"Five threes," Toby snapped, without thinking it through. Then he froze. To win there had to be five threes and ones showing in only six dice. No chance. He had just given the game to Crocker...

"Who's a pretty birdie?" Polly grumbled. She knew he'd lost, too.

"No take backs," Crocker crowed. "Dudo." He jiggled his shoulders.

"Let's see it, Crocker." Dee gestured and Crocker opened his hand. "A five, there's a surprise." Dee looked at Toby as she showed her single dice. "A three."

Uma opened her hand. "Two threes."

Toby swallowed and lifted his own hand from his thigh, where his dice were waiting. "Two ones, Crocker. That makes five for me." He could barely believe it.

"Your last die, Crocker." Dee held out her hand. "Give it here."

Crocker leaped to his feet. "Cheats," he growled.

Uma rose slowly. "How dare you!"

"I saw you look at Toby back then. He knew what you had."

Uma shook her head. "Pathetic. You're out, Crocker. Bring the sausage and eggs to Dee and give us your die."

Crocker shook his head. "Cow!" Then he threw his die towards the sea as hard as he could.

Toby rose and the four of them watched as it disappeared from view.

"You owe me a die, Crocker, and you won't be playing with us again." Dee shook her head. "You're a louse."

"No," Crocker shook his head. "I'm a *man*. And there ain't no one can argue with *that*."

Crocker marched off, his bow legs joggling beneath his windcheater.

Toby turned back to the others. "I—"

"It's all right, Toby." Dee pressed his arm. "One day you'll be bigger than he is, then you can whip him from bow to stern and no one will say a word about it."

"His brother will," Toby swallowed.

Dee pressed a little harder. "By then you'll be able to take him, too."

"Right." Toby glowered down at his feet, too big for his legs; his legs, too lanky for his body; his wrists, too thin for his arms. His shoulders were starting to broaden but everyone still thought of him as a boy. Even Marcus, and Toby had saved his life.

"You know –" Uma's voice came from above him – "I think I'll forfeit. I'm not into the game any more."

"Me, too." Dee smiled down. "Here, Toby." She reached inside her windcheater behind her back and pulled. Toby gasped as her hand came round clutching a short sword. "Take it." She offered it to him and he blinked.

"You're forfeiting?" Toby hesitated and Dee nodded, reversing the blade so that the pommel faced Toby. "It's yours."

Toby's hand closed on the rounded handle. He gave an experimental swish and Polly whistled.

"Ha, I believe your parrot's impressed." Dee laughed. "It's just like your belt knife really." She guided his hand. "Callum can give you pointers next time you have combat training with him."

Toby nodded, eyes bright. "This is brilliant." The blade

winked at him in the sunlight; Dee had polished it to a high shine. The pommel was wrapped in leather. Toby lifted the blade to see it more closely. "Is this...?"

"A phoenix. Well, the best picture of a phoenix I could do with a chisel." Dee laughed.

"It's wonderful. It really looks like a phoenix should." The tail feathers swooped around from the blade into the pommel and the head was held high, beak pointing up to the point of the sword. "She's wonderful."

Uma nodded sagely. "Will you give her a name?"

"A name?" Toby blinked.

"Every great weapon has a name. Ask the captain if you don't believe me."

"Like what?" Toby frowned at his sword. "Betty?"

Dee folded in half. "No," she said when she had stopped laughing. "Like Excalibur, Mjölnir..."

"Or Siegfried's Nothung," Uma put in. "Although I quite like Betty."

Dee glared. "I'll have her back first."

Toby stroked the blade. "How about ... Nix. Short for *Phoenix*."

"Nix." Dee tilted her head. "Which means: 'to make something become nothing'. *I like it.*"

"And in my own country," Uma smiled, "a nix was a water spirit. It's a wonderful name, Toby."

Toby couldn't take his eyes from the sunlight glimmering on the sword blade. He twirled it. "Nix," he said. "She's perfect." He tore his eyes from his prize to look at Dee. "Thank you, Dee."

The captain burst through the hatch beside him, propelling Polly skyward.

"That salvage," he roared, looking for Toby. When his eyes fell on his son, they gleamed. "That salvage is ... wonderful. Enough fuel left in her to get the old engine running for a while and some excellent machine parts. Suitcases full of clothes and –" his beard split in a wide grin – "best of all, she was a Médecins Sans Frontières plane." The crew cheered and Toby breathed out with a blend of relief and joy. "They must have been taking medical supplies to one of the principalities after the war. They had vaccines, penicillin, bandages, painkillers, anaesthetics. There's stuff I haven't even heard of."

Uma was already moving when the captain gestured at her. "The crew is stacking it up below for you, Uma. When you've catalogued it, let me know what we've got."

"Penicillin," she whispered. "Anaesthetic."

"Let me know if there's anything we don't need. Anything we can trade," the captain shouted, as she disappeared below. Then he turned to Toby. "The team is pumping fuel into the lines right now. Well done, son.

You found us a grand prize. Cheers for Toby."

The crew around him raised their voices.

Then the captain lifted a hand. "We have enough fuel to make our objective, so it's time to tell you. The old man we traded with at the last port gave me the location of solar panels."

"Solar panels," Toby breathed.

"Yes, there's a whole cargo container full. The ship went down before the riots, before all the solar panels on land were smashed. No one bothered salvaging it at the time, because the panels were useless without the sun. Now the sun's back. The old man knew where his captain's ship went down, but hadn't the resources to go back for it, so he was willing to trade his notes on her location."

"With solar panels, we can fit the *Phoenix* so she goes and goes." Toby couldn't resist a small cheer.

"That's right. No more reliance on salvage, no more slow sailwork, no more scrabbling for engine fuel. We'll be unstoppable."

"It would change everything." Toby looked around at the ship as if seeing her for the first time. He pictured a solar array on deck, reflecting the sun like a piece of trapped sky, and imagined electric lights blinking inside her dingy passageways. He stared at his hands, closing his palm around the black lines that told his story – he couldn't recall ever seeing his hands clean. No more brushing soot out of the boiler. No more pressure to seek the dwindling combustible junk they needed to keep the boiler running. And who knew what they would find in deeper waters? Acid-free salt, fish that hadn't been poisoned…

"Then we can search for *the island*," Dee added.

"That's right." The captain nodded.

"The island!" Crocker snorted from the back of the group. "Bah, it's a myth."

The captain shook his head. "I don't think it is a myth. When Yellowstone erupted there were several landmasses that rose from the seas and sunk back again, but some of the larger ones remained. We've all heard of the atolls that ringed Hawaii."

The crew nodded.

"Then what's so strange about a whole island rising and not sinking back?"

"It's a children's story," Crocker sneered. "No one's ever found it."

"It's real," the captain snapped. "A whole island, untouched by man, with its own natural resources, free of governments and their military Greymen."

"You just want it to be real," Crocker suggested.

The captain raised his hands. "What do we do if we're not looking for the island, Crocker? Sail aimlessly our whole lives, hiding from Greymen, slinking from port to port? The island is our goal. If you don't like it, I can put you and your brother in at the next stop and you can take berth in another ship. The *Banshee* perhaps."

Toby's heart rose. Were they about to get rid of Crocker and his terrible brother?

Crocker disappointed him. "We can't stay any time on land. You know that, Captain. We're wanted men, me an' Peel. An' we like the *Phoenix*, she's a solid berth." Crocker patted the railing absently. "We're useful to you, ain't we? My brother's the best cook you ever 'ad. An' he saved your life, way back when."

"Then get on board, Crocker." The captain lowered his head. "We're going for the solar panels and once they're installed, we'll be putting all our resources into searching for the island. We'll sail deeper into the ocean than we ever have and further from any port. We'll comb the seas until we find it. Then we'll settle down. That's the aim of the *Phoenix* and that's what we're going to do."

"Here, here," Marcus raised his voice and the rest of the pirates joined him.

Toby couldn't resist. "The island!" he cried, mainly to annoy Crocker.

Toby hadn't been off the *Phoenix* since he first boarded, when he was four years old. He had no idea what it would be like to live on land, couldn't imagine how it would be living without the sea beneath his feet and … he looked around. Who was he supposed to settle down *with*? When they got to the island, he would be the only person his age. His eyes flicked to Rita. Almost eight years older than he was, she was the nearest. But despite her infectious childish giggle, he knew she saw him as a kid.

A gust of wind hit them and Toby inhaled the scent of clean air. Then a shout shattered the crew's celebratory mood. Old Arnav was waving urgently from the crow's nest. Toby followed his pointing arm and his jaw dropped. A false twilight was behind them, and it was gaining fast. The dark sky was broken by lightning so bright that Toby's eyeballs seared with each flash. The storm was almost upon them.

"There must be a bloody hurricane up there for it to be moving so fast," the captain yelled. "Get the sails down, Carson, or we'll lose them." He turned to Toby. "We need the paddles, son. Fast as you can."

"What about the old engines?" Toby was already running for the hatch, Polly gliding at his side. "I can start them up."

"The fuel won't be filtered in time. Focus on the paddles. We can still outrun this, but we have to get some speed on now."

FOUR

Toby tossed an armful of compressed fuel into the burner and flicked some switches on the control panel.

"Are you sure about this?" Polly swayed from side to side on her perch. "You haven't found the problem yet."

"Whatever it is, it didn't stop us reversing." Toby closed his hands around the lever that would open the main delivery lines to the paddles. "I'll get us moving then give her a full work-up." He yanked the lever, which moved smoothly into position, then stepped back to listen as steam sped from the drum into the lines.

Hisssss.

Toby's back straightened. His eyes widened.

"Oh, hells."

"Toby, it's the—"

"*I know.*"

He leaped to pull back on the lever, too late. Four-hundred-degree steam reached the forward delivery line, but it didn't continue along the snaking pipes. Instead, the pressure forced a tiny rupture and steam geysered into the boiler room.

Lungs screaming, Toby backed up and covered his face with his sleeve. For a moment, panic erased everything else. His mind was blank.

"Toby." The speaker crackled. "We aren't moving. Is everything all right?" The captain was obviously putting some effort into seeming calm.

"Polly want a cracker! Polly want a cracker!" Polly wheeled around the ceiling fans, trying to keep away from the insane heat.

Finally Toby moved. He grabbed the lever, which was now a bar of scalding metal. It burned even through the leather of his half gloves and he cried out, but held on. He had to cut the supply to the delivery lines.

The boiler room was swiftly filling with steam. Toby's goggles fogged and sweat pricked every bit of his skin. He released the lever with one hand to lift his scarf over his face then went back to pulling, but the lever didn't want to move – the steam was putting too much pressure on the valve.

"I can't do it!" Toby ground his teeth.

"Call the captain," Polly shrieked. "Get help."

"There's no time! The boiler will be drained." Toby threw his head back, pulling frantically. The lever still did not move. He could feel the muscles in his shoulders tearing, but didn't stop.

"You've got to call him, this isn't working."

Toby saw a blur as Polly flew down. He felt her claws on his fingers. She was trying to help him push. His feet slipped as steam dampened the floor and he jammed his toes beneath the lever base, trying to regain purchase. "If it empties, even a trickle of feed water will cause an explosion that'll take out the hull."

"What about your father's buffering system?" Polly flapped her wings, clearing steam briefly from Toby's face. "He can shut off the passageways."

"It's not enough. We've got to move this lever ourselves."

Toby strained until his muscles popped, but he knew he couldn't move the lever alone.

"Can I help?"

Toby's head whipped round at the unfamiliar voice. He released the lever long enough to wipe his goggles; then he gaped.

A kid was standing there. Smaller than him, a few years younger, dressed in thin clothes completely inappropriate for seafaring. The boy's head was badly shaved and tufts of black hair stuck up in every direction. He was grey with soot, from his eyelashes to his fingernails, and he was cringing from the heat of the steam.

"A stowaway." Toby grabbed the lever again. "You've been hiding out in my boiler room. How...?" He gave his head a quick shake. "I don't care. Wrap your shirt around your hands, grab this lever and *pull*."

The strange boy covered his hands with his tattered cuffs, closed his fists below Toby's and hauled.

"It's moving, don't let go." Polly flapped, helping as much as she could. Suddenly the lever dropped back into position, cutting off the steam's flow.

As the whistling quietened, Toby pulled his goggles off his face and stared at the rupture.

"Ashes," he muttered.

"Toby, the paddles!" The captain's voice was urgent now. Toby grabbed the comms tube, not taking his eye from the stranger who had saved them.

"Captain," he swallowed, "a delivery line ruptured. It must've happened when the *Phoenix* was hit during the salvage."

There was silence from the speaker. Toby f0id0geted. "Captain?"

"I'm thinking," the captain snapped. "Did you cut it off in time, has the boiler run dry?"

"*I'll* check." The new boy ran to the water gauge. "It's reading a third full. That isn't enough, is it?"

"How did you know to do that?" Toby covered the

comms tube as he spoke.

The boy shrugged awkwardly. "Been watching you. Sorry."

"Watching me from *where*?" Toby shuddered. He thought of the boiler room as an extension of himself. Shouldn't he have known that he wasn't alone? Shouldn't Polly have detected the stowaway?

The boy indicated what at first appeared to be a haphazard pile of junk: car bonnets, motherboards, sheet metal, tubing. Toby's hoard of 'things that might be useful one day'. He realized that it had been moved since he had last sorted through, creating a hidden nest. Above the nest the air vent was ajar. Toby blinked, remembering. Years ago he used to slip inside the gratings and travel through the vents, spying on the pirates with no one any the wiser. The captain had put a stop to his travels when, at eight years old, Toby got stuck and had to be cut out of the mess-hall wall. Now those passages were the sole province of the rats and, apparently, a half-starved stowaway.

He exhaled. "OK. I can't deal with this now."

Toby uncovered the tube to address the captain. "It hasn't run dry, but there's not enough feed water. I-I'll have to switch the boiler off to let it build back up. And the line has to be repaired."

"The *Phoenix* can't just sit here," the captain said.

Toby imagined his father's fist almost collapsing the table. From the dents in the metal tabletop Toby could map every setback the *Phoenix* had ever experienced. "If she can't outrun the storm, we have to get to shelter to weather it out. There's a hidden cove near Tarifa that'll take a ship our size."

"What about the plane fuel?" Toby slid a finger under his goggles to rub his eyes. "Is it ready yet?"

"Not even close. It's still being filtered into our tanks. Dobbs is working his team as fast as he can, but I need all hands on deck right now, so he has a skeleton crew. We can't use the sails in this weather – they'd be ripped to shreds. Get that boiler fixed and I'll put more men to pumping the fuel. I'll leave the sails up till it gets dangerous. If that boiler isn't running by then, we're sitting ducks."

Toby hung up the tube then stood stock-still. The boiler was never switched off. Ever. Even in port, a small fire was maintained to keep her low-power systems going. There was only one way to turn the boiler off. He was going to have to put out the *Phoenix*'s fire.

Toby unhooked the blackened fire extinguisher from the wall by the door. With his thumb he rubbed rust from the corroded pin as he strode towards the combustion chamber.

"Stand back," he said to the boy. Then Toby aimed the

extinguisher, yanked the pin and squeezed. Noxious white foam spread over the flames and slowly but surely the *Phoenix*'s heart went cold.

Together the boys stood and watched the embers go out. Combustion fuel broke into small pieces as it cooled and the boiler ticked solemnly.

"OK," Toby said. "Right." He felt off balance. The whole sound of the *Phoenix* had been thrown out. "OK," he repeated.

Polly climbed on to his shoulder and nuzzled his cheek.

The strange boy put his hand on Toby's arm, making him jump. "What do you need to do to fix this?" Big brown eyes stared up at him and Toby exhaled.

"I haven't got anything I can use to repair the delivery line that won't just break or melt as soon as the steam hits it. I need a new line."

"Have you got one?" the boy asked.

Toby's mouth twisted. "Sort of," he murmured.

The boy's eyes widened. "Sort of?"

"The captain's been looking to trade for spares for a couple of months. There is only one other line on board that's long enough."

"And you can't get it?"

"Technically I can." Toby rubbed his eyes again.

"Technically? What does that mean?"

Toby sighed. "It means nothing is ever simple."

The boy lost his footing and grabbed at the feed-water tubes as he fell.

"The sea's getting rough." Toby braced his legs and offered a hand to pull the boy to his feet. Then he began undoing the screws on one end of a delivery line that disappeared into the wall. "What do I call you?" He tilted his head as he worked, examining the small stowaway.

"My name is Sorahiko," he mumbled. "They call me Hiko."

Toby nodded. "You're Japanese."

Hiko shrugged. "My father, yes – not my mother."

"Well, there're not many questions on the *Phoenix* – just what you're wanted for and where. The captain puts back murderers and rapists, but most others get to stay if there's a space."

Hiko looked away. "Do you really think he'll let me stay? I'm not going to be much use. I'm just a kid."

"You've been useful already and I need you right now." Toby dropped the loosened line and gestured to a shovel by the door. "You'll have to empty the combustion chamber for me. Open the porthole, get all that foamed-up fuel out and dump it. Then refill the burner with the dry compressed chunks, over there." He pointed. "Keep an eye on that feed-water gauge so you can tell me how high the levels are. As soon as I get back we can relight the boiler. It's going to take a while to get a head of steam built up. I just hope we've got enough time."

"So, I'm going to be your assistant?"

"I guess." Toby looked up as if he could see through the ceiling and clamped his screwdriver into his belt. "Now I'm going for the line."

"Polly want a cracker," Polly squawked.

Toby stood in the passageway above the boiler room.

"Did you unhook the line I thought you did?" Polly swayed from foot to foot.

Toby nodded. "It's the only one that'll fit."

"You'd better hope the galley's deserted, then." She whistled a short high note. "Peel won't let you just take it."

Toby clenched his fists. "He'll have to. I don't have time to talk him round."

"Talk him round? He'll go ape."

"I'm trying not to think about it." Toby stopped to listen. "I can't hear anything."

"All quiet." Polly shuffled closer to his ear. "All hands on deck, remember? That includes Crocker *and* Peel."

Toby edged to the door and closed his fingers around the latch. His breath quivered on the glass panel, steaming it up, but not before he had peered in. Polly was right – the galley was empty, nothing but shadows in his way. Toby opened the door and slipped inside.

His hand tightened around the moulded plastic head of the screwdriver. He had a job to do; in and out. If he was lucky, Peel wouldn't even know Toby had been there; at least not until he tried to turn on the oven.

The *Phoenix* tilted once more, reminding Toby that he was running out of time. Nevertheless, before he started to work, he gripped the big wooden table and dragged it until it formed a shelter in front of the blackened range.

"What are you doing?" Polly flew on to the table while he moved it.

"Peel may be on deck, but he could come back at any time. I'll feel a lot less exposed with something covering my back."

Polly bobbed a nod and turned to face the door. "I'll keep watch."

"Should I leave it open, or close it?"

"Leave it ajar so I can see." Polly tilted her head. "You don't want him to surprise you."

Surprise was Peel's most effective weapon. Despite his great weight, Crocker's brother moved in a bubble of silence, padding around the ship on the rubber soles of his trainers. So many times Toby had thought he was alone, only to find fingers pinching him brutally tight while he squirmed for freedom.

But he trusted Polly, so Toby turned his back on the passageway and crawled under the table.

The oven ticked in front of him, warm to the touch. Peel was cooking herring. Callum had netted them after a tornado had cleaned the junk from the deeps off Portugal and revealed an actual shoal swimming far beneath the poisoned currents. The crew had salted and barrelled enough to keep them going for several months.

It would be a shame to eat uncooked herring, but with the boiler shut down, the oven would soon be losing heat anyway.

The delivery line that linked the oven with the boiler room was on the back, so Toby would have to slide it out at least far enough for him to wriggle into the gap. He grabbed the metal edges and pulled.

"Damn it."

"What's the matter?" Polly didn't take her eyes from the door.

"It's even heavier than it looks."

Toby put his shoulder to one side of the oven and yanked with all his might.

He rocked it back and forth, the tendons in his neck tightening painfully. Finally the oven lurched towards him.

With a cry, Toby forced it to twist before it dropped. He looked at the result of his efforts. The oven had come out a few centimetres, on one side.

He sighed, moved to the other side and put his shoulder to it.

Bit by rocking bit, Toby pulled out the oven. Every so often the *Phoenix* would pitch at just the right moment, shifting it in the right direction. By the time there was enough space behind for Toby to fit, his breath was coming in exhausted rasps. He wiped the sweat from his forehead, freed his screwdriver from his belt and set to work.

The delivery line snaked from the rear of the oven, an oil-black tentacle. It was firmly fixed into the back with screws that had long ago rusted in place. Toby frowned. He squirted some fish oil from the small bottle in his pouch and began to chip away.

When he had removed as much rust as he could, he nestled the screwdriver back into the head and turned hard. "I *will* get you out," Toby muttered.

With a sudden lurch, the last screw turned. Toby wobbled but managed to secure a grip on the delivery line. Carefully he eased it from the back of the oven. Tendrils of steam emerged. He secured the line on his belt and started to wrap it around his waist, tugging gently as he freed it from the inner wall of the hull.

"Alert! Alert!"

"What the…?" Toby whipped round so fast he cracked his head on the table. Polly was hopping up and down. Behind her, through the crack in the door, Toby could see Peel and Crocker striding down the passageway.

"Why aren't they on deck?" Toby didn't dare pull the line harder in case it ruptured. He held his breath and kept on gently tugging, wrapping the giant tube around his waist as he went.

"Come on."

With a pop, the end of the line came out. Toby had it all. He tucked the free end into his belt, held his breath and turned. Peel filled the doorway. Greasy hair dyed black with squid ink slicked over his balding crown and his nose flared as if he could smell an intruder.

"What's going on in my galley?" Peel stalked forward on his rubber soles. "Why is that filthy bird on my table? Get out, you flying rat!" Toby peeped out to see Polly narrowly avoid Peel's swiping fist. "Catch that bird, Crocker," he growled. "I'm going to make a sodding stew out of it, captain's pet or no."

"Ain't touching that thing. Prob'ly got fleas." Crocker spat on the floor.

"Use the fire axe. Right there. Knock it out of the air."

Silently Toby pocketed his screwdriver so that he could

draw Nix. He had to get past Peel, out of the galley and back to the boiler room.

As Toby's hand closed around the pommel of his sword, Peel halted by the table. Now Toby could see only the stained apron that flapped over his enormous thighs.

"Boo!"

Peel's face appeared right in front of Toby's and he bared yellow teeth.

"Well, well, well. Little Toby, come to the galley at last."

He stepped to the right as Toby moved. "Oh no, you don't. Stay right there."

Toby was caged in. The smell of grease and body odour was overpowering. Toby covered his mouth with one hand. Nix shook in the other.

"Well, little Toby, I see you got yourself a sword. What are you planning to do with it?" Peel squinted. "You going to sink that into old Peel?"

Crocker snorted as he jumped, trying to reach the crimson blur that was Polly flying around the ceiling.

"It's harder than you imagine, little Toby, sticking a blade in something. Tougher than you think. Pointy as it is, you'll need all your weight to get the tip through my leather apron. But it'll go, oh yes, with a pop and a squirt of hot blood all over your hands. You'll have to push in close to get it into my ribs, angle it just right. You'll feel the scrape of blade on bone, you'll have to wiggle and shove to keep it moving. And I'm a big man, little Toby. Yes, I am. I'm not even sure that shaft would reach all the way to my heart. But it might. And you'd feel it – wet, warm blood all over you, like oil. What do you think, Toby? You want to stab me?" Peel cocked his head. "The captain wouldn't like it much, would he? How would you explain it, eh? That you stabbed his old friend in the heart, done for the man who saved his life in Porto Santo? If you killed the cook, Toby lad, how would you explain it?"

"Don't come any closer." Toby gagged. His hand was shaking so hard he could barely hold Nix up. "I have to get back to the boiler room."

"I just bet you do." Peel crouched now, holding on to the table. Rolls of fat rested on his thighs, blubber pushing against his apron. Yet he was strongest on the ship beside Big Pad. He could lift Toby with one hand.

"Is it you that's been stealing my food, little Toby? If you was hungry you only had to ask. I'd be happy to fatten you up."

Another pair of legs added to Toby's cage as Crocker joined his brother.

"The oven's out of place, Peel." Crocker leaned over the table his voice a tobacco-stained rasp above Toby's head.

"Get the door." Peel didn't take his eyes from Toby.

Toby watched, panic stricken as Crocker pushed the door shut. Where was Polly?

"Now…" Peel gripped the table with one hand and dragged it to one side, leaving Toby completely exposed. Peel blinked at the oven, still sat at an angle and ticking quietly as it cooled. "What's wrong with my oven?"

He shot out a hand, but Toby was already racing towards the door. Crocker blocked his way. Crimson feathers brushed the edge of Toby's vision as he reached the butcher's block in the centre of the galley. There he stopped, Crocker on one side, Peel on the other, Polly overhead.

"Don't be mad, Peel," he pleaded and he gestured to the line wrapped at his waist. "I need this to fix the boiler."

"If you've done something to my oven, devil, then the crew'll be eating *you* for dinner."

Toby held out a hand as Crocker slid behind him. "What have you done, boy?" Crocker smiled.

Peel growled as he moved and snatched up a cleaver.

"Wait, you don't understand."

"All I understand is you've broken my oven. The herring'll be ruined. You want the crew to eat raw seagull for dinner? There's no fishing in these parts and raw seagull ain't any kind of edible, especially the way Callum catches 'em." He chopped with the blade and Toby jumped backwards, automatically blocking with Nix as the cleaver

79

whistled past. The blades clanged together. Toby gasped as Peel's blade came within a hair of slicing the precious delivery line.

"It won't be for long," Toby pleaded, trying to appease Peel's rage. "I'll rig something up as soon as I can. There might be something in the plane that I can use for the oven."

Peel slammed his fist on the table with a bang that shook the galley. "Grab him, Crocker."

Thin fingers dug into Toby's shoulder and he leaped to one side with a cry. Polly screeched and Toby ducked as she flew into Crocker's face, claws outstretched.

Crocker screamed and released Toby as he tried to knock the parrot away.

As Peel circled towards him, Toby placed one hand on the edge of the butcher's block. He slid underneath and out the other side just as Crocker dropped to his knees. Blood poured from his torn cheeks and Polly flew upwards with a triumphant squawk.

Toby bounded to his feet in one smooth movement. Peel's fingers tangled in his hair, but failed to get a purchase. With a half-crazed whoop Toby yanked the door open and sprinted along the gangway.

"Get him!" At his back Crocker and Peel fought in the doorway then burst through.

FIVE

Toby wrapped his arms around the line to hold it in place and fled towards the boiler room.

His toes knew the passageways inside out. Ten years of scampering around the *Phoenix* meant that he knew every single nook and cranny. He didn't even need to look where he was going. The comforting lullaby crooned by the creaking rigging when the weather was calm and the shrieking death metal of the ship's rage when she fought a storm were the constant soundtrack to his life.

Polly's feathers brushed his cheek as she bobbed up and down on his shoulder, flapping her wings for balance.

He skidded to a stop at the top of the ladder by the laundry, grabbed the top rung and kicked off. Peel's arms waved above him before Crocker elbowed his brother aside and started to follow, dripping blood on to Toby's upturned face.

Toby jumped the last metre and ran. As Crocker

shouted behind him, Toby threw himself around the corner towards the boiler room.

Crocker remained close on his tail. At any other time, Toby would have found a cluster of crew members and hidden in their midst, but today he and Polly were alone.

Behind him Peel yelled. He had almost caught up with his brother.

Polly screeched in Toby's ear and fluttered from his shoulder. Momentarily blinded, Toby slammed into a solid torso, and bounced backwards.

"Captain." Crocker skidded to a halt at his back and Toby turned. Crocker hunched, trying to cover his blood-splashed cheeks with his shoulders. "That boy has been in the galley, stealing food and *vandalizing.*"

"Stealing food, Toby? Is this the time?" The captain frowned at Crocker's face but said nothing. He reached down and pulled Toby to his feet.

"I never." Toby shook his head.

"Is that the oven delivery line around your waist?"

"It's the only one long enough to replace the ruptured line."

The captain raked his hand through his curly beard. "I came down to see how you were getting on and found a strange boy shovelling ash from the combustion chamber. I assume he can account for the missing food, and *that* covers the vandalizing." He pointed at the delivery line. The *Phoenix* lurched and the captain grunted. "We're almost out of time. The storm's overhead. I've told the crew to haul in the sails."

Peel pulled to a halt behind Crocker and opened his mouth.

The captain held up a hand. "Sorry, Peel, but we don't have time for the tea you were going to brew us all. And we'll be eating raw for a couple of days. Head back up top and help with the sails." He put a hand on Toby's shoulder. "Let's get that boiler fixed."

Behind the captain's back, Peel's civilized face melted away to reveal the monster beneath. He showed his teeth and growled.

Down in the boiler room, Captain Ford rolled up his sleeves. "It's hot in here," he commented. He scrubbed his forehead and put on his glasses, which instantly steamed up. "I'll take out the ruptured line and you start attaching the new one." He removed his glasses and tucked them back in his pocket. "New boy, what is the water gauge reading?"

"I-it's almost half full," Hiko stammered.

"All right. You can refill the combustion chamber with compressed fuel, but don't light the fire yet."

"His name is Hiko." Toby handed his father a screwdriver. "You'll need this."

The captain shook his head. "Got my own." He opened his windcheater to reveal a tool belt much like Toby's. "I'm never without my tools." He grinned. The *Phoenix* rolled until the sea splashed in through the open porthole and his grin widened. "By heaven, I've missed this." He rapped his screwdriver against the attemperator with a ringing clang. "But as the *Phoenix* reminds us, we're on a deadline. Move it."

Even Toby's sea-hardened stomach was beginning to roll as the boiler room tipped up and down. Salt water sloshed around his feet, stinging his toes as it splashed in the porthole with every other pitch of the ship.

"We've got to keep the fuel dry," Barnaby yelled. "Hiko, close that porthole."

"Who's a pretty birdie?" Polly fluttered anxiously, as if it were her claws that were getting a seawater bath and not Toby's feet. She landed on top of the boiler, which was now shuddering hard enough to shake her plumage.

She went silent for a moment then, "Polly want a cracker," she muttered.

"That isn't helping, Polly." Barnaby tossed the ruptured

delivery line into Toby's 'things that might be useful one day' pile. "Toby, pass me one end of the line. I'll attach it to the boiler."

"Hiko –" Toby shoved the line at the shaking stowaway – "take it to the captain."

"I—"

"I don't bite, Hiko." Barnaby grabbed the line from him. "Hold this up here, while I screw her in."

Hiko stood next to the captain, knees trembling.

"Tell me, Hiko, how long have you been on board?"

"Since the last port," he whispered. "I'm sorry."

"Not to worry." Barnaby tightened the last screw. "I'm not going to feed you to the fishes. You've been a great help today. Just keep on being helpful and you can find a berth in the sleeping quarters near Toby's. Eat in the main hall with us and stay out of the vents. I don't want a repeat of six years ago."

"Hey –" Toby looked up from the line – "when are you going to let that go?"

"Six years ago?" Hiko asked.

"Never mind, just stay out of the vents." Barnaby stepped back. "I'm in this end… Toby?"

Toby gave his end of the line a gentle pull. "Secure."

"Then let's check it."

Slowly the two engineers started to walk towards one

another, checking every millimetre of the line for tears. As he walked, Toby kept the gentlest of holds, terrified that he might lose his footing and pull it loose by accident. Hiko crouched on his hands and knees in the wet, no longer able to keep upright on the rolling floor.

When they met in the middle, Barnaby nodded and clapped his son's shoulder. "Good job, there."

Toby grinned.

Barnaby laid his hands on the boiler drum. "It's cool enough so there shouldn't be an explosion when the feed water hits it. Start the fire."

Toby nodded, grabbed his flint and kneeled by the combustion chamber. "Come on," he muttered. Water splashed his hands and he couldn't get a spark. He glanced at his father out of the corner of his eye. "Burn, damn you," he snapped. Finally a spark grew into a tiny flame. Toby leaned in close and curled his hand around it. The fuel started to smoulder as it caught. Then everything went silent as the sea dropped away from the *Phoenix*. Toby opened his mouth to yell as the ship tipped, hit the junk and crashed back. Toby slammed into the boiler. Hiko rolled into his nest and even the captain fell to his knees.

"Are you all right, son?"

Toby opened his mouth to answer, but then rain began to batter the ship like gunfire. Amplified by the *Phoenix*'s metal hull, the sound filled the boiler room.

"We're out of time! The storm's caught us." Barnaby glared upwards as if he could see through the hull. "Carson had better have those sails furled." He whirled to check the water gauge. "She's full enough. Draw that flame through and I'll open the feed-water control valve."

Frantically pressing on the bellows, Toby forced the fire until it roared. He wasn't sure if the pressure inside his chest was from the need to get the paddles running as fast as he could, or desperately trying to impress his father,.

Barnaby opened the valve and the feed water started to run through the tubes. Toby held his breath. Was the drum really cool enough to prevent an explosion, or was the captain just desperate enough to risk it?

On her perch Polly swayed silently then edged behind a pipe. Half hidden by an old car bonnet, Hiko watched with glittering eyes. Toby wished he could hide as well, but knew it would be futile. If it blew, nowhere in the boiler room would be safe from the explosion.

The fire burned hotter and hotter as the feed water filled the boiler. Toby held his breath and closed his eyes. A large hand squeezed his shoulder and he jumped. "It'll be all right, son." Barnaby smiled. "This was kind of fun, eh?"

"Not so much." Toby exhaled shakily. "We're still here though, so I guess the drum was cool enough."

"Told you." His father's smile widened. "I built her, after all."

Toby nodded and glanced at Polly who was edging sheepishly out from behind the pipe, trying to appear as if she'd never hidden.

They strained to hear the sound of the steam drum starting to fill over the rain.

Toby counted under his breath as he waited for the whistle of the steam racing along the delivery lines.

The ship lurched and a crack of thunder reverberated through the metal, sending Hiko completely into hiding. "Listen!" His father's fingers tightened on Toby's shoulder. "Can you hear the steam?"

"I can hear it."

Automatically the pair looked to the new delivery line as it moved and Toby caught his breath. But the steam howled along and it held.

"You did it." Polly hopped on her perch.

"Get those paddles moving, Toby. I have to get back on deck." The captain pulled his windcheater together and tucked his screwdriver away. "See you up there." He slammed through the door and bounded along the rocking passageway.

Toby stood still for a couple of beats. Despite the situation, working so closely with his father was a rare pleasure and Toby wanted to savour it. But there wasn't much time. As he threw switches, he glanced at Hiko. "We'll be moving in a minute. All hands on deck, so you'll have to come with me. You too, Polly." When there was no answer he looked at his parrot. "Polly?" She didn't move. "Damn it." Toby patted his pockets. "I have some pellets here, just wait a second." He pulled a handful from his jacket's inner lining. "Why did you let yourself run so low?" He held the morsels up to Polly. Slowly she lowered her beak to his hand and started to hoover up the granules. Seconds later she fluffed her feathers and flew.

"Who's a pretty birdie?" she asked, as she landed on his shoulder.

"You are." Toby rubbed his cheek against her soft feathers. She was warm from the biomass generator that powered her. It was the tiniest and most efficient his father had ever built. In fact, Polly was the last remnant of Ford's previous life. She was supposed to belong to the Greymen of St George, but on the day Ford refused to make weapons for them, he took his son, the AI and the *Phoenix* together.

And that was why the captain was the most-wanted man on the sea, why the *Phoenix* rarely docked, why Toby wasn't allowed off the ship and why he had a bird as a babysitter.

Polly had originally been a real parrot. Creative

taxidermy had preserved her original body, which was now stretched over a metal skeleton. Polly was more intelligent than half the pirates put together and she wore a faint smell of dusty feathers, metal and preservative. But most of the crew were unaware that Polly was not a natural bird.

"Let's go." Toby gave Polly a gentle stroke. "Follow me, Hiko, it's time to join the rest of the crew."

Hiko looked nervously towards the rain-lashed porthole.

"Don't worry." Toby forced a smile. "It's only a bit of bad weather."

Above deck the full force of the storm almost drove Toby to his knees. He winced as Polly's claws dug into his shoulder, the parrot instantly drenched and half blown away by the raging wind. The sky was near black and the *Phoenix*'s mast glowed with a violet light that turned it into a torch.

"St Elmo's fire," Polly muttered. "Let go of the railing, in case the lightning doesn't ground to the water through the Faraday's cage."

Immediately Toby caught hold of a fibreglass pole to steady himself as he stared overboard.

Behind the *Phoenix* the sea raged with swells as big

as mountain ranges. Long sunken debris was tossed skywards. Toby ducked as a once-red lorry with a Coca-Cola logo was hurled towards them, as though the storm was angry at the *Phoenix* for attempting to outpace it. The pirates at the stern yelled as the lorry splashed down on their starboard side.

Toby gasped as the ship bounced on the shelves created by the deepening waves. Even with the great paddles turning, there was no way they were going to pull ahead of the weather system now.

There was a series of shouts from the port side and Toby turned, face whitening. Three of the main sails had been furled, but the crew was still battling with the fourth.

"If that sail doesn't come down, the mast could break." Toby pointed. "That's where we need to go." He turned. "Hiko?"

Toby realized that he was alone and turned to see the younger boy clinging on to the hatch. Hiko's shirt twisted and flew in the grasping wind and his mouth was an 'oh!' of terror. "Come on." Toby waved him forwards.

The boy shook his head, just as a wave slammed over the side of the ship. Toby already saw what would happen and was moving before Hiko screamed.

He didn't watch the boy get pulled from his feet or torn from his handhold. Instead Toby clamped his own elbow around the railing and caught Hiko as he was swept past.

Polly tangled herself in Toby's shirt as the boy wrapped his arms and legs around him. The three of them hung inside the acid-tinged wave for a long beat, desperately holding their breath, then slammed back on to the deck as it crashed down, exploding over the galley roof in a shower of corrosive spray.

Toby spat out a mouthful of wet feathers and turned his face upwards, so the rain could wash the stinging salt from his face, then he was up, but Hiko remained clinging to him like a limpet.

"Let go."

The boy shook his head, frantic.

"I know you're frightened but we've got to help." Toby pried him loose. Then he realized that he was being too hard on the boy. "Why don't you stay here? You won't know what to do anyway." He wrapped Hiko's hands around the fibreglass pole. "Hold on to this and don't move. I'll come back for you."

Hiko nodded fearfully. His hair lay flat on his head and he was soaked through to the skin.

Toby bit his lip. "I should take you back down." As he turned, a whistle blew, loud enough to make Toby slam both hands over his ears. Hiko dropped to a crouch, shivering.

"What is it?" Hiko whispered.

"Arnav in the crow's nest." Toby looked up, amazed that the old pirate remained so high up. "He's spotted another ship." Toby shaded his eyes and peered out to sea. "Oh, ashes." His face paled.

"What is it?"

Toby turned to the stowaway, his face grim. "That –" he pointed – "is the *Banshee.*"

"The *Banshee*?" Hiko lifted his head to follow Toby's gaze. There in the distance was a former USS Zumwalt-class Destroyer, 180 metres long, bristling with old-fashioned weaponry. Most of it was computerized and therefore long-dead, but cannons bastardized from a Spanish galleon were welded around the *Banshee*'s deckhouse. Blue and violet St Elmo's fire crackled around her hull, which was splashed with red varnish like bloodstains. A painted skull and crossbones gave her eyes of evil.

"The terror of the seas." Toby's voice trembled. "Thank the gods that you didn't choose that ship to stow away on. Her captain is stone-cold. She hates the *Phoenix*. If she boards us, she'll rip us apart, take everything she thinks is useful and feed the rest to the junk pile." His hands pressed against the *Phoenix*'s hull.

"What about us?" Hiko edged close to Toby's knees as if the larger boy could protect him. "What happens to us if they take the *Phoenix*?"

Toby's lips narrowed. "I-I'm not sure. She'll try and collect bounty on the captain and some of the crew, the ones with big rewards on their heads. The rest of us…"

"Yes?" Hiko leaned forwards, rain lashing his face. "What about us?"

Toby swallowed. "Don't worry about it, the captain won't let them board. And they're fighting the storm, too, see?"

The *Banshee* smashed bow first into a mass of junk with the sound of tearing metal and screeching plastic. Lightning flickered among the debris.

The crew of the *Phoenix* watched with grim fascination.

"The *Banshee*'s wail is the sign that they are about to attack," Toby said, without taking his eyes off the sizzling sea. Finally he stiffened his resolve and turned back to Hiko. "If you don't hear the wail, there's nothing to fear." His words were as much for himself as they were for the petrified stowaway.

Hiko's mouth was a thin slash. His terror thickened the air.

"Do you hear the wail, Hiko?"

The boy shook his head.

"Then there's no need to worry." But Toby faced the *Banshee* once more – he could not stop watching her approach.

SIX

The captain was first to recover. His megaphone boomed over the roar of the storm. "Ignore the damned *Banshee*. If we don't get that last sail furled we're doing their job for them. Focus on the task, or we're lost."

Toby tore his gaze from the warship and saw the captain running for the bridge. He was right, the crew had frozen, waiting like junk to be taken as salvage. He offered Hiko a shaky smile. "Everything's going to be fine, but I've got to go. Do you want me to take you back down below first?"

Hiko shook his head. "I'll wait here."

Toby was already backing towards the rigging. "Stay safe." He turned and ran.

Ahead, Carson yelled instructions for tying the sail, and the pirates swarmed up the front port mast to join those who were already wrestling with it. The wind had gripped the silver material and it was being dragged outwards as fast as the crew could gather it in.

The billowing sheet dragged the *Phoenix* to one side and the port paddle began to churn air, uselessly. The *Phoenix* began to turn in a circle.

Toby groaned as several tied loops pulled free. Swiftly he grabbed the rigging and started to climb. Despite the rain lashing his eyes he spotted Dee at his side. She hurtled up the ropes as though the storm was nothing more than a gentle breeze at her back. She swung to catch the next stay, holding it still so that Toby could follow her.

"I'm fine," he shouted.

"I know." Still she made sure that his fingers and toes closed around the hemp before climbing onwards.

On Toby's shoulder Polly made herself as small as possible, tucking in her wings and refusing to allow the wind any purchase. Nervous squawks drove Toby upwards until he reached the sail, wrapped his legs around the fibreglass pole and leaned over to help catch the flying sheet.

Beside him Big Pad grimly reeled sailcloth into his giant hands before tucking it into loops and lashing it tightly. Toby could not imagine the wind taking anything Big Pad had secured. Toby reached out to gather the slick material and began to pass it directly to Big Pad, wordlessly operating in partnership. To his right Marcus and Dee copied their system, Dee leaning over the mast, Marcus tying the gathered sail. Carson gave them a thumbs up.

Slowly the sail began to shrink – the pirates were winning.

A strong gust almost tumbled Polly from Toby's shoulders. He grabbed the parrot and tucked her inside his shirt. "Better?"

She blinked up at him, her eyes glittering in the glow of the storm. "Who's a pretty birdie?" she muttered miserably.

Toby wrapped his fist around another handful of cloth. Exhaustion was setting in, his legs were tired and his perch slippery. But he had to keep pulling in the sail.

Then every pirate froze. The sound they had been dreading screamed across the waves. The *Banshee* was wailing.

Nisha broke first. "We're going to die." She dropped her end of the sail, grabbed the rigging and began to shimmy down the mast.

"Nisha, wait!" Carson reached for the sail she had dropped. The wind caught him as he leaned and pulled him off balance. With a cry, Carson threw his arms around the mast, but let go of the sail.

Toby watched in mute horror as the wind swept beneath the sailcloth. It bulged under the material and yanked it from the hands of the pirates.

"Hold on," Toby screamed. But the pirates had the sail held in loosened hands, their attention on the howling *Banshee*.

Pop, pop, pop.

As each tie was ripped free, the *Phoenix*'s sail opened and the pirates were yanked from the mast with it.

Screaming men and women were hurled into the rigging or smashed into the deck with the crunch of brittle bones breaking.

Dee and Big Pad, on either side of Toby, met one another's gaze with wide eyes. Dee reached for Toby, but before her hand could close on his shoulder, Marcus was torn from his perch by the heaving sail and sent flying into the rigging. As he pin-wheeled, his flying foot caught Dee's shoulder, and she went spinning after him.

The sail reared in front of Toby. He had time to see Dee and Marcus clinging safely to the tangled cord before Big Pad's thick arms wrapped around Toby's waist. For a moment the sail was secure as their combined weight held it flat. Toby let out a sigh of relief.

Then, from behind Big Pad, Ajay screamed. Toby struggled to turn his head and saw Amit topple. Ajay lunged for his brother, who instinctively grabbed the nearest hold – Big Pad's leg. Toby had no time to react. Although Amit quickly wrapped his free hand around the rigging and released Pad, he had thrown them off balance and together Paddy and Toby toppled over. They fell to the tune of screaming pirates, the wailing *Banshee* and the popping of the final ties. The sail billowed free. It whipped into the storm and the mast groaned.

Toby's fall seemed to go on forever. One moment he was looking at the sky, then the deck was hurtling towards him. Abruptly the ship pitched and, for a second, Toby was staring at sea-drowned junk, lit by lightning. Then the *Phoenix* tilted and slammed downwards, bringing the deck back beneath them.

Toby spun again, forced around by the strength of Big Pad's arms. He found his gaze pinned to the silver sail, its NASA logo fully open to the sky.

The impact shuddered through Toby's back and his head cracked against Big Pad's. Dimly he felt Big Pad's arms loosen and release him. His eyelids flickered. Struggling to hold on to consciousness, Toby heard the pirate's screams grow distant and the *Banshee*'s wail fade into insignificance.

But then a new sound grabbed him by the throat. Toby's eyes flew open in time to see the mast crack in two. It fell in slow motion, spinning on its axis as though it was going to be dashed into the sea. At the last moment the wind snatched the sail, brought it back round and slammed it down across the *Phoenix* herself, crushing the bridge like an eggshell under a boot.

The sound of shattering glass and smashing metal seared Toby's ears, but it was the thought of his father, who he had last seen running inside, that finally sent Toby into oblivion.

"Toby, don't be dead." Small hands patted at his cheeks.

"Hiko?" Toby thought he had spoken aloud, but his lips were heavy and he couldn't move his mouth.

"He's unconscious." Polly answered the terrified Hiko and faintly Toby felt her feathers brush his throat as she clawed her way from his shirt.

Then the darkness pulled him back under once more.

"He won't wake up." Hiko's voice again, frightened.

"He's had a nasty crack on the skull. Big Pad's got a chin like granite." Uma. Her voice shivered with grief. "I know you want to stay with Toby, but I need your help. Go to every pirate you see. If they talk to you, leave them, if they seem to be asleep, wrap their red scarf around their leg. Make sure I can see it. That way I'll know who to help first."

There was silence as Hiko moved off. Then hands wrapped round Toby's shoulders.

"Toby, I need to move you. I have to get to Big Pad."

Pain. Darkness.

Thrum, thrum.

The paddles were back in the water, Toby could feel the deep vibration of her roar as the *Phoenix* powered forward. The feel of electricity crackling against his teeth and skin was gone, telling Toby that they had finally outrun the storm, but the rain continued to fall. It no longer lashed Toby's face – now it felt like tears. Relief eased Toby and even the wail of the *Banshee* could not keep him from sliding back into sleep.

Shards of bright pain; lances of light that stabbed Toby's eyes and forced them closed. He lay in self-imposed darkness, his cheeks wet with gentle rain. His head pounded with each thresh of the *Phoenix*'s paddles. His back ached, bone deep, as if he had been trampled by horses. Slowly he raised a stiff arm and shielded his eyes. Then he cracked them open.

"You're awake." Hiko knelt at his side.

Toby shifted as though he would sit, but Hiko's hand on his chest prevented him. The *Banshee*'s wail was even louder now, the sound ringing inside Toby's head. He closed his fists over his ears. "How close are they?" he asked.

Hiko swallowed.

"That close?" Toby slumped, then a memory screamed to the surface and he clutched Hiko's arm. "The captain! Tell me he wasn't in the bridge."

Hiko tried to pull away. "I'm sorry."

Toby groaned and his fingers fell away from Hiko.

Hiko shook his head. "No, Toby, he's alive. He rolled under the table just in time. It protected him. He's at the stern, helping Uma. I was to let him know when you woke up." Hiko looked suddenly panicked.

Toby's heart thudded. "What about Big Pad?"

Hiko wouldn't meet his eyes.

"Paddy?" Toby shouted.

Hiko scooted backwards.

"Son, you're awake!" Barnaby appeared at Toby's side. His glasses were crooked and one lens was cracked right through. Dust was matted into his beard and blood dripped from shoulder to elbow on his right-hand side. Gusts of rain followed him down.

"Where's Big Pad? Is he all right?" Toby gripped his father's hand. "He saved me."

"I know." Barnaby squeezed Toby's fingers. "Uma's with him."

"And?"

Barnaby's nose dripped on Toby's sleeve. "He's alive."

Toby blanched. "But…?"

"Uma thinks his back is broken, she's treating him now. Luckily we have all those new medical supplies. There's some excellent insta-plaster, the first I've seen in years. She's immobilized and drugged him. He isn't in any pain."

"Oh, ashes." Toby glared at the black clouds rearing behind them as Barnaby carefully pulled him into a sitting position and lifted his shirt.

"You're bruised, but no broken bones. I've got arnica, and it's even in date." He started to rub his son's spine. "You'll be black and blue, but it could have been much worse."

"If it hadn't been for Big Pad," Toby groaned.

"Yes. You're a new generation, strong bones, but if he hadn't turned you both, you'd have been a skin bag full of shattered skeleton bits." Barnaby shuddered.

Toby sat miserably as the chill of the arnica eased into his bruises. The sound of the wailing *Banshee* knifed his brain. Although he was almost too scared to ask, he forced out the question that needed asking. "Did everyone make it?"

Barnaby's hand stopped moving on his back and he packed away the cream before he answered. "Everyone's alive. There are a few broken bones. Big Pad's the worst by far, although Uma is worried about Nisha's baby." Toby heard Barnaby sigh. "There's a good reason I don't allow pregnancies on ship." He had to shout now, over the noise of their approaching rival. "Arnav took a bolt of lightning and Peel, a beam to the chin. His head'll be ringing for a week. I'm more worried about the *Banshee*."

"We can outrun her, can't we?" Toby asked. "The *Phoenix*, how bad is she?"

Barnaby's lips pinched together. "We'll need to dock for repairs. But the paddles are working and we're staying ahead of the leading edge of the storm. The *Banshee* might be close, but we're giving her a run."

Beside Toby, Hiko squeaked, his whole body clenched.

"What?" Toby followed the younger boy's gaze. Above the *Phoenix*'s guard rail the *Banshee* loomed.

"Run's over," Hiko whispered.

Toby had never seen the *Banshee* up close. She was a horror.

"See that?" The captain's eyes shone. "A wave-piercing tumblehome hull configuration – she's the only destroyer with that design. Works brilliantly on the junk, but when the fuel crisis reached its peak they ended the building programme."

The *Banshee* looked like a colossal chisel slicing towards the *Phoenix*. Rain splashed from her metal hull, but she was so big and heavy that the waves barely affected her. She powered through the junk, forcing it aside and churning it into debris behind her.

As Toby watched, holes opened along one side and a hundred oars dipped into the water. Ponderously the *Banshee* turned so that she was side-on to the *Phoenix*, showing one empty skull's eye, bloody streaks running down the socket.

Toby ignored the ache in his back and leaned forward, his engineer's brain fascinated.

"What's powering her?" he shouted. "She's got no sail, no paddle. Those oars can't do it all."

Barnaby sneered. "The *Banshee* still uses her original engine. She ransacks everything she can find for fuel. She lives on the very last dregs of the old civilization and she's sucked it dry. She'll be dead in the water soon enough." He shook his head. "If this isn't her final voyage she'll not be far off. Nell's short-sighted in giving her no other means of propulsion. There's literally no fuel left."

Toby stared. "You mean she's running her engines on actual oil?"

Barnaby nodded. "They've increased her efficiency, but

she's a relic, soon to be dead."

"Not soon enough –" Hiko pointed – "look."

All along the *Banshee*, grappling hooks bristled and the cannons on her deckhouse turned to the *Phoenix*.

The captain planted his boots and rose to his feet.

Suddenly the *Banshee*'s wail cut off. The abrupt end of the siren was a shock that made the hissing of the rain seem like silence.

"Toby." Barnaby spoke without taking his eyes from the ship. "Take Polly and Hiko and hide beneath *Birdie*."

"I'm not hiding under a lifeboat." Toby staggered to his feet. "I *can* fight. I *should* fight." He closed a hand around Nix, biting off a grunt of pain. "It's wrong if I don't. Why should the rest of the crew go to battle if I don't? I'm your son – I should be setting an example." He raised Nix defiantly. "I don't want any of the crew to die for me."

Barnaby groaned. "You're hurt and you've never been in combat. I understand your frustration, but you're going to hide so I don't have to worry about you."

Toby opened his mouth.

"That's an order. I'm your captain and I'm telling you, if you don't go and hide right now, I'll lock you in the boiler room until Nisha and Rahul leave the ship and then I'll put you ashore with them."

Toby gaped and all heat fled his body. "You wouldn't."

"Hide, Toby, or this'll be your last voyage on the *Phoenix*."

"Come on." Hiko tugged him towards the launcher. "There's room for us both. Don't leave me alone."

"Everyone else will be fighting," Toby yelled as Hiko pulled him. "I'm in better shape than half the crew."

Polly landed on his shoulder in a flurry of feathers. "Be sensible, Toby." She nuzzled his ear. "This is a job for experienced fighters."

The captain's expression froze and Toby knew there was no arguing with him. Furious, he slid into the crawl space between the launcher and the *Phoenix*'s hull. Immediately he swivelled round so he could see out, kicking angrily at a bolt of waxed cloth at his feet.

The captain removed his glasses and tucked them into his jacket. Then he drew his long knife and blunderbuss, hefting them, one in each hand. "*Phoenix*, I know you're tired but the *Banshee* is upon us. Get up and fight if you can do so, or we're doomed."

A flurry of legs sped by Toby's face as a grappling hook landed on the *Phoenix*'s rail less than a metre from his hiding place. His instinct was to squirm free and cut the rope with Nix, but Dee reached the hook before he could move, sawed through the cable and tossed the hook into the sea.

Now grappling hooks fell upon them like iron snowflakes, clanging on to the deck and hooking over rails, masts and even the pylon that housed the crow's nest. Hiko ducked under Toby's shoulder, his whole body trembling.

Toby tightened an arm around the boy and was about to pull them further into shelter when his eyes met Crocker's and his heart sank. Crocker swung a wicked-looking fishing spear in one hand as he nudged his brother and crouched to peer into Toby's cubbyhole.

"That's right, little boy ... hide," Crocker sniggered. "The grown-ups will protect you."

Toby clenched his fists, but he had nothing to say in reply. He was hiding while Crocker and the others were preparing to fight.

SEVEN

Still sniggering, Crocker and Peel took up a position by the guardrail nearest Toby's hiding place. Peel's bulk blocked Toby's sight of the captain and he wriggled along the launcher to get a better view.

Polly nipped at him and Hiko caught at his shirt.

"Careful," Hiko whispered. "You're exposed."

"I'll be fine." He pushed Hiko behind him. "I need to see."

Arnav, Carson and the other walking wounded were scuttling along the guardrail, sawing at each of the hooks that landed, but the *Banshee* hooked the *Phoenix* faster than they could cut it free.

Toby clapped his hands over his ears as cannon fire boomed and he gasped as a ball of flaming junk smashed through the *Phoenix*'s siding. It dragged a canopy free, scattering the pirates, including Crocker and Peel. Pirates from the *Banshee* immediately began to rappel towards the gap.

Polly squawked and jumped on to Toby's back; she hopped along his spine until she reached his shoulder. "Get back underneath, Toby." She tugged his hair, but he ignored her.

Peel leaped to his feet, his rubber-soled shoes bouncing him on to the gangway. His face wore a snarl of fury as he hefted his cleaver.

The first of the *Banshee*'s pirates reached over the guardrail. With a vicious light in his eyes, Peel whipped his cleaver down, precisely where wrist met hand. The pirate went screaming into the sea. Blood splashed and Peel grinned through the scarlet that now flecked his fat face. Crocker capered at his elbow, stabbing with his spear and forcing invading pirates back off the ship. Like oiled boiler parts, Crocker herded the invaders towards Peel, who finished them off with his cleaver, or threw them overboard.

But the tide of invaders still flowed along dozens of grappling hooks and Toby realized the crew were going to be overwhelmed. With a sound like thunder, the captain's blunderbuss roared from the quarterdeck, spitting nails and other debris. Blood misted the air but the dragoon was a one-shot and the captain was already handing it back to Rita for a reload.

Swiftly, the pirates from the *Banshee* formed fighting

groups and began to head for the remains of the bridge.

Toby's hiding place prevented him from seeing everything, but he kept his eyes on the captain as he moved in and out of view, wielding his long knife as if he had been a soldier all his life.

Dee fought at his side. In her hands she held a metal-tipped staff. When an attacker ran at her, sword raised, Dee whipped her staff straight before her and thrust it towards his face. His head snapped back, his nose flattened, and she whirled the staff to sweep his legs out from beneath him. Finally she cracked his forehead with the butt to knock him unconscious and brought the staff back into a guard position. The whole thing had taken less than two heartbeats.

The crew of the *Phoenix* fought with anything they could get hold of – weighted ropes, fishing spears, rigging hooks, hammers and knives. Even Uma was using her club; applying it to heads and hands with surgical precision. Few of them had real swords though, not like Nix. Toby's fingers closed around his prize.

"I should be out there," he muttered.

"No, you shouldn't." Hiko's hand closed around Toby's leg and Polly squirmed her way beneath his chin.

"You'll have your chance to break my heart," she muttered. "But not today."

Hiko stared. "I've noticed that Polly is not a normal bird," he whispered.

"No, she isn't. Don't say anything to anyone else; they're not supposed to know."

His attention returned to the fight as Marcus fell back, cut from ear to chin. He landed in a tangle of plastic chair backs with a clatter.

The pirate who had attacked him launched himself at the captain, only to find himself knocked aside by Dee's staff and shouldered overboard by Amit and Ajay who were, as always, working together.

"Thank the gods they don't have guns," Toby muttered.

"There aren't many bullets left," Polly agreed. "And guns are no use for close-up fighting anyhow."

Still the *Banshee* pirates were managing to herd the crew of the *Phoenix* towards the shattered bridge and hem them in. Only Peel and Crocker remained near Toby's hiding place.

The pirates from the *Banshee* wore uniforms, Toby realized. Black leather jackets over black trousers. Their heads were shaven, even the women, and every head was tattooed with a screaming skull.

Toby swallowed. They were more organized than the crew of the *Phoenix* and they didn't seem to have suffered in the storm. The *Phoenix* was going to lose this battle.

"Toby!" Polly's warning squawk prevented him edging out of his hiding place as he tried to keep his eyes on the captain.

"Who's this, then?" Hard fingers crushed his throat, dragging him out of his hole. For a second Toby's legs caught; Hiko was trying to pull him back. He yelped as his knees caught on the top of the launcher and Hiko let him go.

He found himself wielded by the scruff of his neck.

"Release the boy."

Toby followed his captor's eyes to find Peel, barely recognizable with a bloodied face, half leaning on the remains of the guardrail with a pile of bodies at his feet. "He's a little bastard, but he's *our* little bastard."

Toby edged his hand inside his windcheater, seeking Nix.

"Cap'n Nell will be happy to meet *you*." His captor ignored Peel and grinned. His tattoo had been applied lopsided so that the twisted skull leered grimly at Toby from one side of his head.

"I said, put the boy down." Peel laboured to push himself straight. His eyes darted sideways to find support from his brother, but the pirate holding Toby snatched a crossbow from a holster behind his back and shot.

Peel staggered backwards as the arrow lodged under his collarbone.

The pirate crowed with laughter but his hand had loosened, so Toby dragged Nix free and stabbed upwards into the arm that held him. The tip of the sword sliced through leather and stuck. Toby recalled Peel's words and pushed hard. He felt the jolt along his forearm as the blade bit bone.

Blood slipped down Nix in oily rivulets. The pirate yelled and opened his fist. Toby remembered to keep a tight hold on Nix as the pirate jerked backwards and the sword came free of flesh with a sucking sound that made Toby want to gag.

Toby scuttled away, but the pirate barely paused before reloading his bow and pointing it at his head.

"You're coming with me."

With a flurry of feathers Polly flew at Toby's would-be kidnapper. The man held her off with his forearm and gestured with his weapon.

Seeing no choice, Toby rose slowly to his feet, still clutching a bloody Nix.

"Captain!" Peel shouted. He forced himself to his knees, ripping out the bolt that protruded from his shoulder. Blood gouted down his chest.

The pirate looked at Peel with a shake of his tattooed head. "Your captain's trapped." He turned back to Toby. "I know who you are, boy. If I get you to Nell, your ship is

114

ours with no more losses on our side."

"No!" Hiko hurtled from beneath the launcher and slammed into the pirate's legs. With a surprised yelp the pirate toppled backwards. His crossbow fired into the sky and with a final grasp at nothing he fell overboard, screaming until he hit the paddle's wheelhouse with a sickening thud.

They both stared at the empty spot. Then Hiko grabbed Toby and began to shove him back beneath the launcher.

Toby's eyes met Peel's and the old pirate sneered as he wobbled to his feet. He straightened his back, ignored his bleeding shoulder and jumped on top of the men surrounding Crocker.

Toby crawled back under the boat as fast as he could. Polly fluttered in and Toby was reaching to pull Hiko beside him when the boy screamed.

Huge hands wrapped around Hiko's waist and dragged him backwards.

Before Toby could wriggle out, the boy had been thrown to another invader who whooped and tossed him to yet another. Toby struggled to his feet and ran after his friend. He vaulted the fallen mast, but the *Phoenix* pitched as he jumped. His feet tangled in the sail and the rigging on the other side. Toby went down hard, his shoulder slammed on a metal spike and he vomited on to the deck as pain twisted his stomach into knots.

He pushed himself up on his hands in time to see Peel lunging after Hiko, too late. Before Toby could rise to his feet, Hiko was rappelled off ship towards the *Banshee*.

Toby gaped as Peel raced to the captain, then he rose shakily to his feet and staggered to the gunwale.

Polly flapped in his face. "Don't do it, Toby."

"Don't do what?" The hook in front of Toby dug into the *Phoenix*.

"I know what you're thinking, but you mustn't." Polly hopped up and down on his shoulder.

Toby turned as a bang and plume of smoke from the blunderbuss obscured his view of his father. The fighting on the quarterdeck was vicious and no one had a glance to spare for Toby. He ached to fight at his father's side, but the captain had his crew fighting alongside him. Hiko had no one.

Toby dragged his eyes from the blur of smoke. "Hiko saved my life, Polly. Twice. The boiler would have exploded without him and that pirate would've taken me."

"You don't owe him anything, he's a *stowaway*."

"He's only a kid. He must be scared out of his mind."

"Send someone else." Polly tightened her claws on his neck, frantic. "Stop trying to be a hero all the time."

"There isn't anyone else." Toby swung first one leg and

then the other over the gunwale, so that he was sitting on the railing. The *Banshee* was taller than the *Phoenix*; it was going to be hard work pulling himself across.

"No!" Polly wailed, as Toby caught hold of the cable linking the grappling hook to its mother ship. He jumped from the *Phoenix*, wrapped his legs around the thick wire and started to drag himself up the steep incline towards the *Banshee*.

EIGHT

"Go back, go back." Polly hopped desperately on the wire above Toby, making it shake.

"Stop it, Pol." Toby ground his teeth. "I'll fall." He looked down and froze. He was already a body length away from the *Phoenix* and there was nothing between him and the paddle cage below. Toby had never worried about heights, he enjoyed his stints in the crow's nest, but this was different.

Between the *Phoenix* and the *Banshee*, colliding junk crashed and smashed in the waves.

"Toby, your heart rate is up." Polly sprung from the cable, making it jerk once more, and flew around him.

"It's so far," Toby muttered. The rain-slick wire began to slip through his hands and he could not tear his eyes from the drop. He clamped his legs more tightly closed, and the thick line bit into the soft underside of his knees.

Then the sea rose, tilting the *Phoenix* and sliding Toby

past her paddle and closer to the waves. Beneath him an ancient washing machine surfaced, door gaping. It dragged a train of plastic bags behind it and seemed to turn to follow him, waiting to swallow Toby when he fell.

Then the washer was smashed between a forklift truck and a transit van. Toby moaned as the sea hauled the two crushing weights apart to reveal the misshapen bulk of the machine, twisted and dented. The washer sank and Toby knew currents of acid waited to corrode it into nothing.

The *Phoenix* tilted once more, tightening the grapple, and Toby was almost flung off the suddenly taut rope. His hands ached with the fierceness of his grip.

All too easily Toby could picture himself slipping from the cable and being impaled on the forklift below. The distance between the two ships suddenly seemed insurmountable. *What had he been thinking?*

"I can't do this." Toby moved a trembling arm to slide back towards the *Phoenix*.

"That's right," Polly crooned. "Go home."

Toby hesitated. If he went back now, he was abandoning Hiko to who knew what fate? The men of the *Banshee* had crawled over the rope. It was possible – Toby should be able to do it.

"I'll get someone, they'll pull you in." Polly fluttered higher.

"No," Toby groaned. "Don't." He set his jaw and turned to look at the *Banshee* once more. "It isn't that far." The cable creaked, drawn tight between the ships.

"It *is* that far, Toby. You're not strong enough."

"I *am*." Toby released one hand, closed it around the cable ahead of him, then heaved himself upwards. He panted with the effort but his body slid a little further.

"I can do this." He pinned his gaze on the cable, then slid his hands higher still and pulled. "I'm going to rescue Hiko."

"You're going to get yourself captured."

"Everybody on the *Phoenix* is fighting." Toby moved again, closer to the *Banshee*. "The *Banshee* will be almost empty and I'm good at avoiding people who want to hurt me."

"Peel's different, Crocker, too. The captain would kill them if they really hurt you."

"Ha!" Toby snorted and pulled once more.

"I'm serious, Toby. You must go back." Polly wheeled in tighter and tighter circles, agitation making her flight erratic. Toby gasped as a gust of wind rocked the cable and he swung sideways. He shut his eyes until the swaying eased.

Polly landed on the cable by his foot, careful not to make it bounce. "Please listen to me, Toby. This is rash.

You haven't got a plan."

"Just let me get there and I'll make one." Toby moved a tiny bit further, pausing as the wind lashed his hair into his face. "I'm not leaving Hiko." Toby blinked a splatter of rain from his eyes. "He's the only other kid I've ever met, Polly. I want him on board."

"Toby, I know that you're lonely..."

"You wouldn't understand." Toby bunched his legs to try pushing this time. He moved further up, then the cable loosened again as the ships anchoring it rocked towards one another. Toby hung like a gull, unmoving, until they pitched sideways and tightened the rope again.

"Toby, I'm the only one of my kind." Polly walked along the cable, keeping close to his feet. "The only one there will ever be." She cocked her head at him.

"I'm not doing this because I'm the only kid on board, Pol – that would be dumb." Toby pulled again. "I'm doing it because I can't just hide while they do who knows what to the boy who saved my life. Can't you see that?" He raised his head and looked towards the *Banshee*. She filled his vision now. "Won't you help me? I can't do this alone."

"What choice do I have?" she snapped, and flew from his feet on to the unfamiliar gunwale. "It's clear." She peered down at him. "You idiot."

Toby grinned, opened his legs and released the cable. His

stomach muscles tightened as he prepared to somersault backwards over the rail and on to the *Banshee*'s deck.

That was when the *Banshee* started to wail.

Toby hung motionless, his ears ringing. The cable in his hands vibrated from the intensity of the ship's howl and his fingers began to slip. He threw his legs back around the wire.

"Is it me? Do they know I'm here?"

The sound had forced Polly to take off and now she landed back on the rail above him. "It's not you, Toby. Look." She tilted her head to indicate a cable running from the *Banshee*'s bow.

A distant fork of lightning lit the sky as a woman in a coat that flapped like the wings of a crow flew along a zip wire to the *Phoenix*'s pylon mast.

At the last second, she released the strap and flipped to touch down on the prow of the *Phoenix*, feet splayed a shoulder-width apart.

The moment she landed, the wail cut off.

Toby dangled in the sudden silence. "Is that…?" he whispered.

Polly fixed her eyes on the *Phoenix*. "Captain Nell of the *Banshee*."

"What does she want?"

"I can fly over and find out," Polly suggested.

Toby shook his head. "I need you here." He completed his somersault on to the *Banshee*'s deck and crouched. He pressed his face against the cold metal of the ship's side, but his brief rest was disturbed by a hiss.

Toby lifted his face to see Polly standing in front of him, her wings spread to make herself as large as possible. In front of them... Toby blinked. In front of them a mangy cat crouched on a bollard. The black feline, fur patchy with scars, stared at them steadily. Then it opened its mouth and started to yowl.

Toby looked around for something to throw at the thing, but the deck was empty. "Shh, puss." Toby made frantic calming gestures with his hands, but the cat's tail shot up behind it and bushed out like a boiler brush.

"Make it stop, Polly."

Its ears flattened.

Polly stamped towards the animal, hissing back at it. The cat retreated, showing pointed teeth.

Toby edged forward. "Shut up, cat. Go away."

Polly made a sudden lunge towards the animal, flapping her wings and cawing. The cat jumped in the air, all four feet leaving the ground. Then it turned and vanished around a corner.

Polly flew on to the bollard the cat had vacated. "I'll find you a hiding place." Her tail bobbed and she flew in the opposite direction to the cat.

Toby crouched, digging his nails into his leather gloves. The deck of the *Banshee* under his bare toes was very different to the *Phoenix*. He could feel her massive pistons chugging beneath his feet, shuddering as she sucked at the last of her reserves.

The *Banshee* was huge. She was a city compared to the *Phoenix*'s small town. Toby realized that he could, for the first time, look at his own ship from the outside.

Toby exhaled. He hadn't even known that the rustproof paint his father had used on the *Phoenix* was orange. The corrosive sea had faded it so that she looked like a shard of sunset floating on the waves. A stylized phoenix decorated her hull and Toby realized that the image on his Nix was a copy. A shout drew his attention to the deck of the *Phoenix*.

To Toby's relief, the arrival of Nell on board appeared to have stopped the fighting. Now both captains faced one another across the quarterdeck. His father waved his hands angrily and Toby saw the crew of the *Phoenix* abruptly raise their weapons and shout. The *Banshee*'s pirates remained unmoving. They had clustered behind Nell, awaiting her orders.

Toby's hand closed on Nix as a sound drew his attention back to his own predicament.

To his right a pyramid of compressed junk balls

was shifting in time with the rolling salt. Netting held them in place, but the top one had thudded to the bottom. Toby blinked: the pyramids dotted the deck, beside cannons that shone black on oiled rollers. The *Banshee* could have destroyed the *Phoenix* at any time, so what were they after?

Now Toby's eye fell on a giant trebuchet that rested on a turntable. The catapult was surrounded by its ammunition: car engines, truck beds, anything big and heavy enough to cause serious damage.

Six men were loading the weapon but there was no joking, singing or complaining as they worked. Their tattooed skulls glistened under the glow of lightning from the storm that was gaining once more on the immobilized ships.

"That's aimed at the *Phoenix*," Toby murmured.

Polly landed beside him in a flurry of feathers. Her processor whirred. "I calculate the payload will hit the main pylon and bring it down on top of the mess hall and pump hatch."

"The injured are in the mess hall. Big Pad…" Toby shut his eyes against the image. "Are they going to fire?"

Polly squawked quietly. "It's possible."

"But not while Nell's over there, right?" Toby spun back to look at the *Phoenix*. He didn't know what Nell was saying, but his father sagged and was caught in Uma's strong arms. The wind carried an anguished wail carried across the sea. "Toby!"

Toby leaned over the side. "What's happening?"

"Your father knows you're missing."

Toby hung his head. "What do I do?"

"Fetch Hiko and return as soon as possible."

"You're not telling me to go straight home?" He raised his eyebrows.

"I should." Polly bit his thumb gently. "But I found him."

"Where?"

"Other side of the bridge. He's in a cage. You're right, we can't just leave the boy."

Toby peered around the deck housing. The bridge was fully enclosed. It hunched towards the stern of the ship behind the trebuchet and its half-dozen guards. The windows of the bridge were narrow but Toby assumed that anyone inside would be able to see out in any direction. The question was – was there anyone inside or not?

He shuffled his feet. "How do I get there without being seen?"

Polly nudged his face, turning him. "I found some passages set into the deck. If you can get into one, you'll be able to get close."

"Right." Toby was about to edge into the open when there was a shout from one of the guards by the trebuchet.

He was pointing towards the *Phoenix*. Slowly Toby turned.

Nell must have signalled because the man suddenly raced towards the prow. He pounded past Toby's hiding place without seeing him. Toby pressed himself against the side of the deck housing, straining to see as the man gripped a winch on the end of the zip wire Nell had used, and started to wind.

On the *Phoenix*, Nell reached one-handed for the strap and hurdled over the side. Toby heard her shout something but the sense of her words was lost as the storm broke overhead once more.

"They're coming back," Polly squawked in his ear. "Move it, Toby."

The crew of the *Banshee* were abandoning the *Phoenix* like rats. Ignoring the driving rain, each rappelled up the cables linking the two ships.

Toby was in deep trouble.

NINE

"This way." Polly shuffled on his shoulder. "Quick."

Now Nell was back on board, Toby didn't dare move. He made himself as small as possible, pressed between the bollard and deck housing, and watched as Nell looked around with her hands on her hips.

Nell looked as old as his father, and her hair was cropped short, streaked with grey and stuck to her forehead by the rain. Her eyes were like shards of ice. Toby shrank back as though she could see him, but her gaze never reached his hiding place.

"Where's Ayla?" Her voice was a low rasp as if, once upon a time, she had screamed so hard it had never recovered.

"She's dealing with the prisoner, Captain. Do you want to see him?" The guard stopped coiling the winch rope and straightened.

"I've more important things to do than meet Toby Ford. Tell Ayla to get the crew below deck." Nell turned her sharp-eyed gaze to the sky. "I've told the *Phoenix* we'll weather the storm and then I expect the coordinates. If they don't give them to me, we'll return the boy to them rather faster than they'd like." She indicated the trebuchet then stretched, wincing a little.

"Some of the men are wondering…" The guard ducked his head as he spoke, but Nell nodded for him to go on. "Are you sure there really are coordinates? The old man was mad and when you're tortured you'll say anything to make it stop." He rubbed a hand over his scarred head. "Isn't it better to strip the *Phoenix* down and take everything they have?"

Nell sneered and looked around at her crew surrounding her. "We've got Ford's son in the cage. He *will* bring me those coordinates. But we won't be letting our enemy go afterwards. We'll have those solar panels and everything else the *Phoenix* has got, too." The crew cheered.

"Everyone get below." Nell curled her lip and directed her attention back to the guard who had winched her home. "I don't like questions. Deliver my message to Ayla, then you can guard the prisoner during the storm."

The man nodded and edged away from his captain. Then he turned and ran towards the bridge.

Toby swallowed. "What does she mean they've got Ford's son in the cage? I'm Ford's son."

Polly nestled into his neck. "The captain doesn't allow kids on his ship – you're the only one. When they found a kid on the *Phoenix*, they assumed it was you."

"But he's younger than me."

"Nell would know that – she's been at sea almost as long as the captain – but she hasn't laid eyes on Hiko yet."

"If the captain believes Nell has me prisoner, he'll deliver our coordinates for the solar panels to the *Banshee*." Toby closed his eyes. "We can't let that happen."

Polly squawked quietly. "What do you want to do?"

A band of uniformed pirates ran past Toby, their shoulders hunched against the worsening weather. He held his breath, but none looked round. Swiftly they vanished into hatches. They were a disciplined crew that made the pirates on the *Phoenix* look like rabble.

Toby inhaled sharply as a gust of wind lashed him with a whip of rain. "We've got until the storm passes, while both crews are below deck. Let's get Hiko, rappel back to the *Phoenix* and tell them to run before all hell breaks loose."

He ducked behind the deck housing again as Nell splashed towards the bridge, her long legs eating up the deck.

Once she was past, Toby edged out. Not far from the winch housing, Toby spotted one of the sunken passages

Polly had mentioned. He lowered himself down with a splash.

Toby held Nix ahead of him and edged forwards. Standing water sloshed around his ankles as he walked. He still hadn't met a crew member, but the longer he went without being seen, the harder his heart thumped in his chest.

"You, there. Stop. All hands below deck."

It was with a kind of awful relief that Toby realized he had been spotted. Even as his heart sunk, he straightened, tightened his hand around Nix and turned.

A single member of the *Banshee*'s crew stood silhouetted above him.

"You're not crew. Who are you?" The voice was high, undoubtedly female. Toby's hand tightened on Nix and he sidestepped as the figure cartwheeled from the deck to land in front of him.

As she flew, a long coat like Nell's flapped behind her. Her booted feet landed with a bone-jarring thud. Next to her the scrawny cat landed on silent paws. Toby watched as it wound itself around his legs, claws ticking through the puddles on the walkway.

Then it went to sit beside its mistress, growling low in its throat, as if daring Toby to move.

As the figure straightened, Toby stared. He was facing a

girl who had to be about his age. His hand loosened on Nix.

All the crewmen of the *Banshee* that Toby had seen so far were shaven and tattooed; men or women, it didn't seem to matter. This girl wore her long hair loose. Tiny braids decorated with beads and feathers kept it from falling into her eyes. Beneath the decoration, her hair was the colour of oil – a shiny black with prisms of colour beneath.

Toby balanced against the rise and fall of the ship and stared. The girl's eyes were shockingly green – algae on seawater. Her face was as tanned as Toby's own, but her skin was not as salt-burned or work-rough. She hadn't the perfect face of the girls Toby had seen in his dreams. Her cheeks were hollow, her nose had clearly been broken at least once and she had a thin scar bisecting her lower lip.

As he exhaled, his breath shivered in the air between them and the girl put her hands on her hips to reveal black leather trousers and a tight waxed jerkin beneath her coat.

"Polly want a cracker," Polly muttered, her warning obvious.

The cat hissed and Polly squawked angrily.

"I told them that boy was too young to be Ford's son. *You're* Toby, aren't you?" The girl frowned. "Then who do we have in the cage?"

Toby growled. "That's Hiko. I'm taking him home."

Finally he stepped backwards to run and the girl grinned.

"I don't think so, *boy*." Before Toby could react, she had grabbed his shoulders, slammed her forehead between his eyes, released him and leaped back.

Toby reeled from the sudden viciousness of the head-butt. Flashes of light burst in his vision and pain stabbed through his head. Half blind, he staggered, secured his grip on Nix and swung blindly.

The girl had already drawn a long knife from her belt. Nix clanged into the knife and struck on the hilt with an impact that shuddered up Toby's arm.

He pulled free. "Sorr—" Half an apology slipped out, but the girl was already taking back her knife and lashing out with steel toecaps. Instinctively Toby blocked with Nix, making barely a dent in her thick boot leather. At the same time he remembered Callum's favourite move from their sparring sessions and stepped in closer to her, his elbow aimed for her face.

The girl blocked with her own elbow and swung her left fist. Toby spun backwards, trying for the leg sweep, but the girl was also spinning, her coat flying behind her with a snap. Both missed.

They paused, panting and glaring at one another. Toby held Nix up and the girl held her knife in one hand, weaving it back and forth in front of her face. The other fist was closed in front of her sternum, protecting herself.

"Who are you?" Toby gasped, but the girl shook her head.

Then they were moving again. She slashed for Toby's throat, but Nix flew, blocking her attack. Toby pressed against her knife and shoved her backwards. Then he lashed out with his feet, trying to plant his heel in her stomach. The girl shifted, but he caught her side. Air flew out of her, then she was already hacking towards his ankle. Toby moved, but not fast enough; pain burned and his blood dripped on to the deck. He hopped, sparing a quick glance downwards. A line of scarlet ran down his shin. He put his injured leg behind him, and raised Nix high, pinning his eyes on the delicate fingers that held the knife.

Polly flapped anxiously and the cat yowled, swiping upwards with wickedly sharp claws.

As Toby glanced towards his parrot, the girl feinted. Toby went to block, only to find a fist hammering into his kidney. It hurt, but he'd survived worse from Peel. He was lucky she had missed his injured rib. Somehow Toby managed to turn his lurch into a low block, caught her next slice on his leather glove, put his back to her and planted his elbow in her sternum.

The girl's howl of rage was silenced by the outrushing of air. As she bent, Toby pressed his advantage by turning and hammering his fist into her side. Then he leaped backwards, leaving her to totter into the hull and lean on the wall, retching.

Toby gave her space. "You know who I am. Tell me who you are."

The girl curled her lip, panting heavily. "I'm the one who'll be taking *you* in."

"Then tell me your name." Toby pointed Nix towards his feet.

Eventually the girl shrugged. "My name is Ayla and I am second in command on the *Banshee*." She raised her knife. "And seeing as you're so fascinated by names, this is Boudicca." She gestured with her blade to point to the cat. "I've been easy on you so far, but not any more. Will you come quietly?"

"Not likely." Toby flicked Nix up and danced out of her reach once more. "How come you're second in command? You're no older than me."

"We don't have kids on the *Banshee*," Ayla sneered. "I'm as good as the old men here and I'm second in command because the captain trusts me." She showed her teeth in a blistering smile. "I am her daughter, after all."

"I'm no kid," Toby spat. "Without me the *Phoenix* is dead in the water. I'm chief engineer."

"Sure you are." Ayla smirked. "That's why you're skulking around over here."

Toby flushed and shoved Ayla so hard that Nix clanged into the wall. Ayla staggered and, as a flash of lightning lit the sky above them, she lost her footing and her head smacked into a protruding chock with a dull thud.

She slid to the ground.

The water in the passageway was flowing steadily. Toby gasped as icy rain filled his lungs.

Ayla rolled face down, the water came up to her ears and her coat began to float.

"Damn." Toby put Nix back in his belt, rolled her over and dragged her into a sitting position, his fingers numb on her narrow shoulders.

The cat hissed, trying to drive Toby away.

Toby caught her coat and dragged it until it hung over the chock to hold Ayla up. Her chin sagged on to her chest and her hair dropped in front of her, the beads chiming.

"She'll be fine." Polly landed on his shoulder and poked him with her beak. "We have to get Hiko and hide until the storm eases enough to escape back to the *Phoenix*. This way." Polly's claws were sharp on his shoulder as she shifted her weight then launched herself into the air.

Toby raced along the passageway after her, splashing through the rising water.

The passageway ran into a hatch and terminated in a ladder. Almost blinded by the rain, Toby looked up. His sodden parrot drooped on the top rung.

"Go on," he encouraged her.

Polly heaved a sigh and hopped on to the deck. There was no cry of warning from above.

"All clear." She didn't land on his shoulder, so much as tumble there in her own small gale. Toby helped her get a grip on his shirt then started up. "How far from the bridge am I? Will Nell see me through a window?" He had to shout now above the wind and rain.

"It's a risk," Polly agreed. "So move fast."

As soon as Toby put his head above the passage his breath was stolen by the gale and replaced by rain. He rolled on to the deck and lay flat; if he stood, there was a good chance he'd be blown overboard.

The sky above rumbled with a deep boom of thunder that shook the deck beneath him and immediately the clouds lit with a bright fork that scalded his eyes.

Polly bit his ear. "You can't stay there."

Toby struggled on to all fours and began to crawl past the bridge.

Polly scrabbled beneath him, claws ticking on the deck. Her feathers were so wet that Toby could almost see her metal casing gleam beneath them.

Just then the *Banshee* tilted as a great wave tipped her and Toby was rolled towards the rail. A coil of rope tangled his legs and he swung round, cracking his bruised shoulders on a cannon and coming to rest against a pyramid of ammunition. He tangled his fingers in the net that held it in place and scrambled to his knees again.

His roll had actually brought him closer to the other side of the bridge. This time he scuttled from cannon to cannon, taking advantage of the netting to provide handholds as the ship pitched. The grappling hooks holding the *Phoenix* in place creaked as the cables stretched to their limit.

As Toby rolled beneath another muzzle, his mind returned to the girl he had left in the passageway. When she woke she would be searching for him. Was she still unconscious? Then he rounded the bridge, saw the cage and forgot about her altogether.

The guard he had seen questioning Nell was crouched against the forecastle wall, gripping on to the bars.

Hiko was huddled as far away from him as possible. Toby could already see bruises blooming on his arms and legs, and his right eye socket shone with a swelling purple lump.

The guard had his head down and his collar up, trying to protect himself from the worst of the weather.

"They shouldn't have left him out in this," Toby growled.

"It works out better for us." Polly wound her way into his shirt. "Even if the guard calls the alarm, who'll hear him?"

Toby nodded.

"Are you sure about this?" Polly nipped his chest, but Toby ignored her and drew Nix.

Remaining low to the deck, Toby crept towards the cage. He got within a body length of the guard before the man looked up.

His bloodshot eyes widened and he jerked to his feet, reaching for the knife in his waistband. Toby leaped with Nix held above him.

The guard's knife clattered on to the gangway as Toby crashed into him and he yelled, but Toby smashed Nix's pommel into his mouth. Toby felt a crunch as teeth shattered under his fist then he grabbed the man and rolled him away from the cage. Polly landed on the cage, chirruping at Hiko.

The *Banshee* rolled again and Toby and the guard slid together, kicking and yelling, towards the rail. Toby wriggled an arm free and bashed the guard with Nix until his grip on Toby loosened. Then Toby jerked free, grabbed the muzzle of the cannon and kicked the guard as hard as he could towards the railing.

The guard clawed at Toby but, with a look of horror on his face, he crashed into the barrier in front of the cannon and flew overboard. Toby's eyes fixed on the guard's with dawning horror as the man plummeted into the poisonous salt. Toby turned his face away as a car bonnet knocked him below the waves. The junk closed over the man's head as though he had never been.

Panting heavily, Toby crawled back to Hiko's cage. The boy was crouched in front of the door, his hands wrapped around the hinges, staring at Polly.

"The girl says they're going to fire me from a cannon," he said.

"No, they won't." Toby examined the door. It was secured with a thick brass padlock. "Do you know where the keys are?" he shouted.

"The girl has them."

"Great." If only he'd searched the girl before he'd left her. "What do you think, Polly?" He rattled the door. "Have I got time to take these hinges apart?"

Polly cocked her head at the screws. "Get moving. Lucky you're still wearing your tool belt."

Toby pulled up his shirt and selected a Phillips screwdriver. He squinted into the rain, and forced the shaft into the rusting head of the screw. Agonizingly slowly, the screw started to lift. "Can you get the rest out with your fingers, Hiko? I'll start on the next one."

Hiko struggled to get a grip on the wet metal, but

eventually wrapped his ragged shirt around his fingers and nodded.

Toby began to unscrew the next hinge. As he worked a crack of thunder boomed overhead. Toby paused, waiting for the lightning, but it was three counts before it lit up the deck.

"The storm's passing." His eyes widened.

"The crew will be back on deck soon." Polly hopped up and down.

Toby shoved his screwdriver back in his belt and caught the screw with numb fingers. It slid between his thumb and forefinger, slicing the skin, but he ignored the stinging pain and forced it to turn. Hiko's screw dropped on to the deck at the same time that Toby's pulled free.

"Step back," he said as he caught the sides of the door and started to lift.

The metal was slippery and almost too heavy for him. He groaned, certain he could hear booted feet behind him.

"Hurry, Toby," Hiko whispered.

Toby nodded and strained. Finally the door lifted free, swivelled on the padlock and tilted to one side, leaving just enough room for Hiko to squeeze through.

Toby grabbed his hand and pulled him out, then started towards the nearest grappling hook that ran right over to the *Phoenix's* pylon.

"Too late," Polly shrieked, as the door to the bridge slammed open. "Hide."

"We can make it," Toby cried, but Hiko was already running towards the stern.

Toby reached for him and missed. The boy slid under a cannon and vanished into the shadows beneath. Toby darted after him. "I'm too big to get in there." Polly flew at his side. "Where can I go?"

"There." She indicated a box sticking out from the decking just a few steps away from Hiko's hiding place. Toby slid into its shelter, just as someone began to shout.

Feeling desperately exposed he looked about him. He caught Hiko's eye and gestured to the wire linking the two ships, but Hiko shook his head and shrank further into the darkness. Toby clenched his fists. He could make the rope if he ran, but he wouldn't have time to drag Hiko with him.

"Find him!" The voice was Nell's.

Hiko's empty cage had given them away.

TEN

The *Banshee*'s wail started up and Toby clamped his hands over his ears. The sound was even worse on the host ship than it had been on the *Phoenix*.

Toby crouched as small as he could. He didn't think it would take them more than a minute to find him, but somehow no one came near. They were searching around the trebuchet, the lifeboats, the sunken gangways, but no one thought to look on the bare stern.

The *Banshee*'s wail cut off and Toby pressed his back against the cupboard that sheltered him.

"What's happening?" Toby whispered hoarsely.

Polly took a chance and glided to the rail. Toby held his breath until she returned.

"Your father is on his way over, on *Birdie*."

Toby clenched his fists. "We can't let him board."

"I don't think we have a choice," Polly muttered, as the *Banshee*'s winches were lowered. "We just have to hope that he has a plan to get *off* this ship as well as on it."

"He won't leave without me. And Nell can't hand me over. It'll be a battle. He'll be killed." Tears filled Toby's eyes. "What have I done?"

Polly crawled under his arm. "It isn't over till the swan sings," she whistled. Then she nudged him until he peered around the stoop.

"Look, most of the pirates are waiting for your father to arrive. They aren't looking for you any more."

"Great." Toby pulled back again. "But now we can't leave." He leaned his head back. His bruised rib throbbed painfully. Toby listened, utterly miserable, as *Birdie* was hoisted over the side of the *Banshee*. Then Nell laughed as his father sprung on to the enemy's deck.

"Where's my son?" he roared.

"I take it you have the coordinates."

"Of course. Where's Toby?"

"You get him after I get the coordinates. Come with me to the bridge." A pause. "Just you, Barnaby."

"Not a chance."

Toby groaned. Marcus was there, too.

"Where the captain goes, we go."

Toby ground his teeth. "That's right, Marcus, you tell her."

"And what do you think you can do against my whole

144

crew?" Nell's voice held a sneer.

"We don't care." Amit. Which meant that the captain had brought Ajay as well. Toby pressed the heels of his hands against his eyes. "You aren't taking our captain off alone. He stays with us, or we go with him." Their feet thudded on the gangway as they climbed from *Birdie*.

"Such loyalty. I see you haven't managed to train your men to follow orders, Barnaby. Fine, come with me to the bridge ... *all* of you."

Amit, Ajay and Marcus – three pirates he thought of as brothers, and his father. Toby hoped that they had an excellent plan.

Silence fell on the deck of the *Banshee* and Toby clutched Nix on his knee. What was going on? Toby closed his eyes. While they were still inside, whatever the captain was doing had to be working. Didn't it? He banged his head on the cupboard in despair, scraping his ear on what felt like a catch. Curiosity made him turn to see a door at his back, too small for a person to fit inside. "What's this, Pol?" he whispered.

Her processor whirred. "On a previous Destroyer class it would have been part of the steering mechanism. I'm sure Nell has made adjustments, but I'd still bet that it has something to do with the steering."

Toby's eyes lit up. "Are you thinking what I'm thinking?"

"I doubt it," Polly snapped.

Toby flicked the screwdriver out of his tool belt and spun it around his fingers. Then he opened the small hatch and got to work.

The abrupt slamming of the bridge door made him freeze.

"I thought you felt more for your son than *this*," Nell was shrieking. "You tried to fool *me*? Did you forget who I am?"

"I know who you are." His father's voice was low. He was trying to calm her down. "Don't hurt Toby."

Toby exhaled. They had a chance. If his father hadn't brought the real coordinates, Nell might send him back to the *Phoenix* to fetch them.

"You thought you could have both your son *and* the solar panels," Nell was saying.

Toby smiled grimly. "That's right," he muttered.

"Stupid, arrogant man." Papers flew by Toby, bundling over the stern like pale birds. Nell had tossed them to the wind. "Were any of those pages real?"

"Some. You have to admit, it was worth a try." His father was attempting to be charming. Toby decided to keep doing his own job as long as he could and switched from his screwdriver to his pliers.

"Not really." Nell tapped a foot. "See, now I get to

destroy the *Phoenix*, kill your son and take the real coordinates from the ruins of your ship which, frankly, I was planning to do anyway." Her voice was a scream as she addressed her crew. "Take them."

"Oh no." Toby looked up again, his fingers numb on his tools. On his shoulder Polly lurched from one foot to the other.

"Wait." Marcus's voice. "I'm a damn good forger, was nearly hanged for it when a client gave me up. How did you know the coordinates were fake?"

An uneasy quiet fell on Toby's ears and he pocketed his pliers.

"Easy," Nell answered eventually. "The coordinates you gave, the place you tried to tell me there are sunken solar panels? I've been there." Toby heard, in her voice, the ghost of a long-buried memory. "There are no solar panels. There's nothing there worth having at all. At least, not since the *Banshee* left."

Toby shuddered.

Marcus grunted. "Damn. Can I show you something before your crew finishes us off?"

Toby leaned carefully around the side of the box. Marcus was handing Nell a flask.

"What's this?" Liquid sloshed as Nell shook the offering. "You buying me a drink, sailor?"

"Not a drink. Open it."

Toby pulled back and pictured Nell unscrewing the cap and putting the flask to her nose.

"Oil." Greed was definitely there.

Toby smiled grimly. "I reckon I made enough mess, what do you say, Polly?" He sat back.

Polly peered over his shoulder. "Put the hatch back and they won't even know why they can't steer any more."

"Right." Toby closed the door carefully and screwed it shut.

"We hit lucky during a recent salvage operation." His father was speaking now. "The oil is in barrels on the *Phoenix*. But there's a lookout in the crow's nest watching us. Anything happens and my second in command has orders to mix the oil with sand."

"Clever." Polly whistled and Toby nodded.

"You wouldn't," Nell gasped.

"We would." The captain sounded smug. "Give me my boy back, send us on our way and I'll make sure the barrels are sent over. I shouldn't have tried to fool you. The oil is yours."

Nell snorted. "Strangely, Barnaby, I don't trust you. Go back to your *Phoenix*, send over the oil *and* the real coordinates. Then I'll return your son. If you don't, I'll

148

have him thrown overboard. It's a long drop from the deck of the *Banshee*."

Toby listened as his father strode back towards *Birdie*. He could hear the frustration in the heavy thud of his father's boots, but he felt a thrill of relief. As soon as *Birdie* launched, Toby and Hiko could run for the cable and rappel across to the *Phoenix*. They might yet get off the *Banshee* alive.

"Captain."

Toby's heart sank. It was the girl he had left in the sunken passageway: Nell's daughter. "The boy in the cage isn't Barnaby's son. He's an imposter, and—"

"An imposter," Nell spat. "I suppose nothing on the *Phoenix* is what it seems, eh, Barnaby. Do you even have oil, or is this flask all there is?" Toby heard the bottle slosh as Nell shook it. "But you care about this boy, yes? Not enough to hand over the real coordinates, but enough to try and save him with fakes when you could have run."

"Don't do something you'll regret, Nell." Toby could sense his father's mind racing. If Nell didn't have his son, where was he?

"Oh, there's only one thing in my long life that I regret, Barnaby." There was a pregnant pause.

It was time to go.

Toby took a deep breath, skidded across the deck, reached

under the cannon and dragged Hiko out by the arm.

"There they are," Ayla shouted.

Toby met his father's eye. Barnaby lurched towards him, but Toby shook his head.

"Use the zip wires," Toby yelled to his father. As pirates from the *Banshee* sprinted towards the stern of their ship, he caught Hiko's wrist and they ran for the cable. "Hold on, Hiko."

"Crackers!" Polly shrieked, as Hiko clambered on to Toby's back and wrapped his legs around his stomach.

Toby didn't even pause at the *Banshee*'s rail. He whipped off his scarf, wrapped it round the cable and, ignoring Hiko's weight, he leaped.

His head jerked back as a pirate's swiping hand clawed at him. For a second they all hung, gasping, over the side, but then Polly flew into the woman's face and she released him with a shriek. Then they started to slide.

Toby looked back to see Ayla crash into the railing. Her oil-black hair flew in a gust of wind and she pushed it back from her eyes, watching him across the waves. He tore his gaze from her and turned back to the *Phoenix*, which was coming up on them, fast.

On the deck of the *Phoenix*, pirates were rushing to the end of the cable he was flying on, already reaching out for him.

"Cut the lines!" Nell's voice carried across the water.

For one horrifying moment Toby felt his cable go slack, but then hands closed around him and he and Hiko thudded on to the deck.

Below him the line slid into the sea. The loosened hook landed on deck, then slithered off under the weight of the line attached to it.

Toby rolled out of its way, Hiko still clinging to his back.

Toby's breath was shallow. "Let go, Hiko," he gasped. Hiko released him and he sat up with tears in his eyes.

"Can anyone see the captain? Rahul, can you see him?" Toby yelled at the crow's nest.

"They're coming, Toby," Rahul cried. "*Phoenix*, get ready to catch them."

Toby whipped round to see the captain, Marcus, Amit and Ajay, all flying along cables towards the *Phoenix*, copying Toby, their scarves fraying as they flew. Polly raced alongside, chivvying them with wild squawking.

Over on the *Banshee* pirates worked, frantically sawing at cables.

Marcus was first to land. He flipped on to his feet and immediately turned to catch Ajay.

The captain and Amit were not so lucky. Their cables split with the sound of cracking wire.

Toby screamed as his father disappeared from view.

He scrabbled to his feet and ran for the railing. Fifteen feet below, Amit was clutching the razor wire of the paddle cage with one hand and the captain with the other. Blood dripped down his arm and beside them their empty cables swung.

"Throw us a rope. *Now.*" Amit's face was creased with agony.

"He's going to lose his bloody fingers." Peel was already tossing a coil overboard. The rope snaked down the side of the *Phoenix* and hit Barnaby in the back. Immediately he wrapped one arm around the rope and the other around Amit, who released the wire. Then Peel started to haul them up.

As the captain was helped on board, Uma grabbed Amit and pursed her lips over his hand worriedly.

"They've got a trebuchet aimed at us." Toby shouldered his way to her side. "If they fire it'll hit the mess hall. We have to run."

The captain followed Toby's gaze over to the *Banshee.* Nell stood next to her daughter. For a long second the two captains stood, glaring at one another. Then Nell raised her hand.

"She's going to fire." The captain burst into action. "Marcus, throw that barrel overboard. Harry, start the engines. Everyone else, find something to hold."

Marcus and Arnav rolled the barrel to the broken rail and tossed it overboard. Toby heard Nell's cry as the plastic shattered against the side of the *Phoenix* and black oil exploded over her hull.

"There's more where that came from," the captain yelled.

"Hold fire," Nell cried. "We need that oil."

Toby spun. "Cut the grappling hooks." The *Phoenix*'s crew were already moving, slicing rope after rope and tossing metal hooks into the sea after the clattering cables.

With a jerk and a purr Toby felt the *Phoenix* settle as her old engines turned over.

"I'm coming for you, Barnaby," Nell howled. "You can't outrun the *Banshee*. And when I board you, the first one on the point of my sword is your son."

The captain looked around at the battered men and women of the *Phoenix*. Most leaned, either on rails or on one another. Weakened bow legs were more splayed than usual. Blood stood out scarlet against skin that was paper pale. Limbs dangled, weighed down by weapons they could barely lift. Exhaustion lined every face.

"We won't win another battle," Barnaby muttered.

The *Phoenix* was already moving. She pulled out from the shadow of the *Banshee* with a crunch of shifting junk.

"After them!" Nell waved. "Prepare more grappling hooks. Destroy them!"

153

Toby closed his hands on the railing, watching the *Banshee*. Her siren chased them across the bouncing waves, but she was not turning. The *Phoenix* loved her old engines and she was flying – ten knots already and heading hungrily for her top speed of fifteen.

Nell's howl of frustration was buried beneath the *Banshee*'s wail.

"Why isn't she following?" The captain leaned over the rail beside Toby. "What do you know that I don't?"

Polly settled on Toby's shoulder and checked that none of the crew could hear. "He wrecked their steering mechanism, Captain. The *Banshee* can move, but not in the direction Nell wants her to go. The only way she'll turn is with those oars and that'll take time."

"You did that?" The captain stared at his son. "I'm not sure whether to hug you or kill you right now." His wrinkles drew into a frown. "You have no idea how it felt hearing that you had been taken to the *Banshee*, so I'm leaning towards murder." Then he glared at Polly. "As for you, you bloody useless parrot. You're supposed to be able to predict his behaviour. Why do I need you, if you're going to let him do things like this?"

"Hormones," Polly muttered, ducking her head. "He's becoming unpredictable."

"You're the most advanced AI there has ever been."

The captain leaned closer and spoke in a low voice. "Factor them in."

He turned to Toby. "Get down to the mess hall and take Hiko with you. You'd better hope Uma gives you a clean bill of health or I'll give you a few injuries myself."

Toby clutched Polly and backed away from his father. Then he caught Crocker's furious glower.

"That's right, Crocker," Toby said, his eyes narrowed. "I went off the *Phoenix*. I sabotaged the *Banshee* and I rescued Hiko. What do you think of that?"

ELEVEN

Hounded by the captain's final growl, Toby and Hiko sped towards the mess hall.

"I didn't think anyone would come," Hiko said, as they jogged past the galley. "Thank you."

Toby stopped. "Of course I came. You're a member of the *Phoenix*'s crew. We're family."

"My family left me before," Hiko muttered.

Toby stared down at him. "Really?"

"My father died and the man my mother was travelling with sold me at the bazaar. She tried to stop him, but he beat her. That was the last sight I have of my mother – it's how I remember her." His eyes filled with pain.

"I'm so sorry." Toby squeezed Hiko's hand. "I don't remember much about my own mother." He shuffled his feet. "All I know is that she didn't come on board the *Phoenix* with us. We waited for her, but she never showed. We never found out what happened to her."

Hiko's brows came together. "She was caught by Greymen?"

Toby shrugged. "I don't know. Maybe she just didn't want to sail with us. The captain doesn't talk about her."

Hiko wrapped his thin arms around his stomach. "Have you looked for her? I'd look for my mother if I could."

"I think the captain did, at first." Toby sighed. "But I've never been off the ship."

Hiko gaped. "Never?"

"Not since we left St George ten years ago. Today was the first time." Toby rubbed his eyes and Polly crooned in his ear. "Yes, Polly, we need to get checked over. My leg needs bandaging." He glanced at his ankle. Blood had dripped on to the top of his foot and dried into a red sock. His rib ached, his back throbbed, his chin was tender and his head hurt. "I need to lie down," Toby mumbled.

Hiko reached up to wrap an arm around Toby's shoulder and pulled him towards the mess hall.

Toby limped into the makeshift hospital and all eyes turned to face him. Uma was bent over Theo, wrapping a bandage around his leg. When Toby entered the room, she dropped the dressing.

"You devil." Uma rushed across the room, the relief in her voice undermining her angry words. "Where are you hurt? Let me see."

She sat him on an empty table and pulled his leg up. "This needs stitches. Hiko, bring me my case."

Hiko hurried away and Toby sagged. "I hurt everywhere," he groaned. Polly shuffled miserably on his shoulder.

"Get off him, you flea-bitten budgie." Uma flapped at Polly. "He doesn't need your weight on his bruises."

"Polly want a cracker!" Polly snapped, but she hopped off Toby to perch on the table by his side.

Uma eased Toby's old shirt over his head and unbuckled his tool belt. She winced when she saw his mottled skin.

"You're black and blue, Toby." Big Pad was watching closely.

"I don't think I can lift my arms." Toby tried to raise them to his shoulders and flinched.

Uma's cool hands pressed his back and ribs. She shook her head. "It's only bruising, but you'll ache for a few days. I'm going to get you some ibuprofen, it should ease the swelling. You should have been resting, not running around the *Banshee*." She tutted. "You could have been killed. I can't even imagine how the captain is feeling right now."

"He threatened to murder us." Hiko had returned with Uma's bag.

"Seems reasonable." Big Pad sighed. "I can't keep my

eyes open, Uma."

"Then sleep, Paddy." She soothed his forehead with her wrist.

"I keep thinking I'll not wake up." Big Pad closed his eyes.

"Go to sleep. You need it." Uma pressed her fingers on his forehead and the Irishman exhaled quietly. "I'll keep checking on you."

After a moment she lifted her fingers and Paddy's eyes remained closed.

"They used to have the technology to fix what's broken in Paddy's spine," Uma whispered. "I'd have had him back on his feet in a matter of weeks."

"But not now." Toby hung his head. "I feel awful. If I hadn't landed on him…"

"Hush." Uma admonished him with a gentle frown. "You won't be blaming yourself for Big Pad. Imagine if it had been the other way around and he had landed on you."

"You'd be flat as seaweed." Hiko looked away, sheepish. "Sorry."

"You're right, Hiko, he would be. Hand me my bag." Uma took it gently from the boy. "You'd better sit, too, and I'll check you over. Goodness knows how long you've been living in the walls."

Hiko shrugged, but he sat.

Uma pulled a needle and thread from her bag. "Let me see that leg, Toby."

Toby raised his leg and looked away, while Uma pushed up his trouser leg. "A clean cut." She pressed his knee. "This isn't going to feel very nice, and I don't want you waking Big Pad or Nisha. Bite down on your glove if you need to."

"I'll be fine." Toby focused on the serving table across the wall where Nisha lay sleeping, one arm curled around her stomach, and Uma started to sew.

The combination of painful pricks and odd tugging swiftly began to make his head spin. Toby thought of the moment he received the injury. Ayla was clearly a trained fighter and Toby had never fought with Nix before. It was incredible that she hadn't managed to inflict worse on him. He had to remember to thank Callum for his lessons in combat.

He pictured the girl cartwheeling on to the gangway, her hair swinging and her coat flying around her. Her eyes were a shade of green he had never seen before, and almond-shaped like Nell's.

"I can't believe she's Nell's daughter," he muttered.

"Huh?" Hiko leaned closer.

"Nothing. The room's going round." Toby wobbled.

"Almost done, Toby, then you can find your bed." Uma

was tying off the thread.

"Right." Toby swayed again and Polly fluttered at his side. He closed his eyes and saw Ayla once more. "I'm never going to see her again, am I?" he whispered.

Ayla's voice rang in his memory. "I don't think so, *boy*," she replied.

Toby was woken by Hiko shaking his shoulder. "The captain says Harry's passed out and the engines are dry, so you need to get the paddles started. And the secondary rudder is a nightmare so you need to prioritize fixing the steering when we dock. And if I don't get out of his way he's going to use me as bait on the next fishing expedition."

Toby groaned. His leg felt stiff and his back still ached.

"Uma says don't I dare wake you up, sleep is doing you the world of good. But I'm more scared of the captain using me for bait, so you do have to get up really." Hiko hesitated. "But not if you don't want to."

Toby rolled out of his hammock and clutched his bruised rib. His eyes were full of grit. He rubbed them and moaned again.

"Are you all right?" Hiko edged closer. "I expect I could get the paddles started by myself if I tried."

"No." Toby stretched and was surprised to find that

he did have movement in his arms after all. "I feel a lot better." He yawned. "How long was I out?"

Hiko shrugged. "Hours. I've been sleeping, too." He nodded at a little nest of blankets on the floor next to Toby's berth.

Toby blinked as he looked at the porthole. "Is it night-time?"

Hiko shook his head. "Day."

"So I slept all night." Toby rose on shaky legs. "Have you eaten breakfast?"

"I didn't dare. The fat man knows I've been stealing food. He doesn't like me."

"Right." Toby pulled on a fresh shirt, wincing as he had to raise his arms. "Let me sort out the boiler room, then we can find something to eat."

Toby exhaled as he entered the boiler room, immediately feeling less tense. The heat soothed his bruises and he stretched. Polly had joined him in the passageway.

"Where've you been?" Toby muttered

"Uploading the captain's log." Polly flew to the top of the attemperator, head cocked to one side.

The *Phoenix* hummed through his feet and Toby nodded. "The captain's right, those engines are about to run dry." Swiftly he switched them off. "It was good while it lasted though, wasn't it, old girl?"

The *Phoenix* grew quiet and Toby yawned once more. "What's the water level?" he asked.

Hiko ran to check. "Over half full." He tapped the gauge.

"All right, let's get some power in those paddles. Give me a hand with the lever." Together Toby and Hiko pulled the lever to divert power from the heating array to the paddles. Steam rushed along the delivery lines and Toby grinned. "Fill the combustion chamber and let's get some more fuel compressed."

They worked quietly until Hiko started humming. Toby listened at first, then started tapping his toes against the fuel compressor.

"I think we've got enough," he said eventually. "Thank goodness the *Banshee* never fired that weapon, or we'd be in real trouble."

Hiko nodded. "They were bad pirates."

"Not like us. We're good pirates, right?"

"Right." Hiko giggled and then threw his hand over his mouth, to hold it in.

"It's OK, Hiko, you're allowed to laugh," Toby said.

Hiko released his mouth slowly. "Never was before," he mumbled.

Toby and Hiko entered the mess hall, their faces and hands grey with soot. All patients had been moved into the sleeping quarters and the room had been returned to its original purpose. Most of the crew were gathered, eating a quiet breakfast.

Toby grabbed two bowls and dragged Hiko to the counter. A vat of watery porridge stood on the bench. Toby sighed and ladled out spoons of the congealing grey mass.

"What's wrong with breakfast?" Rahul stood beside him, looking horrified.

"No oven, is there." Crocker slammed a platter of salt herring down. "Peel soaked the oats in water overnight, it was the best he could do. Cold food till *that* thieving sod gets it fixed." He indicated Toby with a tilt of his head.

"Don't worry about it, Toby." Rahul dangled raw herring from his fingertips, as if it would look better in mid-air. "Better cold breakfast than dead in the water, and we all know what you did yesterday."

"Yeah, well I say we should've left him on the *Banshee*," Crocker sneered. "Would've made a man of him."

"Be quiet, Crocker." Rahul spooned oats into a bowl on top of his fish.

"You gonna *make* me, Rahul?"

"I'll make you," Toby growled.

Crocker laughed. "You and whose army, little boy?"

Glowering fiercely, Hiko stepped smartly up to the smirking Crocker and sunk his teeth into the pirate's wrist.

"Ow, gerrim off," Crocker shouted and tried to cuff Hiko around the ear.

Toby blocked his descending arm. "Let him go, Hiko," he said quietly.

Immediately Hiko stepped back and wiped his mouth.

Toby released Crocker.

"I see you got yourself a dog to look after you, as well as a bird, little boy." Crocker stepped back, holding his arm. "I'll get you for this, just you wait an' see. It ain't over."

Crocker retreated towards the galley and Rahul remained beside Toby and Hiko until he was out of the mess hall.

Then Rahul turned to Toby. "Can't you prioritize that oven, Tobes? Peel's a genius in the kitchen, but there's only so much he can do. If it's raw seagull for lunch, I'll spew."

Toby grimaced. "We don't have the part. The captain is going to trade for it in the next port."

"Well, we're not far from there, thanks to that oil you found, so fingers crossed, eh?" Rahul looked at his breakfast, sighed deeply and went to sit down, just as the captain arrived.

"Morning all." Barnaby stood by the door. "You've

heard the paddles restart and you know what that means – the engines are dry. However, we've been running all night and we're about to reach Tarifa."

"I thought we were going for the solar panels," Marcus called. His cut had been stitched, but he would have a gruesome-looking scar running down his face.

"The *Phoenix* needs repairs," the captain replied. "We can't risk open sea with only three masts and no bridge, especially with the *Banshee* after us. We're still the only ones who know where the panels are, so they'll be there once the *Phoenix* is back in shape."

"Are you talking about docking *in* Tarifa?" Rahul dropped his spoon. "That's a huge risk, Captain, we don't know the portmaster – he could be a government man."

The captain rubbed his beard. "We can't get the *Phoenix* repaired otherwise. It's a risk we're going to have to take."

"Does it have to be Tarifa? Is there a friendly port further round the coast?" Marcus looked at Dee as she entered the mess hall with old Arnav, who still looked shaken. His hair was singed and stood out from his head like frayed wire.

"Navigator?" The captain looked at her.

Dee shook her head and sat on a table next to the captain. "The nearest friendly is three days away at the *Phoenix*'s current speed. And we'd have to go past Gibraltar. It flies its own banner, but still has close ties with St George."

"It's too far," the captain replied. "We've got a head start on the *Banshee*, but she's faster than us. We have to assume she's repaired by now and on our tail. All she has to do is sail the coast in the right direction till she catches up. I want to be on our way out before Nell tracks us down."

"Then it has to be Tarifa." Uma was chasing porridge around her bowl as if stirring would make it less foul. She looked up. "Is it part of Granada at the moment?"

Dee frowned. "Last I heard they were in Cadiz province, but they're always fighting in this part of Spain – the borders keep changing."

The captain nodded. "We'll have to go into port like honest traders, so the Jolly Roger will have to come down."

The crew groaned.

"It isn't all bad." The captain spread his palms. "The portmaster is known to a friend of ours and although we've never traded before, his name has been mentioned in a positive light."

"All our friends started off as strangers once," Theo muttered.

"Exactly."

"Usually you make overtures first – gifts and other offers. And we dock outside their main port." Marcus pressed the heel of his hands over his eyes then looked up. "It's provocative, sailing right into port with no preamble.

It's begging for trouble."

"We have no real choice." The captain started to clean his cracked glasses. "We're badly damaged. We need a new lifeboat, a new mast and materials to rebuild the bridge. Our maps and the protractor were lost in the storm and need replacing. We need a delivery line for the oven and some spares for the boiler room. We have to trade for more food and fresh water. And I need new glasses." He held them up. "We must have somewhere to dock while we make those repairs, so it has to be a main port. If the paddles break down or something goes wrong in the boiler room again, we're dead in the water. We can't move with only two sails. I'm not willing to risk it."

"So, we're honest traders for a couple of days." Nisha leaned against a table. "We can do that."

TWELVE

Toby dragged Hiko up to the crow's nest and the two of them sat curled under the parapet, watching Tarifa change from a grey blur on the horizon to a heat-hazed smear of white that outlined patchy orange hills. Polly stalked the floor, her plumage nodding comically as she bobbed up and down.

"Do you want a turn?" Toby offered the binoculars to Hiko, but he shook his head.

"I've seen Tarifa," he muttered.

"When?" Toby put the binoculars back to his own eyes. "I can't wait to get there."

"After father died, when mother and I were travelling with the merchant who sold me." His voice had gone cold and flat and Toby hesitated, half wanting to ask Hiko more.

Polly squawked reproachfully as Toby altered his position, almost squashing her against the nest wall.

He refocused the binoculars. "Wait, what are those?"

He pointed.

There were rolling hills all along the coast, but behind Tarifa they were dotted with hundreds of spinning blades.

"The reason so many provinces fight over this region." Polly hopped on to the parapet, while Toby trained the binoculars.

"Wind turbines?" Toby leaned forward. "But I've never seen so many."

"You'll understand soon." Polly bobbed from foot to foot. "We're about to enter the straits."

"There's no Junk Dam." Toby stretched to see, disappointed. He had been looking forward to entering a lock and passing through the giant dam that signalled entrance into one of the wealthier ports. They were originally designed by his father.

"They don't need one." Polly ruffled her feathers.

"Huh," Toby grunted, but he quickly shook off his disappointment. "So, Tarifa has power?"

Polly bowed her head. "They invested in wind rather than solar after the crash and had enough power to force-grow food during the Darkness."

Even though Toby had been tiny, he remembered the cold days and even colder nights. He didn't remember his mother's face, but he remembered shivering himself to sleep. The pirates had lived on tiny fish, gull meat and seaweed, supplemented with all the vitamin D tablets they could steal.

Toby had still been small enough to run through the vents when the ash clouds thinned out, growing paler with each week that passed. Dawn after dawn, the crew had watched the sky. Then, one day, the cloud cover fractured like an eggshell. Toby had pointed, although he hadn't needed to. Every eye had tracked the sudden break in the opaque sky, as though the cloud's parting had occurred with an audible *crack*.

It was only a split second before the cloud repaired itself, hurriedly, but it was long enough. Those around the world who, like the crew of the *Phoenix*, were watching the sky had seen the sun.

It was too bright and too yellow. As the cloud cleared more every day, two of the crew spent their whole time staring upwards. One day they found that they could see nothing else, only a glow that encompassed their whole vision. After they went totally blind and had to be pensioned off, the rest of the crew treated the sun with more respect.

Toby had been told that there were sun worshippers on land. His father had seen monasteries where whole communities of sun-blind were praised for their dedication to the orb.

"Why isn't Tarifa the main principality around here?" Toby frowned through the binoculars once more, staring at the spinning turbines with awe. "They must be rich ... *healthy.*"

"It's a small town." Polly examined a claw. "Every governor wants Tarifa's power, so the locals just protect their turbines and pay taxes to whoever occupies the castle. But it's not so great. Half the powered equipment is broken down. Five years ago Algeciras cut the power lines when Tarifa allied with Graada, so two-thirds of the turbines are useless. And, with the return of the sun, Tarifa lost some of its strategic importance. In a few years those turbines will be nothing but rusting junk."

"Yeah." Hiko wriggled by his side. "Tarifans are a bunch of bullies who think they're better than everyone else. They can store food for longer and they've got stupid electric lights. My father said they had a 3-D printer at the beginning, but when it broke there was no one left who knew how to fix it."

Toby's fists whitened on the rail as the *Phoenix* suddenly lurched, blown almost off course.

"We're entering the straits." Polly sounded as though she were grinning.

Hiko huddled behind Toby as the *Phoenix* pitched wildly. "Is it always like this?" Toby yelled.

Polly crawled into his shirt. "For nine miles. It's where the Mediterranean meets the Atlantic. That's why they don't need a dam."

"Nine miles!" Toby rocked to keep his balance as the *Phoenix* pitched the other way. "The paddles are going to struggle."

The *Phoenix* powered onwards. Then the sound of her progress suddenly altered. Heart thudding, Toby leaned out and gasped. "The junk is gone." Sure enough the *Phoenix* was slicing through clear water. "The wind's keeping the straits clear. Look, they're fishing."

A circle of boats was ahead and to the right of them, casting nets.

Polly poked out her head. "There might be tuna on the dock."

"And that's good?" Hiko was getting used to talking to Polly.

"Raw tuna's a lot nicer than raw herring." Toby rubbed his hands. "And it's rare. You don't often get it – and never fresh."

Hiko licked his lips. "I didn't much like the herring," he mumbled.

"No one does, really." Toby's smile quickly faded; the *Phoenix* had been caught by a gust and they were now headed directly for the tight circle of fishermen.

Toby grabbed the speaker. "Course change," he yelled. "Fishing boats dead ahead."

Garbled acknowledgement returned to him through the tube and Toby watched as the *Phoenix* fought the wind, attempting to manoeuvre around the tiny sailboats.

He held his breath – they weren't changing course fast enough. The *Phoenix* was heading straight for the outermost boat in the circle.

"Move," he screamed. The fisherman was frantically pulling his net.

Hiko covered his eyes with his hands, but Toby couldn't tear his eyes from the impending disaster.

At the very last moment a gust of wind swept the *Phoenix* to port. The fishing boat knocked into her hull, but instead of being smashed it was swept into the wake of the *Phoenix*, jostled by waves and half swamped.

Toby exhaled shakily. He turned to watch the fishermen struggling to get control of their boats, which now bobbed wildly in their wake.

"We won't be popular," Toby sighed. "Apart from almost killing them, the *Phoenix* will have scared their catch away."

"The fish will be back though." Hiko fought to keep the boats in view as the *Phoenix* powered onwards. "It isn't as if they can go very far."

Toby returned his gaze to Tarifa. The port was surrounded by whitewashed houses with red roofs. A few trees, barely the height of a man, dotted the roads and hilltops. They had only been growing since the sun's return. In a few years they would provide real shade. He felt tense with excitement – this time he wouldn't be confined to the ship. They were anchoring in port and Toby had proven himself strong and able. He was going to leave the ship and see the trees up close.

On their right, above the port, a giant grey castle stood as custodian over the white houses and sandy beaches that surrounded it. It looked like a stack of boxes, with crenellations slashed all along the battlements. There was a black arched entrance; a gaping mouth, which only half hid a portcullis that lurked like teeth in its recess. It was low, serious and military in appearance. The flag of Cadiz Province flew above the ramparts.

"The Castle of Guzmán el Bueno." Polly poked out her head again and was almost dragged out altogether. She shuddered and hunkered back down. "The governor's seat of residence."

The wind whistled across Toby's face; fresh air filled with the scent of clean sea and carrying the cries of gulls on it. Toby breathed in. "That's what the sea is supposed to smell like, isn't it? Look, is that a…?"

"It's a dolphin!" Even Hiko bounced to his feet.

"I didn't know there were any left." Polly peered out. "It's a bit deformed, but it's a dolphin. Is there a whole pod, can you see?"

"Just one."

"There used to be many dolphins here, and whales. Storks migrated this route, too, before the sun went out," Polly informed them.

Toby looked at the waves splashing against the crumbling sea wall, the grey surf lingering on the brickwork, the sunlight glittering from the blue water. The Darkness suddenly seemed a very long time ago.

Below, the captain emerged from the lean-to that was forming a temporary bridge. He sheltered his eyes from the blazing light and looked for his crew. "All hands, prepare for docking," He looked up. "Toby, get down to the boiler room. I'll need the paddle in reverse soon enough. And furl that Jolly Roger."

"Aye, aye." The pirates leaped into action and Toby reached up to catch the rope that would roll the flag.

"Sorry, Bones," he muttered, as the skull and crossbones vanished. Then he looked at Hiko. "Hop on." Hiko wrapped his arms and legs around Toby and he abseiled the two of them down to the deck.

"I'll learn to do it myself soon, I promise." Hiko

climbed down.

Toby looked at him. Stubble was starting to grow around the hacked tufts of hair on his head, turning his skull a sooty grey. His back was straighter than when Toby had first seen him – he no longer hunched quite so much or flinched whenever someone raised a hand.

"You'll be a great pirate, Hiko, but you don't need to learn *today*." Toby released the rigging. "Come on, we need to get to the boiler room."

"We won't see her dock?" Hiko looked disappointed.

"I never do. When we weigh anchor I have to stay below and clean out the boiler till we leave."

Hiko's eyes widened as he studied Toby's expression. "But not today?"

"Not today." Toby grinned. "I'm going on land."

"Oh no, you're not."

Toby jumped as Dee's hand fell on to his shoulder. "You've already seen how easily someone can control the captain if they have you. He was willing to give up the solar panels to Nell. It took half the crew to persuade him to let Marcus make the fake coordinates. We can't risk you falling into the wrong hands. You have to stay on board."

Toby's face fell. "Are you serious?"

Dee nodded. "You aren't leaving the ship, Toby. You'll be able to see the dock from on board, but if you set a single foot off this ship I will personally cut it off at the ankle." Her teeth flashed in a grim smile and the sunlight glinted from her earrings.

Hiko tugged at his windcheater. "She means it."

Toby snorted. "No you don't, do you, Dee?"

Dee flashed her long knife. "All right, perhaps I won't cut off your foot, but I will chain you up by it. I understand that your confinement to the *Phoenix* is starting to chafe, but now isn't the time to start ignoring orders."

"Come on, Dee." Toby spread his hands and tried a smile that mimicked his father's. "I saved your life, I went on to the *Banshee* and saved Hiko, I'm not a little kid any more."

Dee sighed. "This isn't about your age, Toby. I know you can look after yourself, but if you're captured and ransomed in return for controlling Captain Ford's talent for invention..." She shuddered.

A cold wind touched Toby's neck and he turned. Peel was standing just behind them, listening. Toby shivered and Hiko stepped closer.

"I don't like the fat man," he whispered.

Toby closed one arm around his shoulder and turned his gaze back to Dee. "What are the chances of me being able to change your mind?"

"Zero," Dee said, almost apologetically.

"Then I'll stay on the ship." Toby's shoulders dropped.

Dee touched his elbow, making him meet her eyes. "Thank you. When we've got the panels I'll talk the captain into letting you go on land at a known friendly. How about that? Now get us docked, so we can be repaired and out of here." She glanced over her shoulder. "That castle gives me the creeps."

"I don't like this." Crocker appeared from behind the broken deck housing. "Taking down the Jolly Roger. 'Tain't piratical."

Dee huffed. "Think of it as playing the long-con to get what we want. We pretend to be honest traders, they sell us what we want, and we get out of here with our hides intact."

"I don't like it." Crocker sidled forwards. "'Tain't no sort of luck to furl the skull and bones. An' I'm not the only one thinks this way. That's right, in't it, Peel?"

He nodded. "We're pirates, right enough. No call to be hiding who and what we are. They should do what we want out of fear and treat us proper."

"They've got a bloody standing army, who knows what weapons left over from the riots, and a castle as a stronghold." Dee shook her head. "You want to go in there fighting? You'll hang from those ramparts faster than you can say 'fish bait'. For now we make friends. The captain will offer them some medical supplies from the plane, or repair work on their turbines, in return for what we need. We leave and maybe next time we come in under the Jolly Roger, honestly. Right now we're going in under the radar, and staying there." She fingered her belt where her long knife lay against her thigh. "I don't want you two spreading discord. We've got enough injured as it is. Understood?"

Peel nodded and when his brother opened his mouth to argue he held up a greasy hand to silence him.

"We just hopes you're right, Dee. If this is a bad decision, then we'll all 'ang for it – even the golden boy here." His piggy eyes turned to Toby.

Dee's jaw tightened. "The captain knows what's at risk. This is his ship and I've been on it from the moment he arrived on the dock with Toby sleeping in his arms and said, 'I have to run, who's with me?'"

Dee stepped closer to Peel. "I became his second when we saved Theo from the governor in Sierra Leone and Captain Ford hasn't steered the *Phoenix* wrong yet; not when he gave Uma sanctuary and not when he picked you two up in Porto Santo."

Peel opened his mouth, showing his tombstone teeth.

"No, Peel, I've had enough of your complaining. Head to the anchor – you'll need to do Big Pad's usual job when we dock." Dee turned back to Toby. "You get those paddles stopped, we're getting close."

Toby nodded curtly and ran for the hatch. Dee was right, if he didn't throw the paddles into reverse they would plough straight through the pier and then, honest traders or not, no one would want to do business with them.

Just before he dropped into the hatch he took a final breath of fresh sea air. It was going to be a blazing-hot day. Already the older pirates were wrapping scarves around their eyes to prevent them from going blind. Most had already thrown off their windcheaters, baring arms that still burned easily despite the years in the light. They gathered, ready for docking.

Theo pointed towards two little boats that had appeared from the port and were now heading towards the *Phoenix* to guide her in.

"Toby, we have to slow down," the captain yelled, as he crouched over the rudder.

Toby nodded, opened the hatch and jumped inside.

The *Phoenix* docked with only the lightest of crunching sounds. She scraped her port side along the pier just long enough to make Toby concerned about his new, fragile, delivery line, then she bumped free so the fenders could do their job.

Peel had weighed the anchor and secured the lines and

now Toby stood on deck, Polly on his shoulder and Hiko at his side. The three of them were watching the captain, Dee, Rahul and seven other pirates who had their hair tied neatly under their scarves and sun-gauze over their eyes.

Carson and Oats, who normally joked and laughed their way through every task, were standing seriously.

Dobbs leaned on the gunwale, picking his nails with his small curved knife. Rita stood next to him. She frowned and slapped Callum's hand away as he brushed up against her.

Harry and Simeon brought up the rear. They were the exact same height and build but otherwise like two sides of a coin. Harry was a pale-skinned Welshman; the lightest touch of the sun burned him red. Simeon on the other hand had the darkest skin Toby had ever seen – darker than Rahul's, darker than Theo's. His teeth flashed brilliant white when he smiled and he smiled all the time.

The group were lined up ready to climb down the gangplank that would take them from the *Phoenix* to the pier.

A whole new set of scents had smacked Toby when he climbed out of the boiler room. The sea smell was still strong, but now it was mixed with the reek of latrines, rotting fish and vegetables from the market that lined the marina. Drying seaweed and limpets clung to the wooden pier, steaming and crackling in the sunshine.

Toby gaped. "I've never seen so much wood." He leaned over the railing.

"They had power, remember." Polly shuffled on his shoulder. "Didn't need to burn everything up."

"It's worth a fortune." Toby blinked. "Some of our best trades have been for combustibles."

Polly nodded. "In a few years there'll be enough wood grown back, but right now, it's irreplaceable."

Debris littered the dock; the remnants of the storm that had passed by the previous night. Market stalls lay broken on their sides.

Beside the port stood the remains of a petrol station, torn to pieces long ago, its sign still propped up by a single rusting pump.

Toby raised his eyes to the town itself. Close up he could see the narrow cobbled streets that wound between houses and the faded paint, smears of dirt and poor repair work.

Along the main street a line of military men jogged towards them. Toby's eyes widened; they were big. Even the smallest was the size of Big Pad and they wore peaked caps that protected their eyes from the brightening sun.

"Look at them," he whispered.

Polly leaned to whistle in his ear. "They had food when

no one else in the world did. They still aren't as big as people were before the crisis."

Toby didn't take his eyes from them until they lined up at the end of the pier to await the *Phoenix*'s landing party. In front of them the bustle of the dock continued, tugging at his attention.

The fishermen Toby had seen earlier were tying their boats to the pier, but apart from the soldiers, fishermen and a few overseers, all the other activity on the dock seemed to be carried out by children.

Skinny children with dirty faces and wiry strength unloaded fish and filled barrows. Their high-pitched cries clamoured in Toby's ears – warnings from one to another to catch a load, or step away from a dropping crate; curses when one of them got in the way of barrowloads of moving stock. They scurried between the armed men and women who dotted the pier.

"They're all children." Toby frowned. "Why aren't the adults working?"

Hiko shrugged. "The dock rats are bought labour, like I was."

Polly dug her claws into Toby's shoulder as a scrawny gull swept past, cawing, to swipe a shellfish that had dropped between two planks. A ragged little girl, with shorn hair and sunburnt shoulders, tried to chase the gull off and got a sharp clip around the ear when the bird made off with the morsel. She clutched her hands around her head and ducked away from the fisherman's reach.

Toby raised his eyebrows. "Why do they need dock rats?"

"Use your brain." Polly shoved him with her wing, still keeping her back resolutely turned. "The locals fish, farm, fight and work the turbines. They're rich enough to bring in outside labour for everything else."

Barnaby shaded his eyes again and glanced at his son. "Every port is different, Toby." He lifted his sack of trade supplies. "Of course I'd like to avoid those that use slaves, but we can't always be choosy and, if we were, Hiko wouldn't have been able to stow away." He shook his head. "I can't shield you forever, son."

Then the captain put a foot on the gangplank and looked around his ship. "Right, crew, think 'honest trader'. Marcus, get started on the repairs, hopefully there'll be supplies arriving at the *Phoenix* in fairly short order." He looked over the town and then slowly turned back. "If we haven't returned by nightfall, you'd better leave without us."

"What?" Toby jerked. "No."

The captain looked only at Marcus, and fingered his brass compass as he spoke. "You have my intent, make it happen. If I don't return, then Toby must be protected at all costs. I plan to be back by dusk. If I'm not, then something has gone wrong and they'll be coming for the *Phoenix*, so get her out of here. Crocker knows the coordinates of the solar panels so he'll be in charge of navigation." His eyes flicked to his son. "Everything will be fine, Toby, but I can only do my job if I know you'll do as I say and be safe."

"I'll obey orders, Captain." He saluted, half mockingly. There was no way Toby was going to let the *Phoenix* leave without his father.

"Be sure that you do." His father shifted his sack to a more comfortable position, adjusted his tool belt and put on his cracked glasses. The militia lining the dock awaited them. "Let's trade."

THIRTEEN

Toby, Hiko and Marcus stood in a line along the fallen mast facing Amit, Ajay and Uma. Peel and Crocker were prepared, at the other end, to steady the wood as it moved. The whole crew had tied their scarves around their foreheads and over their eyes. They didn't often labour in such bright sun.

Marcus cracked his knuckles. "One, two, three…"

They all heaved and the ancient telegraph pole began to lift. Sweat dripped from Toby's nose.

"Get under it, Uma," Marcus gasped.

Toby's shoulders popped and his aching ribs strained. Uma slid beneath him and took the weight. Slowly they shifted the mast away from the bridge and pivoted it until it lay parallel to the pier.

As it moved, the silver sail dragged, tearing on glass spears and metal struts. Each ripping sound made Toby flinch.

Finally Marcus indicated that they could drop the mast

and Toby wiped his forehead. Perspiration had pooled under his arms and stained his blue shirt black. Beside him, Hiko was breathing heavily.

"Well done." Marcus rotated his shoulders until they cracked. "Theo and Nisha, can you work on cutting the old mast into tradeable chunks? Draft as much help as you need; I want it off the deck as soon as possible. Break it into as few pieces as you can – the bigger they are, the more they'll sell for. Uma, can you repair the sail?"

Uma rubbed the material and frowned at the long rents. "It shouldn't be a problem," she said eventually. "I can't promise complete wind-worthiness, but I can improve things."

"Do your best."

Uma nodded. "If Toby unties it, I'll take it inside and keep Big Pad company."

Toby looked up from the tie he had bent to unfasten. "He must be bored out of his mind. Why don't we carry him out here?"

Marcus tightened the gauze around his eyes. Sweat was already soaking away its opacity. "Uma, does he need to be below, or can we bring him up to watch the repair work?"

Uma brightened. "Good idea. Peel can bring him up through the cargo hold."

Toby coiled the halyard and pushed the freed sail

towards Uma then he looked back at the bridge. Without the mast plugging the wound, the *Phoenix*'s injuries looked even worse. The fibreglass roof had caved in completely. The windows were smashed and broken pieces stuck up like bones. Papers that had been pinned by the mast now fluttered in the wind, rain-smudged and useless. The captain's sextant was in small pieces, the arc on one side of the bridge, the clamp and index bar on the other. Tiny bits of the horizon-mirror glittered in between.

"Ashes." Marcus stood beside him. "Where do we start?" He rubbed his forearms, which were already glowing pink in the sun. "Right, everyone, let's clear that bridge."

Glass pieces littered the deck. Hiko ran to find a brush and bucket and began sweeping up. Toby joined the rest of the crew, who were pulling apart the housing. Toby's back ached and his skin itched from the fibreglass powder that was working its way into his pores.

"Wish I'd gone on land," he muttered, as Arnav began to cough.

Marcus shoved a fish hook into his hands. "I'll take over here." He pointed at the base of the old mast. "Clear that out, will you."

Toby ran gratefully away from the clouds of dust,

crouched by the mast's soggy remnants and began to work them free.

Slowly the pile of splinters by Toby's side grew and a hole appeared in the *Phoenix* wide enough for a telegraph pole. Eventually he dropped the fish hook and used his screwdriver to pry out the last of the shards. As he was sanding the gaping hole smooth there was a shout from the pier.

Toby raised his head. "What is it?" he asked Marcus.

Marcus adjusted his eye-gauze, peered over the railing and then turned back with a grin. "The bartering must be going well." He waved down to someone and pointed to the gangplank.

"What've they got?" Toby rubbed at the fragments that itched his face.

"You'll see." Marcus stepped out of the way and Toby heard grunting. As he watched, a long pole appeared over the railing. It was being carried above the heads of six dock rats.

Toby stepped back. He had never before met another boy his age and now here were six. Hiko sidled to his side, half hiding behind Toby's back while he stared.

The new boys bulged with muscle. Toby was no weakling, but his strength was wiry. He pulled his shirt down over his elbows, abruptly self-conscious.

"How's the hole, Toby?" Marcus called. "If it's prepped, get that pole in place."

Toby nodded. The visitors looked at him, bullishly silent.

He cleared his throat and pointed. "Can you put it in here for us?"

The boys continued to say nothing.

"Oh … do you not speak English?" Toby shuffled nervously. "Spanish, right? *Buenos Días. Hola.*" He raised his voice to the rest of the crew. "Does anyone speak Spanish?"

Hiko reached up and tugged at his arm. "They speak English here; it's the lingua franca."

Toby frowned. "What's wrong with them, then?"

"They probably had orders to deliver the mast, not help fit it." Marcus looked at the boys. "That right?"

The dock rats nodded.

"Well, you have to put it somewhere." Marcus spread his hands. "You may as well put it in that hole over there."

Still silent, the boys finally nodded and, ignoring Toby, carried the new pole to the hole. Hiko flinched out of their way, hiding behind Toby as they passed.

"Amit, Ajay – rigging," Toby called. The boys holding the back of the mast jerked in surprise when the two pirates immediately shinned upwards holding a noose. The dock rats positioned the end of the mast in the hole and then they tilted it up as high as they could. When the mast had reached a forty-five-degree angle, the boys stood with it balanced on their upraised hands.

One of them grunted, "Now what?"

"Ajay." Toby waved and Ajay threw the noose. It looped around the mast. Toby took a deep breath. He would have to go beneath the dock rats to secure the rope.

He could feel the eyes of the crew on his back, but Toby clenched his fists and ran beneath the arm of the nearest dock rat. Immediately he was assaulted by the stench of unwashed bodies. Toby lived on a ship where washing was a luxury, but these boys smelled even worse than Crocker.

Quickly Toby grabbed the noose and tightened it around the pole, stealing glances at the rats around him as he worked. Close up Toby could see that the boys' muscles were covered in sores and the rags of their shirts barely hid scarred chests and hollow bellies. The one who had spoken saw him staring and grinned slowly, disarmingly. His smile was sweet but his teeth were almost all missing.

Then Toby waved at Amit and Ajay, and the boys watched in fascination as the mast slowly lifted.

Toby helped guide the pole until it was angled correctly. There was a satisfying thunk as it dropped securely into the hole.

The crew cheered.

In a moment of camaraderie, Toby looked at the boy who had smiled. "I'm Toby."

"D'von," the boy grunted. Air whistled through his missing teeth as he spoke. The boy leaned forward, briefly blocking out the light and making Toby tense in fear. "Those big men, they listened to you." The air lisped in and out of the gap, making 'listen' into 'listhen'. It sounded strangely childish, at odds with his frame.

Toby nodded.

"But you're smaller than them." The boy frowned.

Toby shrugged. "Yes, but I know how things work."

"You know how things work?" The boy looked at Toby with what might have been wonder.

"D'von." A snarled order from the largest of the rats forced D'von to back away.

"Goodbye, Toby," D'von lisped. He joined the others and began to back down the gangplank.

"Thank you," Toby cried. He watched as D'von climbed the pier and disappeared into a gang of dock rats who were moving a crumpled canopy.

Then he turned back to the *Phoenix*.

"Good job." Marcus clapped him on the shoulder. "Get some rods hammered into the pole to secure it. We'll be able to furl the sail once Uma has finished the repair work.

At this rate we could be seaworthy before the captain gets back."

"The bridge is clear," Theo shouted from the deck housing. He stood beside a pile of broken fibre boards.

"Good." Marcus buried his knuckles in his back. "Hiko, how's the clean-up coming along?"

Hiko appeared from behind Uma carrying a clanking bucket of broken glass. "Done."

Toby frowned. "What will we do with the rubbish?"

"Chuck it overboard, like usual." Marcus shrugged.

Toby looked to the port side of the *Phoenix* where the dolphin was arcing from the first clean water he had ever seen. Sunlight glittered on its grey back. Even if he never saw it again, the dolphin would live forever in his dreams, a symbol of the possibility of natural beauty undamaged by his species. Perhaps the island, untouched by man, had been found by nature instead.

Toby grimaced. "Can't we store it below till we hit the junk again?"

"Toby's right, we shouldn't litter the port." Nisha caught his eye.

Marcus sighed. "Theo, store the rubbish."

Toby looked at the space where the bridge had been. Next to Theo the primary steering mechanism was snapped in two and the gyroscope wobbled dangerously.

"I'd better go and find something to repair that with."

Marcus nodded. "Crocker, go and barter for something we can eat, will you?"

"Why me?" Crocker spat overboard.

"Just *do it*, Crocker," Marcus snapped. "I want to eat something that isn't salt herring and waterlogged oats."

"Try and find some decent beer, too," Big Pad rasped. He struggled to lift his head and Uma raced to tilt his table. "I'm sick of your rotgut hooch."

Crocker snarled. "I'll be happy not to serve you next time."

"Just find us something to eat and drink, Crocker. And be grateful you're getting out of the hard work." Marcus pointed to the gangplank and Crocker adjusted his scarf then stalked off the *Phoenix*.

Toby kneeled in front of the steering wheel, stroking his fingers over the snapped post. His tools lay at his side, displayed like a surgeon's blades. Beside him he had a selection of wires, poles and hammered metal patches. To his right a small brazier burned. The acrid smell was keeping the gulls away and most of the crew as well. Hiko curled up in the corner, watching him; Polly was a familiar weight on his shoulder.

After a moment's consideration he picked up a metal patch with a set of pliers and held it in the fire.

"What're you up to, boy?" Peel said almost jovially, as he leaned over the guardrail. Toby wrinkled his nose. The man's skin was slimy with the sweat that rolled down the thick folds of his neck.

"Repairing the steering. Shouldn't you be doing something with the food Crocker brought back?"

"Oh yes. We've a nice barbecue going on the prow. We'll have some hot food today at least." Peel licked his slug-like lips. "Just come to let you know, in fact. Tuna's done."

Toby's gut rumbled but he sighed. "I don't have time." He turned the metal in the brazier; it was starting to glow. "Hiko does though. Hiko, go and get some food."

Hiko wiggled his way to Toby's side and whispered in his ear, "I don't like the fat man."

Peel chortled. "No need to be scared of me, Hiko. You just head on up to the prow and Crocker'll see you right. You've had no food before now if you've not had my barbecue. Crocker even managed to score some potatoes."

Hiko looked at Toby, wide-eyed and pleading.

"I'll send Polly with you." Toby shrugged Polly off his shoulder and on to Hiko's.

Hiko licked his lips, hesitated one more moment then

scuttled out from the bridge awning, around the brazier and up to the prow, looking back every few steps.

Toby pulled the metal from the brazier and glanced up. Peel remained watching him with narrowed eyes.

"You think you're special, little boy." Peel ran a single finger along the guardrail. "Just because you went off ship and saved a life? I saved a life. I saved more'n one and I *took* a lot more'n that."

"My metal's cooling." Toby held the spitting metal curl up for Peel to see and the fat man took a step back.

"You're going to fix that steering?" he sneered. "And Crocker tells me you're making clockwork engines. So you're an inventor like the captain? Lot of good that did *him*. You watch out, little boy – there's better to do than invent things that'll get you noticed by governments. You should listen to Crocker and me. Better to be a pirate."

"I am a pirate," Toby snapped.

"You're a boy. An inventor maybe, an engineer perhaps, but you're no pirate."

Toby tossed the pliers and the cooling metal on to the deck, where it smouldered.

"You're a kid and, as long as the captain molly-coddles you, you'll always be a kid. Young'un over there has lived more'n you." He tilted his head towards Hiko, who was now sitting on a coil of rope clutching a tuna steak in one hand and blowing on a potato clenched in the other. "I've seen you train with Callum, seen him go easy on you."

Toby reared to his feet. "Callum does not go easy on me."

"Course he does. I'm the only one trying to toughen you up. No son of mine would be pathetic like you. Saw you when those dock hands turned up – scared as a mouse in a room of cats."

"Well, you don't *have* a son, do you? And you never will. No one would have you. You're bitter and twisted and ... and disgusting."

Peel ducked under the guardrail. "You've been off ship once so you think you can take me on, little boy?"

Toby tore Nix from his belt and held her in front of his face. He was pleased to find that he was barely trembling. "I can if I have to."

"No, you can't." Peel shook his head. "No proper training in fighting, only in fixing things. My son would've been able to take on three at a time by now." Peel stopped so close to Toby that he could smell the squid ink he used on his hair. "I don't have a son, little Toby, that's true. I wanted to. And you're wrong that no one would have me. Remember Carla?"

Toby shook his head.

"Well, she was one of your dad's original ten. She left the year you turned nine – wanted a life on land and a family.

I couldn't go with her. I can't live on land again – I'm what you might call a fugitive. Nowhere left to go."

"So we're stuck with you on the *Phoenix*."

Peel snorted. "I'm the one who's stuck. I don't get to pair up, like those others." He tilted his head at Nisha, who was watching the castle walls as she ate, as though she could see Rahul through the stone. "I don't get to have a son, or teach him to fight, but I do get to see *you* every day, the captain's spoiled brat, reminding me that I could have had a son who would have been everything you're not."

His foot shot out and the brazier wobbled and fell. Toby gasped as burning wood toppled out and flames licked at the deck.

Peel stepped back, a twisted smile on his face.

"Peel, you fool." Toby dropped Nix and tore off his shirt, frantically throwing it over the hungry, spreading flames.

Peel continued to retreat. "Do come and get some lunch when you're finished," he called.

Toby stamped on the fire, bare feet blistering as his shirt began to char. The brazier still smouldered, but now it lay on its side, branding the deck with a stinking mark.

Toby was about to call for help, when he clamped his mouth closed. If he shouted, Peel would have even more reason to think him a spoiled child. He clenched his fists and continued to stamp on the flames until the fire went out.

As soon as the last flame died, Toby grabbed two spanners and used them to lift the brazier back into place. He stood for a moment, ribs heaving, glaring furiously at Peel's back. Then he sheathed Nix, gathered charcoaled wood in his leathered hands and shoved it back into the brazier.

When the deck was cleared he painstakingly relit the fire, picked up the metal patch and began to shape it once more.

FOURTEEN

Toby spun the wheel. The steering mechanism wasn't as smooth as it had been, and it was covered in patches and protruding wires, but it would work better than the secondary rudder which had brought them in. He looked up, wincing as his skin stretched over his sunburnt shoulders. The sun was high in the sky – mid-afternoon.

"Marcus," he yelled.

Marcus was tying the sail back on.

"Any sign of more trade goods?" Toby rubbed his aching back.

Marcus looked over the dock and frowned. "Nothing." He caught some rigging and dropped to the deck. "You're right. We should have seen something else by now. The captain must have been bartering all morning. We should at least have some building materials." He rubbed his red hair so that it stood up like a deck brush.

"So, where are they?"

Marcus shook his head and worry slashed deep lines around his mouth and eyes.

"Do we send someone after them to see what's going on?" Toby frowned.

Marcus bit his lip. "If there's a problem, what can one person do? We wait."

"For how long?"

"You heard the captain, Toby. If they don't come back, we're to sail at dusk."

Toby froze. "You're seriously talking about leaving them … leaving Dee?"

Marcus stood firm. "We have our orders. In the meantime, pray they come back. There's a few hours left, maybe they're drinking in the castle and lost track of time – honest trader stuff, I don't know."

"Ship ahoy." Arnav was in the crow's nest as usual, his bright eyes trained on the ocean.

"What do we care?" Toby shouted up. "We're in port."

"Toby!" Uma was at the bow staring out over the water. "It's *Birdie*."

The crew lined the gunwale, watching as whoever was in *Birdie* tacked through the straits, the metal-bright hull bouncing from wave to wave, the dolphin swimming alongside.

"Who is it?" asked Hiko, clutching the railing at his side.

Toby murmured, "Someone from the *Banshee*, it has to be."

Rapidly *Birdie* drew closer, pushed by a following wind.

The sailor on *Birdie* wore the uniform that Toby had seen on the *Banshee*, a black jacket and a hat pulled down low over their eyes.

As soon as *Birdie* reached hailing distance, the call came. "Hi, the *Phoenix*." The sailor stood with one hand on the jib.

Toby could make out long dark hair escaping from the bottom of her hat. He swore he could see her green eyes sparkling like the sea. "Ayla," he whispered.

"A hand?" Ayla drew *Birdie* to the port side of the *Phoenix* and allowed the boat to bump against the paddle.

The crew stared at her and then Marcus waved. "Send down the winches, at least we've got *Birdie* back."

Toby watched, incredulous, as *Birdie* swung over the deck. Ayla stood in the prow of the boat, but despite her straight back, Toby could see she was exhausted. Her legs shook, her eyes were shadowed and her skin was ashen.

Automatically he reached to help her down. She glared at him with utter disdain and then put one hand on *Birdie*'s prow to somersault perfectly from the side of the boat. Her hat fell to the deck and her hair and coat flew in a wild black tangle.

Immediately she was flanked by Amit and Ajay, weapons in hand.

"What do you want?" Marcus glared.

"Thanks for bringing our boat back, you mean." Ayla curled her lip as she looked around. "I see you've started your repairs. Funnily enough we've been doing repairs of our own." She turned to Toby. "It was you, wasn't it? Very good, 'chief engineer'. But it's got you into trouble."

"With the *Banshee*, I'm so scared. *Not.*" Toby put his hands on his hips and Polly squawked derisively.

Ayla whistled. "Captain Nell wants your body on a spike for our new figurehead. But we're not what you want to be worrying about, right now. You need to weigh anchor and get the hell out of here."

"What?" Toby looked at Marcus, whose sun-bleached freckles suddenly stood out, livid against the paleness of his cheeks.

"That's why I'm here – Captain Nell sent me to protect her investment. She still wants those solar panels. The *Banshee* couldn't follow fast enough, thanks to you, so she sent me in *Birdie*. I was meant to catch up with you before you entered Tarifa, but I couldn't – not in that." She gestured towards *Birdie* and shook out her arms. "Tell me your captain is below deck."

"Why?" Toby rasped.

"Because if he's already gone into port, he's lost."

The crew looked towards the castle nervously.

"Stop this." Uma stamped forward. "This girl is from the *Banshee*. They're our enemy and they want our panels. Of course they don't want us to stay docked. If we get repaired first, we'll outrun them."

Uma glowered at Ayla, who stood watching the pirates panic, her arched brows raised.

"The captain has gone in with a team of ten," Uma snapped. "As honest traders, not pirates. There's no reason for them to be in trouble."

"When are they due back?" Ayla looked around.

Toby opened his mouth.

"Don't answer her, Toby." Uma closed her hand on his arm. "She's the enemy."

Marcus leaned in. "We've already been given a new mast." He gestured. "What makes you think we're in trouble here? What do you know?"

Ayla exhaled. "Put it this way, Tarifa is on our 'stay crap away from there at all costs' list."

205

"You have a 'stay the crap away from there at all costs' list?" Toby stared.

"Yeah, it's on the noticeboard next to our 'people who will one day end up on spikes' list," Ayla growled. "Look, Tarifa is bad news. *Very* bad news. The one time we tried to dock here, we barely escaped. If you think it's possible the captain is still trading, send someone down there with an urgent message to bring him back on board. Then get out of here."

Toby looked at Marcus, who finally nodded. "We've got a mast and some food in storage, the rest of the repairs can wait till the next friendly port. Peel, take that Banshee to the sleeping quarters and watch her, we can't risk sabotage. Theo, go and find the captain. Tell him the team is needed on board urgently. Tell him … tell him Toby's had an accident."

"Is that necessary?" Toby shot.

"Yes." Marcus scrubbed his red hair up again. His freckles were standing out like painted dots. "It's the only news that'll make him drop everything and leave. We'll tell him the truth as soon as he boards."

Toby hung his head. "Fine."

Ayla stood beside Peel. His hand was already closed around her bicep.

"I still don't believe you," Toby muttered.

"As long as Captain Ford gets to safety, I've completed my misson." Ayla tossed her head again. "That's all Nell wants … for now."

"She wants the captain safe?" Nisha cocked her head.

"Of course." Ayla smiled. "Once she's got the coordinates for the solar panels, she plans to kill him herself."

"No one is killing the captain," Marcus growled. "Take her below."

"Marcus…" Theo's voice was an octave lower than usual.

The crew followed the direction of his gaze. Even Peel stood still, holding Ayla stiffly to his side.

Dee was crawling up the metal gangplank, her face bloodless. At the first sight of her Marcus started running.

Dee's hand closed over the gunwale and she pulled herself to the deck, her legs dragging behind her, useless. She clutched one hand to her side. With a sort of sluggish horror, Toby realized that she had left a crimson trail up the gangplank behind her.

"Pull the plank," Big Pad cried hoarsely. His table was angled so that he could see the dock. "Pull it *now*."

Amit and Ajay moved as one, Toby on their heels.

They reached the entryway as Dee toppled into Marcus's arms. On the pier a squad of soldiers raced for the *Phoenix*. Dee's blood stained the hand and grey sleeve of the piggish front runner.

Amit and Ajay were already grabbing the gangplank, but the first of the soldiers reached it before they could pull, and held it in place. His fellows grinned and put their feet on the slope. Theo and the twins heaved, trying to shift the plank against the weight at the other end.

Toby ran to his brazier and grabbed the metal bowl. His leather gloves didn't protect his hands completely, but it was enough. The soldiers were already a quarter of the way up.

"Out of the way, Theo." With a yell Toby tossed the contents of the brazier downwards. The soldiers howled and batted at their faces and chests. They dove off the plank and retreated.

"Destroy the gangplank," Toby gasped, dropping the brazier. Theo nodded and Amit grabbed a sledgehammer while Ajay wedged a fishing hook under the hinges. Ajay levered the plank upwards and Amit smashed the connectors holding the plank to the *Phoenix*.

Angry shouts from below intensified as, with a furious heave, Amit and Ajay managed to toss the gangplank away from the deck. It clattered down the hull and splashed into the sea by the pier.

For long seconds the crew of the *Phoenix* was suspended between relief and the horror-struck realization that Ayla was right – the landing party were in deep trouble.

"Oh gods, Dee." Marcus was on deck, cradling his partner.

Uma shoved her way through the pirates. "Let me by, you idiots." She crouched beside Dee and pulled her clenched hand from the injury. "It's all right, Dee. I can fix this," she hissed. But Toby saw the lie in her face. "Lay her down, Marcus, and for the gods' sake, get pressure on that wound." She pulled her own scarf from her eyes and pressed it into his hands. "Make that into a pad, put it on and press, hard. Hiko, get my black bag from the mess hall, fast as you can."

Hiko sprinted for the hatch. Stunned and unable to move, Toby watched him go and realized that Ayla still stood on the deck. At least she had the grace to remain quiet.

"They'll be trying to get on board," Toby rasped. "We need lookouts on the bow and stern."

"I'll watch port side." Big Pad's voice was thick with grief. "I'm already here and not going anywhere." He shifted his gaze to watch Amit and Ajay separate, heading to opposite ends of the ship.

"What happened?" Nisha stood behind Toby, her whole body vibrating with her fear. "Is Rahul all right?"

Toby dropped to his knees and squeezed Dee's bloody hand in his own. Dee opened her eyes.

"Toby…" After saying his name she fell quiet, her chest labouring painfully with each breath.

"It's all right, Dee, you don't have to talk." Marcus stroked her face and Dee closed her eyes.

Nisha's eyes flashed. "Yes, she does," she snapped. "I'm sorry, Dee, but it *isn't* all right. We need to know what happened down there."

Toby squeezed her fingers once more. "Can you hear us, Dee? Nisha's right."

Dee forced her eyes open. Toby could see how much effort that simple movement cost her. She sought Marcus with her gaze and then shifted to look at Toby. When she spoke her voice was barely a whisper.

"They played us." She swallowed and blood flecked her lips. "They were trading with us, trading honestly – we got the mast and they seemed to be agreeing to the other items we need."

Toby's vision blurred and quickly he dashed tears from his eyes, jumping ahead in his mind.

Dee's head rolled back and Marcus caught it. Uma took the pad from him and pressed it on the wound herself. Arnav rushed over with a cup of water. Uma nodded her permission and Marcus held it to her lips.

"Cadiz is a front," Dee choked eventually. "The governor is in the pocket of St George. The portmaster knew who we were the whole time. His men attacked us when we were toasting a deal."

"But you escaped," Marcus murmured.

"What happened to the others?" Nisha pleaded.

"Carson and Dobbs are dead," Dee managed, and the crew drew together. "Last I saw, Rita and Harry were injured, but moving. Rahul, Callum, Simeon and Oats were protecting the captain, but they were all being herded into the dungeons below the castle." Her bloodshot eyes pinned Toby's. "I tried, Toby, but the captain ordered me back here to warn you. I would have fought for him, but he made me leave."

Toby nodded. "You did the right thing. Otherwise the soldiers would've been on board the *Phoenix* before we knew different." But as he spoke, all he could think about was his father, locked in a dungeon.

"What now?" Nisha looked around at the other pirates.

Peel shoved through the crowd, dragging Ayla behind him. "The Banshee was right all along." He gave Ayla a shake and she glowered at him. "It's clear 'what now'. The captain won't be back by dusk, we're about to be boarded by the Tarifans and nine of our crew are lost. We set sail, now, before we lose any more."

"Eight." Reluctantly Marcus dragged his eyes from Dee and rested them on Peel.

"What?" Peel snapped.

"Apart from the captain only *eight* of the crew are lost." Marcus squeezed Dee's limp hand. "Dee's going to be fine. Right, Uma?"

Uma looked up, her hands bloody. "Where's Hiko?" she muttered.

The small boy slid through the legs of the pirates and plunged to her side, already opening the bag. Uma pressed his hands on the bloody pad. "Hold this and don't move." She squinted into her bang and grabbed her needle and thread.

Amit shouted from the prow. "They're coming."

Theo ran to the gunwale. "Don't let them board."

"I can fight." Ayla yanked her arm free of Peel's grip.

Toby stared at her. Ayla rubbed her arm where Peel's sweaty hand had been and she swayed gently in the wind – it was clear that only pride was keeping her on her feet.

Toby cursed. "Go to the sleeping quarters." Ayla opened her mouth to protest and Toby raised a hand. "All we're going to do is hold them off. Get some rest – didn't you chase after the *Phoenix* all night?"

Ayla glowered then nodded.

"We don't trust you," Toby heaved a sigh, "but when we need you to, you can fight."

"There's no reason for any of us to fight the bleedin' Tarifans," Crocker shouted from his brother's side. "Why don't we just *set sail*?"

Toby swallowed. He remembered Marcus's determination to obey even though it might cost him the woman he loved. "We have our orders." Toby rubbed his eyes. "If the captain isn't back by dusk, we set sail."

"Why not leave now, little boy?" Peel's fat face was red, incredulous. "Why risk more death? Who put you in charge anyway? Marcus is acting captain."

Marcus didn't even look up.

Toby clenched his fists. "What if the captain escapes and finds the *Phoenix* gone without him?"

"He's not going to escape," Dee's voice was a bare murmur, yet Toby heard her. He shut his mouth, feeling like he'd swallowed ice.

"Ashes," Paddy breathed. "There're dozens of them, they're almost here."

"We should leave," someone shouted.

"I'm not starting those paddles," Toby snapped. "The *Phoenix* isn't going anywhere."

Ayla crossed her arms. "Before you all die, I think you should share the true coordinates of those solar panels. I did come to warn you after all."

Theo laughed harshly. "Sorry, love, couldn't if we

wanted to. The captain is the only one who knows where we're headed."

The rest of the crew remained silent at the lie.

Ayla groaned. "In that case," she said slowly, "I'd better go and rescue your captain."

Toby blinked. "What?"

"My orders are to make sure Ford is safe." The beads in her hair chimed as she shook her head. "If I go back and tell Captain Nell he's in a Tarifan dungeon and I've no idea where the solar panels are, she's likely to keelhaul me."

Toby leaned closer. "She's your mother, she wouldn't."

"You don't know Nell." Ayla suddenly looked tired. "I'm going below." She allowed Peel to guide her towards the hatch, but then she stopped him with an imperious wave of her hand. "But when I'm rested, I'm going to rescue your captain. So, *Phoenix*, don't set sail without first putting me ashore."

FIFTEEN

Before anyone could respond to Ayla's wild request, they heard the clattering of boots from the pier. Toby clutched the gunwale beside Paddy and watched a small army coming down the jetty towards the *Phoenix*.

They joined the militia already gathered around the remains of the *Phoenix*'s gangplank.

The crew ran for their weapons.

"We need someone on the starboard side, too." Toby pointed. "They might try and sneak round in fishing boats."

"Hiko can go." Uma looked up briefly. Her hands were red and she pinched a bloody needle between her fingers. She gave the boy a gentle nudge.

Hiko scampered across the deck and Toby returned his attention to the pier. A group of Tarifans, three deep, now faced the ship.

The crew of the *Phoenix* bristled with hooks, hammers,

215

knives and staffs. They looked fierce, but the confrontation with the *Banshee* had left its mark. Bloody bandages dangled from beneath shirts, insta-plas supported more than one leg and weapons shook in hands that trembled with exhaustion.

"We won't win another fight, Polly," Toby whispered.

Polly said nothing. The pirates and Tarifans stared at one another and the sun blazed down, hotter than ever.

Eventually a young officer stepped to the front. "You're under arrest. Governor's orders," he shouted. "Lower your weapons and surrender your ship."

Theo brandished his fish hook. "Bite me."

"We're happy here, thanks," Amit called.

"If you want us to lower our weapons, you can damn well *make us*." Crocker capered by the railing, apparently cheered by the prospect of spilling blood.

"We'll be doing that shortly." The officer nodded. "We've gangplanks of our own. Surrender now and we'll go easier on you. Your captain awaits."

"Our captain told us to set sail," Peel shouted.

Slowly Toby closed one hand on the railing of the *Phoenix*, his heart racing. "I have a counter-offer for you," he called. "Return our captain and crew by dusk, otherwise we set sail." The crew of the *Phoenix* muttered over the soldiers' laughter but Toby leaned forwards. "I'm not finished. I said *we set sail*, but we won't be leaving straight away. First thing we'll do is we'll ram our ship through that valuable wooden pier of yours. You can see our hull, it's an ice-breaker. The *Phoenix* will go through it like a knife through fish guts. It'll be years before you have enough wood to rebuild. So if you don't want your dock to be a pile of splinters by nightfall, you'd better do as *we* say."

The pirates stared at Toby.

"Ajay," Toby snapped without taking his eyes from the Tarifan line, "let's show these *pendejos* that they're dealing with pirates. Unfurl Bones."

For a heartbeat the pirates made no movement but then Amit started to whoop. Soon the whole ship was jeering at the soldiers. Only Marcus sat silent, his arms around Dee, his chin lowered.

Toby held his breath, waiting for an attack, but the soldiers on the dock remained still. Finally the officer lowered his eyes. "This is not a decision I can make," he growled and the pirates jeered louder.

As Ajay climbed into the crow's nest, Toby found himself seeking Ayla. She stood by the open hatch with one hand on the railing and the other resting on her weapon.

Toby's hand crept behind his back, automatically

checking for Nix. The pommel slid into his palm.

Ayla's glance slid to the fluttering Bones, then back to Toby.

The crew's cheers bolstered him and he was suddenly hopeful. The Tarifans would return his father and the rest of the missing crew and then they would set sail. Toby's heart skipped as Ayla turned her back and climbed into the hatch.

"I've done all I can." Uma's voice broke into Toby's thoughts. He turned as she tied off Dee's stitches and sprayed the wound with disinfectant. "Lie her down, Marcus."

Toby turned away from the bleakness in Marcus's expression. Dee would recover and take her place as second, Toby told himself. They would salvage the solar panels and after that … the island.

Toby closed his eyes, allowing the noise of the *Phoenix* to wash over him as he tried to imagine a sandy beach and abundant resources, free of government interference. But the picture wouldn't form. His back ached, his ribs throbbed, the stitches on his leg were tight and his hands and feet were blistered.

He leaned over the railing and saw a soldier running for the castle, presumably taking his ultimatum to the governor.

"It was a clever threat, Toby," Polly whistled in his ear.

Toby stoked her plumage. "Do you think it'll work? Will they free the captain?"

She didn't answer.

The pirates stood waiting along the railings, but tiredness was making them sag by the time the soldier returned.

Toby watched him deliver a message to the uniformed officer. "Well?" he shouted. "Are you returning our captain?"

The officer shook his head. "The portmaster has a better idea. For every hour that you do not surrender, he will hang one of your pirate crew from the top of the castle ramparts. How do you like that?"

Toby caught his breath and the crew drew together.

"While you're thinking of your answer, by the way, we are awaiting some more useful weapons. You've heard of bows and arrows, have you not?"

"This is bad." Theo edged to Toby's side. "We need shields."

"I've got piles of junk in the boiler room," Toby said. "Take anything you can use."

"Stop this." Nisha was hysterical. "We have to surrender. What if they hang Rahul?"

Toby swallowed. "We can't discuss it now. They'll hear us." He looked over the side; the soldiers were smirking at the pirates' disarray. His voice quavered. "Pad, let us know if they try anything. Everyone else, come away from the railing, and keep your voices *down*."

"Toby?" Polly cut into his racing thoughts. "This isn't on you ... Marcus—"

"We can't ask Marcus, look." Toby gestured towards the tragic tableau on the deck. Marcus had torn his scarf from his scarred throat and added it to the blood-soaked bandage around Dee's waist.

Nisha reached the bridge and stood on the captain's old table, making sure that her voice was the first one heard. "We have to surrender," she repeated. "A fifth of the crew are down there, including the captain. You want to watch them die one by one?"

The crew shuffled, awkward, but Crocker leaned on the deck housing. "Surrender? Then what happens? I'll tell ya – the captain goes to St George, those of us with 'dead or alive' on our heads go to the hangman, the rest of ya get jailed as pirates, sold for slaves, maybe hung for fun. You and Rahul don't get no happy ending if we surrender, Nish. 'Tain't no solution."

"What is the solution?" Toby leaned forward, hoping against hope that Crocker actually had an answer.

"We sail." Crocker folded his arms. "We sail before we lose any more crew. We ram 'em, just like you said, boy, for revenge. Then we go get those panels and find the island."

"You want to run," Toby shot back.

"None of us *want* to leave the captain, Toby." Ajay gestured at the miserable crew. "What other choice do we have? If we surrender we lose the *Phoenix*; either way we've lost our captain. We've *lost*, Toby. I know he's your father, but if we run, at least some of us remain."

Toby brightened despite the pirate's doom-laden words. "They'll have to sail him to St George, right? We can lie in wait outside the straits, maybe rescue him on his way."

"They'll kill the rest of them," Nisha wailed.

Tears of frustration filled Toby's eyes. "Maybe they won't," he said desperately. "If we just set sail there's no *reason* to execute the others, is there?" His mouth twisted. "There has to be another way." But he knew he was begging.

"There is." The quiet voice came from the port side of the ship.

"Hiko?" Toby craned to see his friend, who was attempting to both watch the sea and speak to the crew at the same time.

"Why not do what Ayla said?" Hiko gestured towards the closed hatch. "Why not rescue the captain?"

His words hung in the air and then the crew began to laugh, bitterly.

"We can't fight our way through a whole town, into the castle and down to the dungeons, rescue the captain and the surviving crew members, get them out and back to the ship without all being killed on the way," Amit said.

"I don't think we should *fight* our way in," Hiko said. "I think we should *sneak* our way in. Like how I got on board the *Phoenix*."

The crew wavered, silenced. Then Amit stepped forward. "Tell me how and I'll go."

"And me." Nisha's eyes had lit with hope.

Hiko shook his head. "Even if you could get off the ship and on land without being spotted you'd be done for as soon as you were seen. There's only one group of people who can move about the dock without suspicion, who are all different colours, shapes and sizes."

Toby gasped. "Dock rats. He's right. They've got slaves from every principality, but one thing is the same about all those rats. They're kids. So there's only two of us can go on a rescue mission. Me and Hiko."

"Three." Crocker shoved his way to the front. "That girl from the *Banshee* is young enough. And she *wanted* to go."

"But what can you *do*?" Nisha stamped her feet. "Even

if you get off the *Phoenix*, you can't fight your way into the castle."

Hiko smiled sadly. "Dock rats can go anywhere, no one notices."

"So you, Ayla and me disguise ourselves as rats," Toby said, "sneak off the *Phoenix* and the pier, then walk into the castle. All right. But even if we manage to work our way into the dungeon and release the captain –" he exhaled shakily – "how do we get out again?"

Hiko sagged. "You're right, it won't work."

"Barrows," Marcus spoke up.

Toby jumped. It was as if a statue had suddenly come to life and entered the discussion. "Take barrows into the castle," Marcus continued, still refusing to take his eyes from Dee's bloodless face. "Hide weapons inside and hand them to the crew when you find them. Rita and Harry can be transported back inside them if they're too injured to walk and the rest can fight their way out. Even with Carson and Dobbs gone, that leaves five pirates, armed to the teeth, coming from a direction they won't expect. In the meantime we'll hold off the soldiers. And if I can kill the bastard who stabbed Dee..." He trailed off, raising his head to look at Toby. Murder shone in his bloodshot eyes. This was not the Marcus that Toby had rescued from the sea.

"The captain won't like it," Uma said eventually. "If we get him back, he'll likely throw us overboard for sending his son in alone, with nothing but Hiko and an enemy pirate to protect him."

"I don't need protecting, Uma," Toby snapped. "We've under an hour before they hang one of our crew and this is the best plan we've got. I'm going to speak to Ayla. If you come up with something better while I'm below deck, let me know. In the meantime, make sure they don't board while our backs are turned."

The sleeping quarters were silent. Toby tiptoed in and found the girl from the *Banshee* fast asleep in his own berth.

Her face was utterly relaxed, making her look younger and her hair fanned over his pillow.

One hand was curled under her chin, her fingers loosely furled. The other hand was hidden beneath Toby's blanket, which, despite the heat, was pulled high over her chest.

Ayla's breath shifted strands of hair like spiderwebs against her lips, and her eyelids flickered.

Toby stepped nearer and raised a hand to shake her awake. But before he could touch her Ayla was gripping his wrist in her fist. The tip of her sword pressed against his chest, leaning on his solar plexus. He held his breath. Green eyes glared into his, demanding an explanation.

"I was just coming to wake you." He spoke with the barest movement of his lips and tried to pull back, to show his good intentions.

Ayla released his hand, but kept her sword pointed unwaveringly in his direction. "What do you want?"

Toby gestured to Rahul's bunk. "Mind if I sit down?"

Ayla shrugged and Toby sidestepped then sat.

"I'm sorry to wake you," he said at last, "but we have a time limit. They're going to hang a crew member for every hour we don't surrender."

Ayla nodded. "Makes sense, it's what Nell would do." She swung her feet so she was sitting up and dropped her sword point. Her hand trembled as she leaned the tip on the hard floor.

He hesitated and wondered if he could really ask her to go with him on the rescue mission. He imagined her rowing through the junk-filled darkness, ploughing through obstacles as she chased the *Phoenix*.

"Why were you sent after us?" He frowned suddenly. "Surely someone older ... stronger?"

Ayla bristled immediately. "I told you before, I'm the captain's second for a reason."

"But..." Toby bit his lip – he couldn't find a way to

avoid offending her. "To send you alone…"

Ayla exhaled and refused to meet his eye. "I wasn't alone. Rochelle was knocked overboard by junk that swung past us in the dark. I don't know what it was, we never saw. Ricardo made it as far as the straits, but then he wanted to take over the mission."

"What happened to him?"

"I clobbered him with my oar." She shook her head. "Nell won't be pleased – they were two of her best. So I'd better return with the captain, or the directions to those solar panels, otherwise…"

"Otherwise what?" Toby whispered.

"You've seen the cage she uses for those who've displeased her." Ayla tried to look nonchalant, but Toby saw her lip quiver.

"So you were serious about rescuing the captain?" Toby leaned forward. "If you were, we have a plan and, to be honest, we need you."

Ayla tilted her head. "Of course I'm serious. But why do you *need* me? What kind of plan would rely on a rival pirate for its success?"

"A crazy one." Toby brushed his hand through his hair. "But it's the only one we've got."

SIXTEEN

There was a pile of junk on the deck, everything from car bonnets to hubcaps. Each of the pirates sifted through, looking for something to protect them from the coming attack.

"Gods," Nisha muttered. "This is madness." She gestured to the port rail where Toby and Ayla were preparing.

Without her leather coat and black trousers Ayla looked smaller. Now she wore one of Peel's shirts. It was long enough to reach past her knees and voluminous enough to hide the sword she refused to relinquish. Her hair was pulled into a loose tie and she had removed the beads but insisted on keeping her boots. Hiko had argued until she had removed the laces, so that they flapped around her ankles, loose and tired-looking.

She scowled at Toby, who had been allowed to keep a pair of trousers, but had on a shirt so ragged that he might as well have been topless.

Hiko edged up to them with a knife in his hand. "Your hair." He winced when Toby stared down at him.

"What's wrong with it?" He ruffled his hands through his messy hair.

"It needs to go."

Toby looked at Hiko's roughly shaven head and sighed. "You're right."

When it was done, Toby rubbed a trembling hand over his bare skull.

"Now this." Uma opened a pot of stinking cream. "That sea looks clean, but there'll still be poisonous currents. You'll need protection."

Toby nodded, remembering Uma's barrier cream from his swimming lessons, and the three of them covered themselves as best they could.

"It'll wash off eventually, so don't spend too long in the water." Uma put the lid back on.

Toby took a deep breath. "Let's go and get them out of there."

With a cry, a pirate fell from the rigging to crunch on to the quarterdeck. An arrow stuck from his neck like a signpost.

"They're attacking," Theo cried. "Man the rails. They can't be allowed to board."

Toby, Hiko and Ayla stood out of view of the pier. It was a long way down into the water. Toby wrapped one hand around the rope he had prepared. "Get on, Hiko. It'll be just like when we came down from the crow's nest."

The younger boy's arms tightened around his shoulders and Toby winced at the added weight. Ignoring his discomfort, he swung his legs over the side. Ayla too had wrapped a rope around herself and a pack of weapons bristled on her back.

An arrow whistled between them and Toby ducked. The crew of the *Phoenix* were lined up along the railing, shaking with fear, frustration or fury but unable to do anything but stand guard.

"Theo," Toby shouted, his eye caught by the remains of the junk pile Theo had created on the deck. "Throw that junk at them." Theo brightened and Peel joined him in dragging chunks of scrap metal to the gunwale.

Ayla put her boots on the *Phoenix*'s hull and began to abseil towards the sea.

"Save Rahul, Toby," Nisha called. She had a plastic chair back in one hand and a curved blade in the other. Toby nodded before he followed after Ayla, wishing he felt certain it was a promise he could keep.

Toby didn't look down; he stared instead at the hull of the *Phoenix*. The faded colours of the bird greeted him as he jumped, easing the rope through his gloves.

The weight of Hiko on his shoulders made Toby's back scream and, as Toby moved lower, rust and flaking paint reddened his bare feet. Finally his soles felt the cool wash of the water. He looked down. One more jump and then he could release the rope.

"Toby…" Hiko's voice in his ear.

"What is it?" Toby jumped for the last time and slid on a patch of slimy weed. He winced as his toes bumped barnacles.

"I can't swim."

"Are you serious?" Alarmed, Toby tightened his fists on the rope, he had almost let go.

Ayla splashed into the water and Toby held his breath. The shirt ballooned around her. She rolled and gave him a thumbs up, then her booted feet began to kick as she headed for the prow and around to the quay.

Toby swallowed. With the open sea dangerously clogged with junk, the captain had periodically flooded the wreck room so that the pirates could learn to swim in safety.

"I can pull you, Hiko," he said. "But you mustn't fight me. If you struggle we could both drown." Immediately he regretted his words, as Hiko's arms tightened. "Ashes, we don't have time for this. Polly, can you watch Ayla?" The parrot flew around his head then sailed after the girl.

Instead of jumping free as he had planned, Toby lowered himself carefully into the water. Hiko's legs wrapped around his waist as soon as the waves touched his feet.

"Gods, Hiko, why stow away on a ship if you can't swim?" Toby floated with one hand still closed around the rope, keeping them both above the waves, careful not to swallow any water. "You have to let me go," Toby cajoled him, but the boy didn't move. "I can't move with you like this."

Slowly Hiko unwrapped his legs.

"See. You're safe, we're right against the ship. Can you feel the water?"

Hiko's legs swung freely in the water like seaweed. "It's cold." His teeth chattered.

"Use my arm," Toby urged him. "Hold on to it, but edge out, away from me."

"Don't let go!" There was panic in the boy's voice and he had tensed once more. Hiko crept along Toby's arm until he was hanging from his wrist, his face pale.

"Now lie on your back." Toby kept his voice low and calm. "Relax, feel the waves bobbing you up and down."

Hiko rolled, but the moment water splashed his face, he spun back and grabbed at Toby.

"Hiko, you have to do this." Toby agonized – he needed to get beneath the pier. Ayla would already be climbing out.

He could sense the younger boy trying to gather his courage. "It's only water," Toby pleaded. "Lie back and then I can drag you." He changed tack. "You were amazing on the *Banshee*, you sank your teeth into Crocker, you stowed away on a ship even though you can't swim. You came up with this plan. You're braver than I am, so if I can swim then you can, too. Just relax."

Finally Hiko lay back in the water and let Toby wrap his arm beneath his chin. When the younger boy seemed comfortable, Toby released the rope. Both of them dropped and the salt washed over Toby's face, terrifying Hiko, but the boy remained lying flat.

Relieved, Toby started to pull him towards the jetty.

As he reached the *Phoenix*'s ice-breaker Polly whisked into sight. "Stop," she squawked.

Toby put a steadying hand on the hull and trod water. The metal was hot and Hiko lay behind him, rigid with terror. Polly circled out of sight once more. Soldiers were watching the sea. Toby's heart thudded; his body was chilled now and he was starting to shiver. The water should be warm, with the sun blazing as it was, but the wind kept it endlessly churning, always cold.

Toby wasn't used to long stints in the water and he was already tiring, his skin starting to tingle as the barrier cream washed off.

Finally Polly flew back round. "Quick," she squawked. Toby swam as hard as he could towards Polly, and relied on her to lead him in the right direction. His arm ached as he reached forward again and again, propelling himself one-handed through the dragging tide.

Suddenly a shadow fell overhead and welcome shade blotted the glare as he swam beneath the jetty. Footsteps shook the pier and told Toby the soldiers were already receiving their backup. Quickly he searched for Ayla. She was perched on a piling in the centre of a shaft of sunlight, watching him with narrowed eyes as she squeezed water from her hair.

"What took you so long?"

Toby guided Hiko to a post of his own and Ayla nodded. "Oh."

"I thought you might have gone without me."

"Had to dry off a bit." Ayla shrugged. "Wet dock rats would be suspicious, don't you think?"

She shook her hair out and it started to fluff. The wet shirt that stuck to her body like a second skin was beginning to dry out. Toby forced himself to think of other things.

"Didn't your boots make it?" He looked at her bare feet. Her toes curled around the pile. She nodded and raised a hand. She held her boots in the warmth, the leather cracking as they dried.

"All right." Toby hauled himself out of the water and dragged Hiko after him.

To Toby's surprise, Ayla moved over and pulled the boy into the sunshine. She rubbed his shoulders with one hand, drying him.

With all of his soot washed off, Hiko looked even paler. Toby frowned. On his right arm was a dark smudge that had not been removed by the sea. "What's that?"

"What?" Hiko looked at his own arm. "My tattoo? I've always had it."

Toby edged closer. On Hiko's right forearm was a cross-hatch of lines. Toby counted eight horizontal and eleven vertical, with what looked like two tiny arrows beside.

"What does it mean?"

"Nothing. It's the same as my father's, a copy." Hiko covered his marked arm with his other hand and Toby looked up again as marching boots rained dust from the boards above them.

They would have to find a place to climb up on to the deck and hope they weren't spotted.

He pointed to a likely piling, with pitted grooves that could be used as footholds, and Ayla nodded.

Polly flew beneath the pier and landed on his shoulder.

"You can't take that thing." Ayla acknowledged the parrot with a tilt of her head. "It'll draw attention."

"Her name is Polly," Toby growled. He stroked her with one finger. "She's right though, Pol. Can you keep an eye on us from somewhere else?"

"Why're you talking to it like that?" Ayla sneered. "It's only a bird."

"She's cleverer than your dumb cat," Toby snapped, as Polly flew a jeering wobble above Ayla's head then swooped out from under the pier again.

"Are you sure you're ready for this?" Ayla paused with one hand on the wooden pillar.

Toby nodded.

"Then let's be dock rats." Ayla hopped on to the shorter post. She put her boots back on and then shinned up the column, digging in her fingers and using her arms to pull herself up. Hiko followed, more slowly, then Toby. His toes found every nook, his fingers every cranny. It was easy as climbing the pylon to the crow's nest.

When Ayla reached the top of the jetty she put her arm up for the wood, paused and listened for activity above her head. Then she swung herself out and up as fast as a snake.

Toby heard her land on the pier, hesitate and then patter out of his way. Hiko went after her.

Toby took a deep breath. This was it, his first time on land since he was small. He judged about half an hour, maybe forty minutes, before the first of the crew was hanged. He balanced with his knees tight around the post, reached up, wrapped his hands around the landing and let go.

The wood was slippery, but his fingers adjusted to find purchase. He swung one leg up and paused for breath. Then he rolled his whole body on to the pier.

"What're you doin', Toby-who-knows-things?" The voice was low, curious. "And what've you done to your hair?"

SEVENTEEN

A curse slid from Toby's lips before he could stop it. He rolled on to his knees and looked into the face of a smiling, toothless dock rat.

"D'von," he gasped. His eyes flickered and roved as he searched for Hiko and Ayla. Hiko was crouching behind a blackened aluminium barrow. Ayla rose up behind the teenage dock rat with her sword raised.

"Ayla, wait." Toby lifted a hand to stop her and Ayla hesitated, staring at him in disbelief. Swiftly Toby took stock. They had emerged on to the pier behind a pile of stacked crates, only D'von had spotted them and he stood now, waiting for Toby to explain himself. Toby licked his lips. Was he making a mistake? Should he let Ayla cut the dock rat down?

"Toby?" D'von's smile was slipping.

"D'von." Toby rose to his feet. He gestured and Ayla lowered her sword with a scowl. "My friends and I have something important to do. You've seen all the soldiers – they want my ship. We're trying to stop them."

"If the soldiers want your ship, you'd better give it to them." D'von's brow creased. "Soldiers are bad news. Do what they say for an easy life." He nodded earnestly.

"I'm not after an easy life, D'von," Toby snapped. "And I won't allow my ship to be pulled apart for scrap or sold to St George." He spread his hands. "Listen, we're going to the castle to rescue our landing party. Just pretend you haven't seen us."

D'von's frown cleared. "I can help you." He smacked Toby's shoulder with a loud crack and Toby suppressed a wince. D'von was already picking up a crate and dropping it into Toby's arms.

Ayla hesitated and then she sheathed her sword.

"What do I do with this?" She swung the weapon pack from her shoulders.

"Into the barrow?" When Hiko spoke D'von blinked, noticing him for the first time, but Toby shook his head.

"Tie it under the pier and we'll come back after a recce."

Ayla nodded and hung the pack from a bollard so that it dangled beneath a loose plank. To the casual observer it was hidden but if anyone looked hard enough…

"It'll have to do," she said critically. Then the breath

was almost knocked out of her, as D'von shoved a crate into her arms.

Hiko was already picking up a box, his wiry muscles bulging with the weight. He slotted neatly into D'von's world, a smaller dock rat – nothing to worry about.

As Toby took his first step, he staggered. His feet, used to the endless rocking of the *Phoenix*, were caught out by the unmoving boards beneath them. His ankles jarred and he almost fell.

Ayla's hips swung ahead of him as she too overcompensated for the change from sea to land, but as he watched she swiftly gained her land legs.

Hiko shuffled worriedly beside him as Toby took another awkward step. This time his toes expected the ground to come up to meet him and he found himself missing his step altogether and tripping over his own feet.

"Toby!" Hiko shifted his crate under one arm and caught Toby with the other.

Toby's eyes widened. "How can I rescue the crew if I can't even walk?" Alarm raised his voice and Ayla turned around to shush him. She saw him tottering and frowned.

"Just take a moment," she hissed. "Go slow. It'll come to you."

Toby shook Hiko off. "I'll catch you up." This time he placed each toe carefully and slowly his body began to get the idea. By the time he reached the main part of the pier he was growing steadier.

Toby's ears were assaulted by the noise of the dock – the sounds of rapid-fire Spanish mixed with heavily accented English, the thudding of feet and the barking of stray dogs.

"Crates and boxes over there," D'von shouted. "Over there, you got it? All of them. Out of the way of the very important soldiers."

Toby blinked as D'von swept his arm over the dock. Toby, Hiko and Ayla had managed to emerge from the sea at perhaps the only spot on the jetty that was not crawling with militia.

The soldiers were not only clustered in the shade of the *Phoenix*, they also gathered around the dock, ready to relieve the fighters. They leaned on stacks of crates and jeered at the dock rats. When one tripped, they laughed and placed bets on how hard the overseer would hit him.

Toby held his breath as a small boy flew past him, arms pinwheeling and a bruise already flowering on his cheek.

A crash and loud cry from the direction of the *Phoenix* made Toby look. An old car engine was rolling across the dock, bowling soldiers to either side. One of them was lying still; blood staining the timber beneath him.

Just ahead of him Toby saw a trio of soldiers glance at Ayla. Immediately she compressed herself, her shoulders drooped and her knees caved. Toby's eyes widened. It was as if she had put on a cloak of invisibility, dropping below the soldiers' line of sight.

Hiko, too, was moving in a low scuttle. He ducked beneath swinging hands and avoided pinches and tripping legs with years of expertise. He moved as if he knew where he was going and no one looked at him twice. Immediately Toby realized that he was sticking out. Quickly he hunched like Ayla, pulled his crate closer to his face, and followed D'von.

As he hefted his own load, D'von nodded at other dock rats. Three big lads that Toby recognized from when the new mast was delivered to the *Phoenix* were carrying the broken hull of a fishing boat. Toby held his breath, but not only did they not recognize him, they barely acknowledged his existence.

Hiko sensed his surprise. "Dock rats are always changing, Toby. Traded in and out, grown out of the cages, sold or killed. They assume you're new traded." Relieved, Toby nodded.

When Toby dumped his crate on the pile at the end of the jetty and shifted his gaze to the castle, D'von cuffed him around the ear. "Get more crates."

Toby rubbed his ear. "We have to get to the castle," he whispered.

Next to him Ayla was placing her own load. "We're being watched."

The trio of soldiers who had spotted Ayla earlier had rotated to watch the four of them place their cargo.

"If they call an overseer, we're toast." Hiko came up to Toby's elbow. "*Keep working.*"

Toby ground his teeth, tore his eyes from the open portcullis and headed back to the jetty for a second crate.

"I'm not here to shift crates," Ayla growled, but she followed him, stamping crossly on the wooden planks.

"Hey, you." It was the soldiers. "You, there, with the boots."

Ayla strode on mulishly keeping her head down, pretending deafness.

"Stop."

"He means you," Hiko supplied. Ayla stomped to a halt and Hiko skirted around her. "Keep moving," he muttered to Toby. "A real rat wouldn't wait around to be included."

"But—"

Hiko shoved him from behind. "You don't know what he wants. Don't look back."

D'von crowded him on the other side. "He's right. The girl will be fine." He paused. "Probably."

Hiko pushed again. "Move, Toby."

Toby raced to the crate pile and picked up the nearest box. It brimmed with clams and filled his nose with the stench of seafood left too long in the sun. The traders had been chased off the dock by the soldiers. Toby turned and took the walk back more slowly, giving himself the opportunity to watch Ayla.

Ayla remained still as the soldiers surrounded her.

Her hands clenched and unclenched and Toby could see that she was barely stopping herself from grabbing her sword from beneath Peel's shirt.

"Take those boots off," the smallest soldier said. He kicked at her toecaps. "They look about my size."

Ayla's shoulders grew tight and Toby could see that she was about to explode. There was nothing he could do. In his head he offered her all the boots she could ever want, if she would just take off her own and give them to the soldier without starting a fight.

He edged closer, the crate clutched to his chest. He tried to meet her eye, but Ayla was glowering at the soldier who had kicked her.

Toby coughed. Her green eyes flicked towards him and her face hardened. Then, slowly, as if she was handling an unexploded mine, she bent down and pulled her boots from her feet. Then she threw them at the soldier.

They bounced on the planks, two hollow thuds, and came to rest beside him.

The soldier curled his lip. "Rat! Pick up the boots. Hand them to me nicely."

Hiko ran behind Toby, carting a crate almost as big as he was. "Don't get involved," the small boy muttered, as he went past.

Ayla bent, picked up the boots and held them out to the soldier, her face sullen.

The soldier stroked his moustache and took the boots, holding them up to his friends. "Damp," he sneered. "Still, pretty good. How did you get away with keeping such good boots? The overseers are getting lax." He leaned forward to stare into her eyes and raised his eyebrows, his cheer at his good fortune making him abruptly friendly. "Maybe you charmed him with your pretty green eyes, huh?" He reached out his free hand and his fingers raked through Ayla's hair. He leered and said something in rapid Spanish. Ayla tensed and Toby could see that she was about to fight.

Taking a deep breath he ran into the soldier and spilled his crate of clams down the front of his uniform. The soldier jerked back. All three soldiers turned on Toby and Ayla was forgotten.

"Sorry, masters. Sorry, clumsy of me." Toby ducked, covering his head as they aimed blows at him.

Ayla edged backwards until D'von caught her arm and, from under his, Toby saw him driving her back to the crates. Then he cried out as one of Ayla's boots, swung in an uppercut, smacked his already tender chin. He wobbled backwards and saw stars long enough for the soldier to grab him by the arm and shove him in the direction of the crates.

"Get back to work and be more careful from now on, you filthy vermin." The soldier spat.

Ayla ignored Toby as he staggered up – she was standing her ground against D'von.

"You're too pretty," he was telling her. "You need messin'." He grabbed her arm in one hand and with the other, began to rub fish guts into her hair and face.

Hiko ran around to Toby. "Crates." He nudged Toby into action, then stopped and stared at Ayla. Brown goo was slimed down her cheeks and her hair was now a clumped mess. His lips twitched into a grin. "Much better," he snickered. Then he grabbed the lowest box, shouldered it and started to scuttle back to the edge of the jetty.

"He's right." Toby couldn't help himself. He grabbed a box to avoid Ayla's furious glare. But then he looked her in the eye. "Thank you, by the way."

"For what?" Ayla snapped. Her bare feet fidgeted on the wooden planks.

"For giving him your boots."

"It's my own fault. I should've left them on the *Phoenix*." Ayla picked up her own crate. Then she stopped. "You tried to protect me."

Toby shrugged.

"No one ever did that before."

"Not even Captain Nell?" Toby was shocked.

"You keep saying stuff like that, as if you think I receive special treatment. Maybe that's true on the *Phoenix*, but the *Banshee* isn't like that."

"How come…" Toby gestured at Ayla's hair.

"There is that." Ayla grinned. "I don't remember much about life before I got on the *Banshee*, but I remember throwing the mother of all tantrums when she tried to cut off my hair. Eventually she let me keep it. Maybe when I disappoint her it'll go."

Toby tilted his head. "Why would you disappoint her?"

"Everyone does, in the end." Ayla sighed. "I've learned not to get too close to any of the crew she takes on. It's easier." She looked him directly in the eye. "Still, I've learned some useful stuff over the years. You think that soldier could've laid a hand on me if I didn't allow it? I don't need a sword in my hand to defend myself."

Toby swallowed. "Well, it was less suspicious for me to

take a thumping than three soldiers to get beaten up by a dock rat. Come on, we've got to get to the castle."

The pile of crates was growing smaller and Toby's nerves were wound tighter as each moment passed. He found himself glancing at the castle walls again and again. He was terrified that he would see one of his friends flying rope-necked from the ramparts.

"Watch for me," he murmured to Ayla and she immediately busied herself in front of him, stacking the final crates as she kept watch.

When she indicated that the coast was clear, Toby retrieved the pack of weapons and tossed them into the bottom of the barrow Hiko had hidden behind. Then Ayla helped him load it up with dripping plastic crates. One of the boxes, laden with bitter, soggy oranges, had a piece of sackcloth tossed over it.

"Careful with that, rat."

Toby looked up, sharply.

"That's mine. And once that damned pirate ship is boarded and they let us traders back on the wharf I'll be checking every bit of stock for damage. I'll remember your face, rat."

Toby didn't answer – he ducked his head and picked up

the cloth-covered box, putting it on top of the pile in the barrow. Then he hefted one handle and Ayla the other. Together they wobbled back towards the new pile of crates that was growing on the very edge of the wharf, out of the soldiers' way.

At the pile of crates, Toby unpacked all but the weapons, then Ayla laid the cloth back on top. Hiko skidded to a halt at their side. "Is it time?" the boy asked, his face screwed up against the sun's glare.

Toby nodded and caught a flash of Polly's wings in the sun as she flew skywards.

At that moment, the pirates on the *Phoenix* began beating their shields on the gunwale.

"Toby…" Hiko's eyes were round and Toby followed his pointing finger. Every dock rat on the pier, D'von included, had stopped what they were doing and watched as a squad of grey-uniformed militia, elite Greymen, jogged over the cobbles. In their hands were blackened pistols.

Toby gaped. "We're running out of time. The *Phoenix* can't defend against them."

"They can and they will," Ayla snapped.

"Get off the jetty." Muscular overseers started yelling and waving their arms. "Soldiers only, now. Dock rats back to your cages. You'll have to do double work tomorrow."

Toby placed a palm on Hiko's shoulder. "This is our

chance. No one is watching us."

Ayla picked up the barrow again. "Let's go."

D'von, who had started to move with the rest of the rats, looked at them, his big face creased with concern. He hesitated, then broke away from the main body of queuing, grumbling rats.

"I'll take you." D'von spread his big arms and herded them towards the end of the pier. "I'm big – overseer-size almost."

"You'll get in trouble." Toby objected.

"Dock rats off the dock with no overseer telling them what to do? That's not normal. I'll have to be your overseer." D'von nodded.

"He's right, let him help." Hiko scurried beside D'von.

A flash of colour above him made Toby look up. Polly was gliding close by. A gunshot rang out behind them and he gasped.

"Don't look," Ayla said. "First lesson from the *Banshee*. Keep moving forward, don't look back."

EIGHTEEN

Four dock rats proceeded towards the castle. Two of them pushed a barrow, the littlest walked to the side holding a crate, and the biggest harangued them in low tones.

As the front wheel bumped over the cobbles and threatened to overturn its cargo, Toby mused that the important thing was to look as if you knew where you were going and what you were doing.

He glanced sideways at Hiko and tried to emulate the way the smaller boy moved – head low, feet quick, steps small.

Ayla grunted as the barrow wobbled dangerously. "Stop that," she snarled, righting it and gripping her handle more tightly.

"I'm trying not to get caught." Toby gritted his teeth.

"Well, a barrow of weapons spilling on the cobbles will be a wonderful disguise," Ayla retorted.

"Shut your mouths," D'von rumbled. "You don't talk, I talk. You're not allowed."

Toby pressed his lips together and glared at the girl by his side. Her face was sticky with sweat and fish innards and the scar on her lip stood out against the sunburn on her hollow cheeks. He realized that she hadn't eaten since she'd arrived on the *Phoenix*, yet she made no complaint.

Toby looked up. They had left the promenade now and were passing houses. Every other one looked derelict, but there was a smithy and a bakery, both lit by the glow of large fires within.

Spicy cooking smells tinged the air, making Toby's mouth water and his eyes caught the flickering of bulbs in dark rooms.

A little girl peered from between curtains in one house and pulled a face at him. "Yuck, dock rats!" she squealed.

A boy grabbed her by the shoulder and swung her around. "It's your turn to be the volcano," he shouted. "An' I'm the lava."

"Boom!" she shrieked. "Get Mama."

They ran out of sight and Toby stole a look at Ayla.

"What are they doing?" she murmured, half to herself.

"They're playing," Toby said, surprised. He caught her disgusted expression. "You don't get much leisure time on the *Banshee*, huh?"

Ayla looked resolutely away from him. "Waste of time," she muttered. "She should be learning to fight."

"Shut your mouths." D'von clipped Toby around the ear.

Toby clamped his mouth closed and shook his head, then glanced across at Ayla. She was staring back at the house with the little girl in it. He set his face forward. The castle was straight ahead now, the portcullis open. More soldiers were emerging from the entrance. The officer called to someone then jogged forward, sword at the ready, towards the four dock rats and their barrow. It seemed to Toby that Tarifa had an endless supply of soldiers.

"Hold it," D'von grunted and Toby, Ayla and Hiko froze.

Toby's hands closed tight around the barrow. If one of the soldiers kicked it the weapons would be spilled to the ground.

"Out of the way, rat," the officer snarled, aiming a swipe at Hiko. The boy hopped sideways and Toby and Ayla laboured to move the barrow off the street. The sweating men pounded past, ignoring them.

A gust of wind brought the sound of gunshots and yelling to their ears but Toby set his jaw, refusing to look back. They were running out of time.

As soon as the last of the soldiers passed, Toby dragged the barrow back on to the cobbles and stepped up the pace.

Just ahead Polly swooped through the portcullis and

was swallowed by the gloom. As the wheel of the barrow reached the castle's shadow Toby hesitated. He glanced at Ayla just as she raised her head. Their eyes met.

"The mission," she said, like a vow, and he nodded.

D'von was first beneath the portcullis. Hiko tiptoed anxiously at his side, and Toby and Ayla followed into the darkness, balancing the barrow between them.

Toby stood, blinking, forcing his pupils to adjust to the shadows. After seconds that seemed to take hours, he was able to look around. He tensed, waiting for someone to shout at him, but the courtyard in front of them was deserted.

Suddenly D'von gestured. "Back, back."

Toby and Ayla retreated into the shadows. Hiko crept under Toby's arm.

D'von, however, was ahead of them, and didn't have time to follow them into shelter.

A man dressed in a long red jacket with a high collar appeared from the archway to the right of the courtyard. His hair was braided in a low plait at the base of his neck. Toby guessed this was the portmaster.

He spotted D'von. "What are you doing, rat? Sent to help with those pirates? Get down to the dungeons and ask for instructions. We'll be doing the first hanging in –" He consulted a gold watch that dangled from a chain in front of his chest – "twenty minutes." He rubbed his hands and looked at the sky. "What a serendipitous day, Ford falling into my hands like that." He glowered at D'von. "Still here? Are you stupid? *Go to the dungeons.*"

"Should I take a key?" D'von asked. He held his hand out to the man and Toby's heart filled with affection.

"No, idiot. The keys are in my office. Why would you need keys? Just go and find the officer in charge." The man shook his head. "Those overseers spend too much time hitting you rats on the head. You're good for nothing once they're done with you." He looked D'von up and down like hanging meat. "Although you'd probably make a half-decent soldier. If I remember, I'll mention it to your overseer when the cages are next cleaned out." D'von ducked his head. "Why are you still here?" The portmaster almost shrieked.

"Which way?" D'von asked.

The portmaster rolled his eyes. "Past the kitchens and keep going down. When you can't go down any more, you'll be at the dungeons. You'll like it in there, it's just like home." His moustache squirmed as he sniggered.

D'von marched in the direction of the portmaster's pointing finger. Open-mouthed, Toby watched him go and then the portmaster swept past them, never suspecting that even more rats were hidden in the shadows.

When he was gone, Ayla stepped into the light. "Quick."
She gestured in the direction the portmaster had appeared
from. "His office has to be this way." There was a small
staircase.

Claws closed around Toby's collarbone and he nuzzled
his head into Polly's familiar weight. "Glad you're here."

Ayla rolled her eyes. "What are you waiting for?" She
ran up the stairs, already unsheathing her sword. "We have
less than twenty minutes."

Toby swung the weapons pack on to his back and tipped
the barrow on its side in an attempt to hide it.

"Let's go." He motioned for Hiko to follow him.

Toby stepped into the office and shut the door quietly
behind them. There was a narrow window that overlooked
the straits, but it was too small to allow much light in.

"Here, Toby, you can do the honours." Hiko stood by
the wall. Toby looked quizzical and Hiko gestured again.
To his left was a dented plastic panel with a dirty switch.

Polly hopped off his shoulder and flew on to the desk,
her left eye on Toby, her right swivelled towards the door.

Toby put a finger on the plastic switch and pressed.
There was a crackling hiss then a bulb flickered and lit
with a fluorescent glow. "Electric light."

"All right, all right, twenty minutes, remember? Let's find those keys." Ayla was already rifling through a box on a shelf against the wall.

Toby was looking at the room. In front of him there was an actual wooden desk covered in what looked like a lifetime's supply of precious wood-pulped paper.

"That's a month's wages there, right enough." Ayla was next to him. "I'm tempted to take them for Nell."

"Keys?"

Ayla shook her head. "Let's try in the desk."

Toby yanked at the top drawer, but it didn't move. "Locked."

Ayla elbowed him out of the way, shoved her sword into the top of the draw and levered her weight down on the end. Polly skittered off the desk and the draw opened with a splintering of wood and popping metal.

Toby peered in. "No keys." Then his eyes widened. "But look what we do have." He grabbed a handful of yellowing paper.

"What?" Hiko ducked under his arm and Ayla leaned in, her eyes sparkling.

"Maps," she breathed. Then she shook her head. "Not the mission."

"But look. Planned trade routes, suspected shipwrecks, desirable salvage. Everything we need to last for years at sea. No wonder the portmaster wants the *Phoenix*. He could use these maps and be rich. Gods, Dee will go wild for this." He stammered to a halt, remembering his last vision of her, bloodied and crumpled on the deck.

As he hesitated, Ayla swept up a handful of maps and shoved them into his pack. "Here, then, take them. We don't have time to read now."

She dropped a curled map on to the desk. Hiko rolled it open.

The boy's eyes saddened. "Hey, I haven't seen this writing since I was sold. This is my father's first language. He taught me some before he died." His fingers stroked the ink. "Look, someone's been trying to translate it ... badly."

Toby leaned closer, interested. "What does it say?"

Ayla rolled her eyes and started pulling out more drawers.

Hiko pointed at what to Toby's eyes was a bunch of scribbled shapes. "Island." Hiko stroked the word.

The second word looked to Toby almost identical.

"Volcano," Hiko said.

Ayla froze and Toby's lungs stopped taking in air. "Volcano island?" he whispered. "Are you sure?"

Hiko nodded. "Island – volcano."

"It's a map to the island." Ayla exploded into action. "Give it here."

Toby blocked her. "You can't read it. It's no use to you."

"It bloody is." Ayla's hands turned into claws and Polly flew into her hair with a screech.

Ayla batted the parrot back and stepped away from Toby, her hands formed into fists. "Give. It. Here."

"I found it." Hiko clutched the map to his chest. "You're not having it."

"We don't have time. I'm putting the map in with the rest. We'll sort it out on the *Phoenix*. We have to find those keys."

Ayla took her fists to her sides. "Fine, we'll sort it out on the *Phoenix*." Her eyes tracked the map as Hiko rolled it tighter and slid it between a sword and hammer on Toby's back. The small boy looked at Ayla as he did it, narrowed eyes warning her that he would know exactly where the map was at all times.

She turned her back on him. "Where are those damn keys?"

The keys were in the last drawer. Gathered on a giant ring, there was no way to tell which were for the dungeon and which were for the kitchen cupboards. Toby pocketed the whole ring and made to leave.

Hiko, standing in the doorway, waved frantically. "He's coming back."

"Ashes." Toby and Ayla glanced at one another then,

as one, they grabbed Hiko, shoved him through the door and ran down the short stairwell with his feet tripping between them. They flattened themselves against a side wall, just as the portmaster put his foot on the bottom step.

The portmaster paused on the second tread and checked his watch. He muttered to himself and then proceeded to climb.

Toby exhaled. They had only moments before the alarm was raised.

"The dungeon, quick," Toby gasped.

NINETEEN

The pack bounced on Toby's back and the keys jangled in his pocket as he ran. Ayla kept pace with him, and Hiko sprinted just behind.

His nose told him they were approaching the kitchen and his heart slammed as he saw figures beyond the open door. But steam billowed outwards as they approached and no one saw them run past.

His ears rang with the pounding of the blood in his veins, but he was certain he could hear shouting in the courtyard. An opening beside the kitchen led on to stairs that disappeared into dank dullness. It had to be the way to the dungeon.

Without missing a beat, Toby grabbed the lintel and swung on to the top tread.

The staircase was narrow and twisting, lit by flickering bulbs that buzzed in the darkness, and finally Toby was forced to slow. His feet slipped on the uneven spiral stone staircase and, as they climbed lower, Toby found that his hand was coming away from the brickwork slimy and damp.

He could hear the sound of banging from the floor above. Someone was on their tail.

Finally the stairs stopped at a gaping archway and the stonework dripped into slimy puddles that pooled around his toes. To his right was an alcove packed with metal slop buckets, brushes and shovels and through the archway Toby could see what appeared to be a large storeroom filled with crates. Beyond was a series of thick doors striped with bars.

His heart rose – D'von stood in the corridor, his face turned to one of the doors, his eyes fixed to the dusty grille.

Toby jerked as if to run towards the captive pirates, but Polly nipped his ear. At the same time Ayla put a hand on his shoulder, holding him back. His eyes found the sitting area at the end of the corridor. Crowded with guards, it was open and would easily allow them to be seen if they moved into a bulb's guttering light.

"What do we do? There're too many of them," Hiko whispered.

"We don't have time to mess around. Be ready." Slipping from shadow to shadow, Ayla vanished into the storeroom.

"What's she doing?" Hiko tried to follow her, but Toby shook his head.

"Stay here."

Hiko looked at the stairwell, the pounding footsteps and echoing voices getting louder. "We'll be caught." He sounded terrified.

Polly hopped off Toby's shoulder and into the alcove. She perched on a shovel handle, head cocked. Swiftly Toby dragged Hiko inside. He stepped over mops, almost tripped in a grating that was set into the floor and pushed the two of them flat to the wall.

The smell from the grating gave away the sewers below his feet and Toby covered his mouth. He was so close to his father, but time was running out. How could they fight ten guards, plus however many more that §were coming down the stairs?

"Move over, quick." A figure appeared in the entrance to the alcove – Ayla. She put a finger to her lips.

Suddenly the light in the corridor jumped. A yellow glow swayed on the wall. Hiko coughed and Toby felt his throat start to close up.

"You set a fire," Toby whispered.

Ayla nodded. "A distraction."

The first of their pursuers appeared at the bottom of the steps and Toby crushed Hiko against the wall. They watched as the guards spotted the flames. They yelled and the guards at the other end of the corridor looked up.

Cards scattered and tables rolled as the men sprung to their feet. The two groups converged on the storeroom, feet clattering over the grates. D'von didn't move from his post.

As soon as the last of the men vanished into the storeroom, Toby flung himself towards the locked door and his father.

"I watched them for you, Toby." D'von nodded his head vigorously.

"Thank you, D'von." Toby didn't even look at the bigger boy. He closed his fingers around the bars and pressed his face to the gap. "Captain?"

The room beyond was dark, lit only by the bulb that swung in the corridor, but Toby knew his father's figure.

"Toby, is that you?" Barnaby's hands closed around Toby's. "Get out of here."

"Not without you. We've got keys. Weapons, too." He shrugged the rucksack from his shoulders and started to empty it. Hiko helped, passing the weapons to Toby as Ayla watched the blazing room, making sure the guards remained within.

The captain closed his hands around a giant hammer. "Let them try and hang one of us now, eh?"

"Is Nisha all right?" Rahul's face appeared beside the captain's.

Toby nodded as he pulled the ring of keys from his pocket. "I don't know which it is." The keys jangled as he passed them into Rahul's palm.

"Toby, you're a wonder." The captain hefted his hammer. "Can I smell smoke?"

Toby nodded. "We set a fire to distract the guards."

"In that case, get the hell out of here. We'll follow."

"Works for me." Ayla nudged him. "Let's go."

Metal rattled as Rahul tried the first key in the lock. The sound echoed around the corridor.

Two guards emerged and Toby realized they would be spotted.

"Prison break!" The guards' screams brought others running.

Ayla's sword appeared in her hand and Toby groped for Nix with one hand, shoving Hiko behind him with the other.

"Grab the bag, Hiko," he snapped. "And get behind us."

Polly cawed and focused on the guards running down the corridor.

"Polly! No!" Toby yelled, but she was already launching.

"Get back in there and fight that fire, or we're all dead." The officer shoved half his men back inside and turned face first into the parrot that was coming for him.

D'von banged on the wooden door. "Give me a weapon,"

he shouted. "Quick."

The pirates returned a crowbar through the grille – D'von closed his hands around the weight and swung experimentally.

Polly had inflicted bloody claw marks down the officer's face and now he covered his ears, leaving her free to rake him across one eye. A lucky swing and he knocked her off, but Polly glided back round to strafe him again.

"I'm not letting your bird have all the fun." Ayla ran to meet the lead guard.

As he saw her coming and lifted his sword, she dropped and spun into a rear leg heel-sweep that put her head below the level of his swing and knocked his feet out from under him. As he fell with a surprised grunt, Ayla jumped forward. She landed with her legs on either side of the guard and stabbed downwards. He died with a choking cry and a look of shock.

Toby stared. She had killed the man without a second thought and was already moving past him towards the next.

With a yell of his own, Toby threw himself forwards.

"No! Toby, get back." The captain rattled the grille. "Open this door, Rahul."

"I'm trying." The ring rattled again as Rahul tried another key.

265

D'von looked anxiously at Hiko, who cowered against the door with the paper-stuffed pack clutched in his fists. Then the large dock rat ran forward, swinging his crowbar like a club.

Ayla faced two guards; the rest were trapped behind her in the bottleneck of the corridor. She glared from one to the other, waving her sword in a figure of eight. The one on the right rushed her, while the other shouldered past to reach Toby.

As Ayla's sword crashed into the guard's, Toby ducked under a swipe aimed at his head. He raised Nix and their weapons clanged. The vibration of the guard's sword against his shook his arm.

He found himself back to back with Ayla, both of their arms hampered. "Swap," he cried.

Without missing a beat, Ayla spun around him and drove her sword into the side of his opponent, while Toby twisted around her to complete the same move.

Nix sliced easily through the guard's shirt; then stuck. As the man screeched and swiped wildly downwards, Toby sidestepped. He retched, but forced Nix to keep cutting. Peel was right, this was truly horrible.

The man Ayla had stabbed was down, clutching his bleeding stomach. "Finish it, Toby." Ayla was already rolling into the legs of the soldier beside the officer, using her heels to deliver a vicious double kick to the groin.

Toby twisted Nix and pulled. The sword came free with an arc of blood. Warmth splashed his face and lips and he gagged again as the guard fell to his knees. D'von smashed his crowbar across the man's head, finally putting him out.

The officer slashed a sword at Polly, but the parrot swooped on to Toby's shoulder.

"Are you all right, Toby?" Polly nipped his ear and Toby shook his head, staring at the blood coating his hands.

The officer and guards were more wary now, lined up across the corridor. Blood dripped into the officer's eyes and he wiped it with his sleeve.

Toby stood next to Ayla, panting. Smoke entered his lungs and he coughed, his eyes welling up. The corridor grew dark, filling with smoke.

D'von stood just behind them, his crowbar swinging in one hand.

Toby straightened his back and curled a lip. "Come on, then," he rasped.

The officer gestured and the three guards stepped forwards as one. Again Ayla went low, so Toby went high. She threw herself into a slide, slashing at knees, wrecking the guard's careful formation. As they hopped and slashed downwards, Toby whipped Nix across the corridor at neck height, forcing them to duck and scatter.

Breaking through the line, Ayla attacked the officer, leaving Toby and D'von to press the three guards at the front.

D'von smashed a sword with his crowbar, snapping it at the hilt. The guard stood, shocked, and stared at the dock rat.

"B-but you're rats!" he shouted, as he retreated. He met the officer and they both ran towards the stairs.

Only two guards faced the pirates now. One limped on an injured leg and the other held his throat where Nix had cut him.

Toby's lungs tickled again and he almost doubled over with a cough. Behind him he could hear Hiko's higher-pitched hacking. Ayla held the collar of Peel's shirt up over her face.

"Polly want a cracker!" Polly squawked.

Inside the storeroom the fire leaped higher.

"Do you know what you've done?" the officer shouted from the stairwell. "If that fire doesn't get put out…"

"What do I care?" Toby coughed. He slashed downwards. His sword caught and he yanked as he landed, pulling it free to the noise of an injured howl. The guard whose shoulder he had sliced staggered into the wall and D'von hammered the crowbar into his stomach, then brought down the bar once more on his head.

The single remaining guard called out towards the storeroom. "We need help here."

The reply was panicked. "We can't put out the fire! Get out!"

The guard turned, wide-eyed, then sprinted away from them.

Toby rested with a hand on his knees. The guards fighting the fire were running into the corridor now and heading for the stairs. "Why are they running?" he whispered.

The cell door slammed open and the crew of the *Phoenix* appeared.

"Captain." Toby turned.

Barnaby strode down the corridor and wrapped his arms around his son, forcing Polly into the air. Toby felt the prickle of his beard and his father's brass compass pressing against him.

"I'm all right," he said. "We've got to get back to the *Phoenix*."

Rahul limped to Toby's side, clutching his torso. Behind him Callum was trying to move Rita, but struggling with his own injury. Hiko dropped the pack and put his arm around her. Rita's chin rested on her chest and her legs dragged. Blood dripped from her arm to the floor.

"Simeon needs a hand with Harry." Rahul coughed.

269

D'von tossed the crowbar with a clang of metal and walked to the cell. He lifted the injured pirate over his shoulder.

Simeon nodded and staggered into the corridor followed by Oats, who was bent over his arm, his face deathly white.

"What about Dee?" the captain asked.

"She made it back." Toby blinked sudden tears. "It's bad. But the *Phoenix* would've been boarded if—"

"Toby, we need to move," Ayla interrupted.

"Is that…?" Barnaby stared at Ayla.

"Later." Toby strode towards the stairs.

Suddenly the flames in the storeroom jumped. Fire spurted and lit up the corridor and a bulb exploded above Toby's head, raining broken glass and forcing the pirates to duck.

Toby found himself and Ayla bundled towards the archway, Polly flapping wildly in his face.

"Move," Barnaby roared, as Ayla tried to free herself.

Rahul turned and put his arms around Hiko, Rita and Simeon, forcing them forward. D'von broke into a run and Oats and Callum lurched after, bumping from wall to wall as fast as they could.

Flames licked at their feet, catching on anything that would burn. In the alcove, metal buckets spat.

As they reached the staircase, Hiko was shouting.

Toby couldn't work out what he was saying. Then Ayla twisted out of reach.

"You dropped the maps?" Her face was furious. "You stupid little..." She leaped down the steps, shouldered past the others and ran back through the archway into the corridor. Toby's pack lay smouldering against the cell door.

"Ayla," Toby yelled. "Leave it! There's no time!"

As Ayla's hand closed around the pack, the smoke seemed to be sucked back towards the storeroom. Barnaby threw himself over Toby, closing his arms around his son's head.

"Ayla!" Toby screamed.

Polly flew towards the girl, wings pumping and Toby wriggled, trying to see.

An explosion slammed into him, forcing him downwards. Stairs punched him in the gut as a sun-bright flare burned his eyes. A squawk penetrated the ringing in his ears and his heart stuttered as Polly's feathers were seared to nothing. She flapped once more and tumbled to the ground.

"Polly!" he screamed, but all he could hear was the endless rumble of collapsing stone as the corridor vanished. A second, more-muffled explosion was followed by the rattling of brick and a final deep thump.

Then silence, broken only by the fizz of electricity inside a single swinging bulb.

Toby raised his head. The staircase above was completely blocked. He turned with difficulty. Behind him there was no corridor, no Polly, no Ayla – only a pile of broken masonry and a single dusty hand reaching out from under the brick.

TWENTY

"There were explosives in the storeroom," Rahul said again, as if by saying it he could begin to believe it. He was staring at the blocked stairs, his face bloodless beneath its layer of dust.

Toby said nothing. He sat between Oats and the captain, his shoulder missing its familiar weight, his eyelids prickling. His hands kept forming fists and then falling open. His gaze returned to Callum's bloody hand where it protruded, claw-like, from the pile of brick behind them.

Hiko huddled next to him. "It's my fault," he whispered. "If I hadn't dropped the maps, she wouldn't have gone back for them."

Toby shook his head, opened his mouth, but still said nothing.

"Toby." Barnaby shifted in the small space until he squatted in front of his son. "Polly's gone, but you're all right… We're all right."

Toby looked up. The captain wore a thick patina of brick dust with trails of blood running through it. The bulb flickered briefly and went out, sending them into darkness. There was a collective inhalation of breath and then power surged and light splashed their cave once more.

"Don't forget Ayla," Toby whispered eventually. "She's gone, too."

His mind's eye flashed a picture of the girl. In his head her hair was once more plaited and beaded and the jewels in her braids clattered.

Toby felt a tear track through the dirt on his face.

"How much stone do you think there is?" Rita was staring at the blocked staircase. "Can we dig through?"

The captain shook his head, but Rahul rose unsteadily to his feet. "We have to try," he grunted. "We have to get back to the *Phoenix*. They're under attack, right, Toby?"

Hiko replied for him. "The soldiers have guns and everything." The younger boy wiped his nose.

"We have to get back," Rahul said again and, moving like an automaton, he began to pull bricks out of the pile on the stairs. For a moment Rita watched him, shuffling her feet in the blood pooled around them, then she lurched to her knees and weakly started to help him dig with her bare hands.

"We survived because we were under the archway,"

Simeon said. He sat at Harry's side, one shoulder supporting his semi-conscious friend. He looked up as if he could see through to the top. "There could be as much as ten metres of stone above us."

"Or there could be less than one. Come on, Simeon." As Rahul glanced back, Toby saw the panic on his face.

"I don't want to die down here." D'von was crouching alone in the archway, his face screwed up, fear thickening his accent.

Simeon leaned Harry carefully against the archway and pushed himself to his feet. Moving closer to the bricks he shook his head. "I'm not sure we should even touch this. Captain?"

Barnaby exhaled. "What choice do we have?" He patted Toby's knee as he too stood. "If we don't run out of air we'll be dead of thirst soon enough. We dig."

Toby's nails were broken and his hands were bleeding from a hundred cuts. Behind him a pile of stone was growing, but it seemed as though they had made no difference to the blockage. He handed another stone to Hiko and swayed, suddenly light-headed. He clutched his head and turned to see Rita sag on to her heels, her hair dangling in tangled rat's tails over her eyes.

Rahul's breath was coming in thick pants. Even the captain was leaning against a wall, gasping.

"Toby…?" Hiko's voice was faint.

Toby reeled round to see the younger boy topple over. Hiko tried to lift himself but only managed to press his elbows against the floor. "What's happening?" he pleaded.

"We're running out of air," the captain groaned. "Dig faster."

D'von threw his arms around a giant stone sticking out from the avalanche and began to pull.

"Wait," Toby cried, but with a great heave D'von yanked the rock free and teetered round with a look of triumph in his bloodshot eyes.

The pile began to shudder and Toby dived for Hiko. He dragged him back under the archway, which was now partly blocked with dug-out rubble. With a sound like thunder, the stones shifted and tumbled in towards the pirates, who yelled and threw themselves after Toby. A cloud of dust and the rattle of pebbles finished the second rockfall and Toby opened his eyes. The space the eight were crouched in was even smaller than before.

"Ashes." Oats glared at the stone. He was struggling to clear the rock using one hand. Where his other hand had been, only a bleeding stump remained – a reminder to Toby of the extreme situation that had put them there.

Rahul groaned. "We're trapped," he said at last and his head fell into his hands.

"There's no way to let the *Phoenix* know not to wait for us," the captain murmured. "How long before she sails?"

"She'll hold out till dusk," Toby whispered. "If she isn't boarded before then."

They were all silent, their breathing the only sound in the darkness. Then D'von began to weep, great heaving sobs that were muffled by the brickwork. They huddled together and listened as each cry was sucked into the dust.

Toby's head now lay on the captain's knee. Hiko leaned on his legs and Rita's arm pressed against his. Harry and Oats were propped on Simeon, one to each side, and Rahul curled up on the floor, staring blankly at the blood that dripped from his nose on to his fingers.

D'von had fallen silent, his lament drying up as the air grew thinner and drew the volume from his lungs. Now he was folded into a corner, his head on his knees.

"You know," Toby whispered suddenly. "It's almost as though I can still hear her...?"

"Who?" The captain stroked Toby's stubbly head.

"Polly." Toby closed his eyes. The squawk of his parrot seemed to come from far away. Perhaps she was calling him back to the open sea. He closed his eyes and drifted, took himself to the *Phoenix*. Now he was sitting in the crow's nest. In his hand one of Peel's rare sugar biscuits. He stared into the sunset as the sea air filled his lungs and junk rose and fell beneath him. On his shoulder the familiar weight of his oldest friend warmed him and her feathers tickled his ears.

Polly's squawk was closer. Toby's chest hurt, his lungs laboured and he gasped like a netted fish. He tried to lift his head, but dizziness forced it back down. He went back to the *Phoenix*. He wasn't meant to die on land, so he would spend his last moments at sea.

"Who's a pretty Polly?"

"You are," he muttered.

"Sounds like Polly," Rita giggled drunkenly.

"Wait." Toby blinked. "You hear that, too?"

Barnaby's hand tightened in Toby's hair. "That *is* Polly. She was on the other side of that explosion. Where is she?"

Toby blinked again. Thinking was almost impossible. He kept drifting back to the rocking *Phoenix* and his mind moved like treacle.

"The alcove," he said, finally, "it might not have collapsed. She has to be in there."

"She's getting louder." Rahul's bloody fingers twitched.

He was right. With a great effort Toby dragged himself away from the *Phoenix* and back to the present of the airless dungeon. Polly's chattering was getting louder – she was coming closer.

Callum's buried hand suddenly twitched. D'von squealed hoarsely and toppled backwards. Hiko struggled to move, but could barely lift his head.

Toby could not tear his eyes from the macabre sight. The hand jerked and twisted and then dust lifted into the air around it, motes hanging in the flickering light from the bare bulb. Pebble-sized pieces of stone rocked and began to slide down the pile of bricks, then a larger piece of stone moved and Polly's beak appeared.

Toby watched as his parrot struggled her way through the hole that she had made between Callum's body and the fallen stone.

Finally she tumbled out, hooting as she bounced down broken slabs to land on her back on the rocky floor.

"Polly?" Toby whispered.

Oats was already struggling to the hole Polly had made, putting his mouth to the space and gasping for breath.

"Take turns." The captain pulled him aside and dragged Hiko into his place.

Toby flopped on to his knees and lifted Polly.

"Pellets," she cawed, and then she went still.

Toby held her loosely. His Polly was gone and in her place was a brass-coloured skeleton with one blue eye, going dim, and one broken lens. Tiny rivets held her together and the remnants of charred feathers that clung to her tail were all that told Toby this was still his Polly. Her breastplate was dented and her head was scraped and misshapen. Dust and soot blackened her shine and Toby rubbed her wing gently with his sleeve. He pulled crumbled pellets from his belt and held them to her beak.

A click, a whirr and they were inhaled. Toby watched, fascinated. He could see the glow as Polly's biomass generator lit inside her chest. Her single operational eye glowed brighter and she came back to life.

"Who's a pretty Polly, then?" she mumbled. Then she held out her wings, looked at herself and shook. "Sod it," she cawed. "The game's up."

"You're still my pretty Polly." Toby's voice caught in his throat and he tightened his hands around her. "Are you hurt?"

"I can't be hurt." Polly nudged him. "But I am damaged and I'll need some attention from Captain Ford. There isn't time now – I calculate ten minutes before you have no air. So, who wants to get out of here?"

D'von and the other pirates stared at Toby. It was Rahul who finally spoke. "What the hell is that?"

280

"According to Polly, we should dig in that direction." The captain pointed towards Callum.

Toby tried not to look.

"Use your weapons to shore up the hole, pull Callum out and you'll be able to crawl almost all the way through." Polly flexed her blunted claws. "Get to the alcove and there's a grate. Time is getting short."

Toby remembered the alcove. "She's right, there was one near Ayla…" His voice dropped. "I mean, near your cell." The possibility of escape tightened Toby's chest. "Will it lead us out?"

Polly's wings clattered as she shrugged. "Better than staying here." She glanced at the other pirates and almost apologetically squawked, "Polly want a cracker!" Then she shuffled on to Toby's shoulder. "Sorry. Built in."

Automatically Toby went to stroke her, but stopped as his fingertips met not soft feathers, but metal. Polly nudged his head. "It's still me."

"I know." But Toby's fingers dropped.

"Let's work." Rahul was on his feet.

"There's not room for everyone." The captain glanced at Callum's corpse, then at Toby. "And there's no time for arguments. Hiko, D'von and Toby, get to the back with

Rita, Oats and Harry. The rest of us will pull him out. Polly, you keep an eye on the tunnel and let us know if it's going to collapse."

Toby left Polly with the captain and retreated to the rear of the space. He sat with his knees up, Hiko huddled next to him and D'von on his other side. Harry still drifted in and out of consciousness.

Rita offered a tiny half smile. "It'll be all right, Toby."

Toby nodded and, despite the heat, he shivered. The captain was grunting with effort now, pulling one of Callum's arms. Simeon had the other. Rahul was trying to dig around the body as the others pulled.

"Carson, Dobbs, Callum, all dead," Rita said quietly. "Callum was an idiot." She picked at one of her nails as she watched his torso sagging out of the widening hole.

Toby swallowed as Callum's head flopped. He looked away again.

"Always trying it on," Rita continued talking absently. "As if I wanted to get pregnant and leave the *Phoenix*." She shook her head, but there were tears in her eyes. "He was an idiot," she repeated, but she did not take her eyes from his face.

Finally Callum's legs slithered from the hole. The captain bundled the fallen pirate to one side, pulled off his own coat and covered the body. Then he gestured to the hole. "Hiko, Toby, you're smallest, you go first."

Hiko crawled forwards, but Toby held him back. "I'll go first ... just in case." He looked at the hole. Hammers, crow bars and blades held chunks of rock in place and prevented the roof from collapsing, but he could imagine how it would feel to get inside and then have the whole thing crack and crumble, burying him just like Callum.

"We're running out of time, Toby," Rahul coughed. "Think of the *Phoenix*." He wiped sweat-caked dust from his forehead. "Every minute we're in here is another minute they have to fight."

Toby nodded. He tried to take a deep breath, but dust clogged his lungs. He kneeled down in front of the hole.

On the other side he could see the alcove. Beyond was more fallen stone, but the storage space had remained mostly clear. Toby placed his hands on sharp-edged brick. Lying down flat, he scraped his stomach and chest by commando-crawling into the hole. Above him he could feel the weight of shattered stone and deep darkness pressing down, trying to crush him. He wriggled as fast as he could and toppled out on the other side, falling in a landslide of pebbles on to the grate in the alcove.

"Toby, are you all right?" The captain's voice floated through the hole.

"I'm fine." His shout pulled dust down on his head and

Toby covered his face with his hands and coughed.

The alcove was dark. The only light came from the bulb that swung on the other side of the narrow tunnel. Still, Toby could feel the grate beneath him. He rolled and gripped it with his fingers, pulling as hard as he could. It shifted with the creak of breaking rust-seal and a rush of fetid air. But at least it *was* air.

"I've opened the grate," Toby choked. Then he stood next to the hole, hands outstretched, ready to catch Hiko, but it was Polly who came next. She jumped into the alcove, cocked her head then hopped towards him.

Hiko followed, wriggling to get through even faster than Toby. Toby gripped his wrists as soon they appeared and dragged him to his feet. Hiko doubled over, gasping.

"Who's a pretty Polly?" Polly squawked from below. "Send him down, Toby." Toby peered past the grating. Her single blue eye glowed up at him, a firefly in the darkness.

"Ready?" he asked. Hiko nodded and Toby grabbed his wrists again. Hiko stepped into the hole and Toby lowered him. He had to drop to his knees and then lie on his front before Hiko called out that he could feel the ground. Toby released him and listened for the splash as the boy landed.

"Are you all right?"

Hiko retched. "It stinks down here" he choked. "But there's air."

The little light they had was blocked out as someone else started through the tunnel. Toby reached blindly into the hole, feeling for hands to pull. When he felt someone he heard them gasp, then fingers closed around his. He pulled and, as the person slithered into the alcove, light followed to show D'von.

"Help me down?" Toby asked, nodding towards the grate and holding out his hands. D'von gripped and lifted Toby as though he was no heavier than a crate.

Toby's feet dangled over the hole and D'von began to lower him. Toby held his breath. When Hiko's fingers touched his toes he gulped and found himself swallowing air that tasted of faeces.

His tongue shrivelled and he flopped like a fish as Hiko guided his feet to the ground. As soon as D'von released his hands, Toby covered his mouth. His naked toes squelched in something slimy and he gagged again.

"I'm standing in a sewer," he groaned.

"Aren't we all?" The voice was neither Hiko's nor Polly's and it came from the pitch dark just ahead.

"Say that again," he rasped.

"You're not the only one in the blasted sewer." The voice was shaky, yet achingly familiar – enough for his heart to leap into his throat.

"Ayla?" Toby whispered.

"Who else!" she snapped.

"How?" Toby stuttered. "We thought you were killed."
He held his arms out towards her voice, but felt nothing.

"I should have been. The explosion knocked me into
the cell, where your parrot thing found me. I managed to
clear the nearest grate enough to climb in. Then it went
back for you."

Polly squawked acknowledgement and Toby shivered.
"I'm so glad you're alive."

Ayla grunted, paused then spoke again. "I-I feel like it's
my fault." Her voice floated on the rancid air.

Toby shook his head, although she couldn't see him.
"We had no other choice. There was no way for you to
know there were explosives in that room."

He somehow sensed her sag. "Was anyone killed?"

Toby didn't reply.

"Who? The captain?" Her voice was carefully neutral.

"No. His name is … *was* … Callum."

"I didn't know him."

"You wouldn't have." They remained in awkward silence.

Then Toby heard Ayla shuffle closer. "I thought you
were dead, too," she whispered.

Toby reached out once more and this time he felt Peel's
shirt with the tips of his fingers. He edged closer and felt
his way until he found the top of an arm. Then he pulled

gently, giving her every chance to tear away.

She didn't.

To Toby's shock, Ayla allowed him to step in close, until his toes found hers and he could wrap both of his arms around her. There they stood, breathing in the darkness, trembling in one another's arms.

"I didn't want to die alone in the dark," she mumbled. Her breath brushed against his ear.

Toby tightened his arms and Ayla hissed and jerked. Toby immediately released her. "What's the matter?"

"Nothing." Ayla's voice had suddenly weakened.

"The girl has a broken arm and third-degree burns to her shoulder. She has first-degree burns elsewhere. She has not allowed me to examine her properly." Polly's damaged voice processor made her sound almost like Uma.

Toby bit his lip, hands hovering. "Are you…?"

"I'm fine, forget it." Ayla stepped away from him again. Toby was about to follow when a splash behind him made him spin.

"Who's that?" Hiko whispered.

"Rita." The pirate's voice was dull with pain. "My wound's open again and, gods, this smell."

"Can you come to the sound of my voice?" Toby reached out a hand and Rita grabbed it.

It felt like forever before the captain finally stood with the group. He had waited till last, but now they were all free. Lost inside a pitch-dark, stinking hole, but free nonetheless.

"Polly, how's your night vision?" The captain cracked his knuckles.

"Operational." There was a mechanical whir and a clank as Polly tried to fluff her non-existent feathers.

"So, which way?" The captain prompted, as he lifted her on to Toby's shoulder.

Polly looked one way, then the other. "This way."

The pirates formed a chain with Toby and Polly in front. Ayla put one hand on his shoulder, Hiko behind her, then D'von and the others. At Polly's prompting, Toby started to slide one foot in front of the other.

Inside the sewer the darkness was a presence of its own, pressing in on all sides. Toby breathed as shallowly as he could.

"Stop," Polly rasped. She scrambled around on his shoulder and looked up. Toby followed the tiny light of her eye. Overhead was the grey outline of a manhole.

"How do we get up there?" Toby stretched, but his hand came nowhere near.

Simeon scuffled to the front, picked Toby up and balanced him on his shoulders.

This time when Toby reached, his hands touched the ceiling.

"How do we know we won't climb out into a load of soldiers?" Ayla muttered.

Toby dropped his hands from the grille. "She's right, how do we know?"

"We don't." The captain spoke from the back of the line. "We'll have to take the risk."

Ayla touched his ankle. "Do it, Toby."

Toby reached up and gripped the grille. Simeon pushed him from below and he heaved.

TWENTY-ONE

When the manhole cover lifted, Toby pressed his eye to the gap. At first he was blind. His eyes had become accustomed to the dark and the hot sun washed everything out to pale nothingness. He could hear though, and when the screams and clashes of a pitched battle floated through the gap, Toby shivered.

Claws dragged on his back, scoring marks on his battered skin, and Polly scratched her way on to his shoulder.

"Polly want a cracker," she muttered.

Frustration burned Toby and he closed his eyes then opened them again. He tried to force his pupils to adjust. Finally the world came into focus and he could see. The hole opened out on a road leading to the port side of the jetty. To his right stood the pile of crates that he, Ayla, Hiko and D'von had helped to move from the pier. Behind the crates traders huddled angrily, trying to watch their goods and avoid fallout from the battle at the same time. The back end of the pier was almost empty. As Toby watched, a soldier pounded towards them with paper in his hand – a message from the castle. He ducked as the man ran along the road, but the Tarifan didn't notice the open manhole.

It was the front of the wharf that Toby was interested in but he couldn't see far enough. He rose to his knees on Simeon's shoulders, lifted the grille still further and his heart sank. Soldiers swarmed around the *Phoenix* like fire ants. Arrows filled the sky in a deadly hail that hammered on her deck and the Tarifans were throwing themselves up makeshift gangplanks, trying to board.

"Can you see?" The captain shoved his way to the front of the line. "Has the *Phoenix* been taken?"

"It looks like they're holding them off." Toby crouched on his toes now, Simeon a solid base beneath.

"Can we get out of here?" Ayla hissed.

In answer Toby shouldered the grille aside and lifted himself on to the road. Polly fluttered awkwardly from his shoulder to the dirt verge as Toby checked around him, slithered on to his belly, rolled and held out his hand for the next pirate.

As fast as if they had practised it, all the able-bodied pirates excluding the captain took up position around the grating. Toby, Hiko, D'von, Simeon and Rahul crouched around the hole, half of their attention on the road, half on the next of them to emerge.

Rita was the first of the injured to come into the light. The captain lifted her as high as he could and Simeon caught her armpits. She collapsed when he pulled her out, one hand around her stomach wound, the other covering her eyes from the brutal sun.

Harry followed. He was barely conscious and Simeon had to prop him against D'von before he turned back for Oats, who had almost pulled himself clear.

Finally it was Ayla's turn. Toby found himself unable to look away from the hole as he waited for her to emerge.

"Get off me," she hissed from below. "I can manage."

"Stupid girl, I can see those burns, let me lift you," came the captain's voice.

"I'll climb."

"You will not."

"Ayla." Toby lay on his stomach. "Can you reach my hand?"

"No," she snapped.

"D'von?"

The dock rat understood what Toby was thinking and lifted him by the ankles and dangled him over the hole. Nix shifted in Toby's belt and he grabbed the sword with one hand. With the other he reached out as D'von lowered him.

"Now?" He stretched and his fingertips touched skin.

A splash and a surprised grunt from the captain. Then Ayla's fist closed around his wrist and Toby gripped her forearm.

D'von started to lift them up. Toby felt as if he was being pulled in two, but eventually he lay on his stomach with Nix twisted uncomfortably beneath him. Ayla dangled from his hand. He hauled and she came into the light.

Their eyes met. Ayla's were glazed with shock. Her hair frizzed out, singed and shorter on one side. Where Peel's shirt was not scorched, it was grey with dust and, as she lurched to her knees, the arm that Toby was not holding flopped stiffly to her side. The skin was red raw and blistered.

"Gods," Toby murmured.

"It could've been worse." Ayla twisted awkwardly, trying to stop him from seeing and Toby's eyes fell on the backpack that hung from her good shoulder. Charred paper curled inside.

"You still have it." Shock garbled his words.

Ayla nodded and edged away from him. "The map's mine now." Her good hand closed around the pack. "I earned it."

293

"I…" Toby stopped himself. "Now isn't the time to talk about it."

"There's nothing to talk about. You've got your captain back and I have the map, so back off."

Below they could hear the captain take a run and leap for the hole. Simeon caught his arm and helped him out. They were free.

Tearing his gaze from Ayla, Toby looked quickly around. A few traders had spotted them but none of the soldiers had been alerted yet.

"Now all we have to do is get through that lot." Rahul gestured to the battle.

"Our weapons are buried beneath the castle." The captain pursed his lips. "We can't fight past."

Toby regarded the pier thoughtfully. "We were dock rats before, we can be again."

"That'll work for you and me, Toby, but what about everyone else?" Hiko asked.

"Look." Toby pointed. Next to the crates was a stack of deep aluminium barrows like the one they'd used to get the weapons to the castle. "They're big enough for a man to curl up inside."

"Then what?" Ayla cradled her broken arm gingerly as she spoke.

"The girl is right. We can't take wheelbarrows up the

gangplank in the middle of a war," Simeon rumbled.

"We only have to get close enough to the *Phoenix* to swim for it without the soldiers seeing us." He pointed to the place where they had climbed up the pilings. "There."

The captain twisted his compass in one hand. "It's worth a try." He pointed to a palm tree beside the road. "We'll wait there. Leave Polly with me and bring the barrows."

Toby held out his arm and Polly walked along it, metal wings gleaming in the sun, and hopped on to the captain's shoulder.

Then Toby, D'von and Hiko set off and Ayla followed.

"Wait a minute." Toby spun on his heel. "What are you doing?" He stared at Ayla, who was tottering along the road after them. "You're not coming."

Ayla's eyes widened. "You did *not* just give me an order." She tightened her fist around the backpack. "I'm not getting taken anywhere inside a barrow. I'm as useful as you are."

"You're injured. Rita and Harry are happy to wait, why can't you?"

Ayla closed her eyes and opened them again. "I've been injured before. Pirates don't show weakness, especially in front of the enemy."

"Be sensible," Toby pleaded. "The soldiers haven't even spotted us."

"I'm not talking about the soldiers," Ayla said wearily. "I'm Banshee, you're Phoenix."

Toby opened his mouth and closed it again.

"I'm Nell's second," Ayla sighed. "You think she'd be OK with me curling up inside a barrow and being tipped into the sea like old junk?"

Toby spread his hands. "How would she know?"

Ayla shrugged. "I learned early on it's best to assume that she knows. Whenever you think she doesn't, somehow she always does ... or she finds out."

"But you're injured," Toby repeated.

"And I'll get medical attention when I'm on the *Phoenix*. But I'm getting on board on my own damn terms." Her jaw set firm and Toby realized there was no point in arguing. Ayla had to be in shock – when it wore off the pain would overtake her and force her to slow down. In the meantime he would have to keep her safe.

"Here. Barrows." D'von stopped and gestured, as if he was gifting them to the pirates.

"What are you doing?" A red-faced trader stamped forward. "There's no one meant to be on the pier. Where did you come from?"

Toby rubbed his aching head, his thoughts slow and unresponsive. Would they have to fight the traders now?

"We have to load the barrows and take them on the

dock," D'von rumbled. "I don't question orders. I do as I'm told."

Hiko capered at his side, the picture of sun-stroked idiocy.

"Stupid dock rats." The trader growled and he aimed a kick at Toby. Toby ground his teeth and allowed the man's foot to connect with his calf. Then he hopped backwards, making himself ignore the man's self-satisfied smirk.

"You be careful of our goods. Don't go near them."

D'von grumbled as he rolled the first barrow to Toby.

Toby gripped the unsteady barrow and started to roll it back towards the waiting crew. The trader glared after them. "What are you loading into them barrows?" he shouted.

Toby froze, his mind racing.

"Spies," Ayla said solemnly. "Dressed as pirates. They'll sneak on the ship and take it from inside."

"Of course. There's no chance of surrender any more, not now their captain's dead in the explosion." The trader nodded sagely then stared at Ayla's arm. "What happened to you?"

Toby could see him putting two and two together – an explosion in the castle and a burnt girl.

"She wouldn't stop talking," Toby said quickly. "Overseer stuck her in the fire. Shut her up right quick."

The trader relaxed with a snort. "Better learn that lesson, rat."

Ayla's mouth twitched, her scarred bottom lip narrowing. But she nodded and picked up one handle of a barrow. Hiko took the other and they started to teeter after Toby. D'von followed with the last cart, ducking his head.

Toby could feel the man's gaze burning into his shoulder blades.

"Trouble?" The captain fingered his compass.

Toby shook his head. "They all think you're dead in the explosion so no one's looking for you. The trader thinks you're all spies getting ready to take the *Phoenix* from inside. He won't raise the alarm."

"Clever." Oats was crouched over his stump, his head bowed. He lifted it now to look at Toby. "Who goes first?"

"The injured have to go last." Toby dropped his cart and rubbed his hand over his stubbled head. "You can't climb the pilings without help from below."

"The captain goes first." Ayla gestured at her barrow. "That was my mission – get the captain back."

"The captain, Simeon and Rahul first. Rita, Harry and Oats on the second trip." Toby nodded.

Rita didn't look pleased, but eventually she leaned on the tree. "We'll just wait here, then." She looked at Harry and Oats. "You know that if we get caught we can't protect ourselves."

Ayla sneered. "I'll take that risk." She cocked her head again. "Are we doing this, or not?"

The barrow was almost too heavy to move with Rahul inside and Toby found that it caught on every single bump on the ground. With each step it threatened to tilt in a different direction and his arms ached with the effort of keeping it upright. He heard D'von grunt and knew that even the experienced dock rat was having trouble. He closed his ears to Ayla's laboured panting. She and Hiko were sharing a load and she held her side of the barrow one handed, so the steering was all down to Hiko. The captain and Polly were both inside their barrow and it was the one most likely to tip over. Toby hardened his heart, forcing his eyes to remain straight ahead.

Underfoot the road turned to planks and suddenly the wheel of the barrow rumbled as if it was on tracks. As the wheel caught in warped timber and stopped abruptly, Toby and Rahul both grunted. Toby took a deep breath, wiggled the wheel free and then looked towards the *Phoenix*. Just ahead of him, close enough that Toby felt engulfed by the noise, the battle raged.

Toby could see Amit and Ajay holding a car bonnet over Nisha's head while she tipped burning fuel pellets over the gunwale. Arrows snapped on the metal of the ship as charred combustibles from the boiler cascaded down the nearest gangplank, burning soldiers who plunged into the water with screeches of their own.

Bullets pinged from the *Phoenix*'s hull as Theo and Marcus defended the head of another gangplank, holding hubcaps and long salvage hooks.

Toby looked higher. Arnav had abandoned the crow's nest. The *Phoenix* had not yet spotted its returning crew.

As Tarifans screamed and yelled, officers ordered more arrows to fire and the *Phoenix* fought on.

Toby kept his legs moving forward. Ayla and Hiko skirted the twisted board and drew level.

"Nearly there," Hiko gasped.

Toby looked at him. The younger boy was red-faced and struggling for breath. His knees shook as he walked. They stopped on the edge of the pier. Still no one stopped or even looked at them – every eye was on the resisting pirate ship, the enraged officers and the falling arrows.

Toby knocked the side of his barrow and Rahul sprung out, leaped over the side and crouched on the jetty. D'von tipped Simeon out of his and the captain emerged more slowly, clutching Polly. He nodded thanks to Hiko and Ayla and his gaze rested for a long moment on his desperate ship. His beard twitched as his lips narrowed.

"Better get back on board." Toby gestured, and Barnaby turned to him.

"I wish you didn't have another trip to make. I'd do it for you if I could," the captain said.

"We'll bring the others as fast as we can. Go." Toby pointed.

Simeon and Rahul were already slipping over the side of the pier and wrapping their legs around the pilings. Barnaby nodded, turned and slid his legs over the water.

"Quick, then." He looked at Toby. "I'm proud of you, son, but we'll not make a habit out of this."

Toby's eyes suddenly widened. "We don't have any of Uma's barrier cream to protect you from the water."

Barnaby nodded. "I think we'll be all right – this is the cleanest salt I've yet seen."

Toby nodded as his father disappeared beneath the boards.

"Come on, Toby," D'von prompted him. He was already turning his barrow and jogging back along the pier.

Oats lay in Toby's barrow, curled over his missing hand. Harry slumped in the bottom of D'von's, barely breathing. Rita climbed into Ayla's cart, meeting her eyes with a warning look as she ducked inside. Toby threw sacks over them all and once more they made the trip, passing the anxious traders and rumbling on to the floorboards without being stopped.

Then a squad of soldiers ran past, headed towards the castle.

Toby ducked his head and kept facing forwards. The officer stopped. Toby glanced at him from the corner of his eye. Sweat dripped down the man's face and his uniform was ripped and bloodstained at the shoulder. Suspicion twisted his eyebrows.

"What the hell are you doing on the pier?" The officer fingered his blade. "The rats were meant to be locked up an hour ago."

Inside Toby's barrow, he felt Oats shift but there was nothing the pirate could do.

The officer stepped nearer. "I asked you what you were doing, rat."

Toby forced his jaw to drop, his eyes to go vacant, his shoulders to slump – the very image of a worker switched off.

Behind him Hiko, too, stopped his barrow and dropped his arms to his sides, massaging his fingers. He kicked Ayla in the shin, making her drop her own handle.

"What've you got in those barrows?" The officer shifted closer and D'von edged out from behind his own load.

"Got to tip cage rubbish into the sea," he said. "Rinds, rubbish, crap. Then we put the barrows away. Then we go back to the cage."

The officer's lip curled as he sniffed and retreated from the barrows. "Smells like it." He shook his head. "But this is not the time. Go back." He pointed. "Get off the pier."

"Got to," D'von pressed on. "Orders."

Hiko nodded vigorously. "Don't want to be beaten again, oh no."

Ayla twisted her arm into view, her face morose. "Or burned," she added.

The officer flinched at the sight. "*Madre de Dios.* But there's a battle going on, dumb rats. Get off the pier."

"Last load, then we're gone." Hiko looked pleading, his eyes giant in his pinched face.

"Last load." Toby repeated, stupidly. He shuffled stubbornly in place.

"Lieutenant, they need us at the castle." The soldier behind the officer looked anxiously down the road.

"You're right, I have better things to do than deal with this." The man spat on a board and turned his attention to D'von. "You get yourselves killed it's not my problem. One last load, then get the hell off the pier."

D'von nodded and Toby and Hiko picked up their

barrows. Heads down, eyes on the floor, they rolled away from the officer as fast as they could.

"Is he still watching?" Toby hissed.

Ayla peered under her arm. "No, they're legging it to the castle."

Toby stared then a snort forced its way out of his nose. Another exploded from his chest and abruptly he was shaking with laughter. "Moving crap," he sniggered.

Ayla giggled, D'von rumbled deep in his throat and then they were all hysterical, the carts wobbling dangerously as they broke into shambling runs which ended at the pier edge.

Toby put down his barrow and helped Oats to his feet. D'von lifted Harry and Rita groaned as she rolled on to the boards. "Idiots," she muttered.

"Toby, is that you?" The voice came from beneath them.

Toby sobered up. "It's us," he hissed. "Are you ready?"

"Send them down." Simeon's face appeared, one of his arms held him on to the piling, the other reached up. "I'll take Harry."

D'von dropped the pirate into Simeon's arm then the captain took his place. Polly still perched on his shoulder, claws wrapped in his shirt. Her eye whirred as she focused on Toby.

"Give me Rita." The captain held up a hand and Rita

crawled to him. Toby noticed that she left blood behind on the splintered planks as she rolled over the pier edge, trusting the captain to catch her.

"Which leaves me with you, Oats." Rahul grinned. "Coming?"

Oats threw his own legs over the pier edge. Rahul just had to give him a guiding hand. There were three splashes as the pirates all hit the water.

"Now us." Toby looked at Hiko. "Over you go."

"I … I still can't swim." Hiko bit his lip.

"D'von, can you?" Toby looked up. D'von was sidling backwards, his sunny smile vanquished.

"Can I what, Toby?"

"Can you swim?"

D'von nodded. "But I've got to get back to the cages now. There's a big beating waiting for me." He shuddered.

"What do you mean?" Toby was blind-sided. "Why are you going back?"

"I helped, yes? But you don't need me any more, so I'll go back to my cage."

"Don't you dare." Ayla trembled. "If the *Phoenix* won't have you, the *Banshee* will."

"She's right." Toby stepped towards him, hand held out. "You're coming with us."

D'von's toothless mouth slackened. "You don't want to

send me back to the cage?" His lisp was more pronounced than ever.

"You're our friend, D'von." Toby caught his big hand and pulled, forcing the teen to step closer once more. "If you want to come, you're welcome."

"I can live on the ship?" D'von looked nervously at the raging battle.

"For as long as you like." Toby smiled. "Now, can you swim?"

D'von nodded again.

"Then can you take Hiko?"

"Ha." D'von's back straightened as he wrapped one arm around the smaller boy. "Already I'm a better pirate than you." And with that, D'von jumped off the pier, Hiko held firmly in his arms.

Ayla gasped and Toby looked over the side. He watched D'von bob to the surface, dragging a spluttering Hiko behind him. The other pirates were treading water, waiting for Toby.

"Our turn." Toby held a hand out to Ayla.

"Wait." She swung the bag from her shoulder and tried to stuff the maps inside and secure the opening one-handed. "I don't want it to get wet."

"Let me help." Toby edged closer.

"Back off," Ayla growled. Finally she wrestled the flap

shut and pulled the plastic zip.

"Are you at least going to let me help you swim?"

Ayla closed her eyes. When she opened them again she looked utterly defeated. "You'll have to. I won't get far with this arm," she muttered. Then she brightened. "You can catch me when you get down there." And she turned and launched herself from the jetty.

Sunlight tangled in her hair and her pale legs flashed beneath Peel's filthy shirt. As she hit the water she tucked in her arm, but the impact still shocked a scream from her and Toby saw her face crumple as she sank.

"Stubborn fool." Toby jumped after her.

He splashed down almost on top of the spot she had gone in, but Ayla was still underwater when he surfaced.

"Damn it." Toby dived and forced his eyes open. Ayla struggled, trying to reach the surface with only one arm, but the water that pulled at her broken wrist caused her to twist in agony. Toby closed his fists around her billowing shirt and kicked towards the sky. Spikes in his shoulder made him wince – Polly had hold of his shirt and was pulling, hard. They broke the surface together. Ayla's arm floated in front of her.

"Gods, it hurts," she choked.

Toby caught her shoulders as she kicked weakly. He held her close, squashing the bag between them and forcing

Polly to climb to the front of his shoulder. Ayla panted desperately, trying to breathe through the pain her crash into the sea had caused.

"I've got you." Toby's legs were tiring, but he forced Ayla's chin above water.

"Toby." The captain swam to them, one arm around an unresisting Rita. "We'll have to swim around the *Phoenix*."

"There's only one problem." Rahul kicked closer. "How in all the hells do we get back on board?"

TWENTY-TWO

"Can't your parrot-thing fly up and tell them to lower the ropes?" Ayla gasped.

"Of course she can." Toby nudged her but Polly gripped his shirt harder. "Go and tell Marcus we're here, Polly."

Polly hung her head. "My pinions were burned off, Toby. I'm broken. I can only glide from a height – I can't fly up."

"Oh," he said tiredly.

"We'll have to get to the other side and yell." The captain was tiring, too, fighting the tow of his own heavy clothing and boots.

"They won't hear us over the noise of battle." Rahul was pulling Oats behind him. Like Ayla, the pirate was trying to swim with one arm; the other was tucked beneath his shirt, hiding from the fish that already crowded around his stump.

"We have to try." Toby tugged Ayla flat, and started to

swim out from under the pier. Ayla kicked and they moved quickly together towards the *Phoenix*.

D'von and Hiko drew level. D'von faced forwards and panted like a dog as he pulled Hiko.

As they reached the ice-breaker hull, the shade of the *Phoenix* fell on the group and the water noticeably cooled.

"Watch out." Ayla jerked in Toby's arms as an arrow splashed into the water a bare finger-width from her leg.

"Have they seen us?" Toby squinted up, but no further arrows came. Polly's eye swivelled outwards and she shook her head as she zoomed in on the dock.

"Just a bad shot, I think," Barnaby huffed as he dragged Rita closer to Toby. "Keep swimming."

Slowly the pirates made their way around the *Phoenix*. As soon as the pier was out of sight, they started to yell.

Toby kept their heads above water as Ayla waved her good arm. "*Phoenix!*" she shouted. But there was no response.

"They're all port side, holding off the soldiers." Rahul kicked more vigorously, forcing his shoulders above the water, as though the extra lift would raise his voice. "Nisha … *Nisha!*" Still no answer from the deck high above them.

"What now?" Hiko's voice was small and shivery.

"We keep shouting. Ho, *Phoenix!*" Toby waved.

"Look, there's someone." Ayla pointed with her good hand and Toby squinted up. The sun haloed a figure leaning over the gunwale, then he moved, his gait a familiar limping roll.

"It's Crocker," Toby said.

"Crocker! Crocker!" The pirates yelled his name as loud as they could and Toby saw him hesitate. He knew then and there that they had been spotted.

Then Crocker walked away.

The pirates were silent.

"Did he just…?" Ayla murmured.

"He's an evil-minded, vicious son of a toad," Rita spat. "If he leaves us down here to drown or be picked off by arrows, I'll … I'll—"

"You'll what? Die." Simeon shook his head. "I didn't come this far to drown in reach of the *Phoenix*." He made a fist and started to bang on the hull. "Come on," he yelled.

"It won't work." Toby shook his head. He tensed as he began to tingle, the sea's poison finally starting to irritate his skin. How long did they have?

"Can we climb the paddle cage?" Rahul looked doubtfully at the razor-sharp wire designed to catch and dice any junk that might block the paddle, then at the injured pirates that they dragged behind them.

The captain shook his head. "No. Crocker saw us – someone else will, too. I don't know why he isn't lowering

Birdie, but there'll be a good reason. Maybe he's in real trouble up there. Keep shouting."

Simeon hammered harder on the hull and Rahul joined him.

The crash of their fists on metal rang through the water and reverberated on and on. The water sloshed beneath Toby and a current started to pull at his legs. Suddenly he thought he heard a new sound.

"What's that? Stop," he shouted.

Simeon stopped hammering and Rahul raised his fist from the hull. But another noise – a tortured metallic scraping sound – continued.

Toby felt the pull as he and Ayla were dragged back towards the ice-breaker in front of the ship.

"Brilliant!" the captain yelled suddenly. "Back to the prow. Crocker's opening the hull. We can swim straight into the wreck room."

As the *Phoenix* continued to crack, and water poured past him, Toby half swam, half floated on the current. He reached the splitting ice-breaker as it stopped moving, leaving a gap just wide enough for them to enter. He grabbed the hull with one hand, and pulled Ayla into the wreck room beside him.

The other pirates followed and flopped, exhausted, on to the salvage platforms.

The water continued to pour in.

"We have to close her before she sinks low enough for the soldiers to climb on board." The captain was already on his feet. "Toby, you have to get to the boiler room as quick as you can. Simeon, wait by the pump and when Toby powers her up, empty this water out. Harry, Rita and Ayla will stay here, everyone else on deck. We'll sail as soon as we can."

Toby nodded and released Ayla, then rose wearily to his feet. Ayla used her good hand to drag herself on to a ledge. Her hair hung in front of her face, a dark curtain that closed her off from the world. She tucked her broken arm into her shirt then puffed loudly and stood up.

"What're you doing?" Toby stared. "You heard the captain. Stay there."

"I'm going on deck." Ayla settled the bag on her shoulder and hefted her blade with her good hand.

"You can't be serious." Toby appealed to his father, "You told her to stay there. She should stay, right?"

The captain wrung water from his shirt as he regarded his rival's daughter.

"I have no authority over the girl," he said eventually. "I don't think she should fight, but I can't stop her. You don't have to fight for the *Phoenix*, you've done enough – rest."

"Until you're safe, my mission isn't complete." Ayla's

313

voice was a weak imitation of her earlier bluster. "I can't stay down here while you fight up there."

The captain sighed. "What mission?"

"I have to make sure you're safe." Ayla swung her sword wearily. "Nell has plans for you, Captain Ford."

"Of course she does," Barnaby replied. "Come, then."

"We need weapons," Rahul growled.

"Take whatever you can use." The captain gestured around the wreck room and the pirates split up, digging through lingering piles of unsorted salvage from the plane.

Armed with broken wing pieces, curves of metal from seat sides and shards of propeller, the pirates climbed out of the water and up the ladders towards the hatch. Toby followed Ayla with Polly on his shoulder. Hiko and D'von were right behind him. When Toby reached the hatch he looked down. Rita and Harry lay on the highest salvage platforms; the rising water already submerged their feet.

"How fast can we get powered up?" the captain asked.

"Depends how quickly the combustion chamber can heat the feed water." Toby drew Nix. "It'll be faster with Hiko's help."

"All right, then. Hiko, you're with Toby. Oats, take D'von and show him how to operate the winches, together you can get that hull closed. Ayla, Rahul, you're with me. Let's go."

Toby climbed out of the hatch and Hiko stayed so close to his legs that he bumped the younger boy with every movement. Toby's face was almost pressed into the bag on Ayla's back, but that gave little protection from the battle that roared from prow to stern.

"They've boarded," Toby breathed.

Ahead of him the captain thudded on to the gangway with a roar.

"The captain's back! He's not dead." Word spread around the deck and Toby took advantage of the brief lull to sprint around his father's legs and duck towards the *Phoenix*'s second hatch. D'von and Oats were right behind him, heading for the winches.

"Toby," Hiko shrieked. Toby turned just in time to see a hubcap whip across his vision, slamming aside the arrow that was headed for his face.

"Thanks, Theo!" he wheezed.

"Welcome home." The big man knocked a soldier across the deck with a backhander that made Toby's muscles shiver. "Just in time – we're about to be overwhelmed."

"I'll get us moving." Toby dropped beneath a sword swipe, grabbed Hiko and slid the last metre to the hatch. "Just a few more minutes, Theo." He grabbed the mechanism, turned the wheel and tore the hatch open. "Hold on," he yelled and leaped feet first into the darkness.

Toby and Hiko clattered along the corridor and skidded into the boiler room. Toby was tossing Nix aside and dragging on his goggles before his feet had finished sliding.

Inside, the room was dark and quiet. He was home.

The pirates had made a mess of his 'things that might be useful one day' pile. It looked as if a storm had wrecked the room. But there was no time to take it in – he had to get the ship moving.

"Hiko…"

"I know – the boiler needs fuel." Hiko was already hauling an armful from the compressor and staggering towards the combustion chamber. Polly jumped from Toby's shoulder on to the steam drum and he relit the burner, cursing as the flame guttered before taking. Then he ran to check the water-level gauge and the feed-water control valve. A flick of his wrist and the boiler drum was filling.

Toby pulled levers, making sure power would go straight to the paddles. They could pump the wreck room once they were away from the jetty and out of range of the Tarifan's missiles.

Agonizingly slowly, steam began to build, whistling as it entered the delivery lines. "Come on, come on," he urged it.

Hiko danced from one foot to the other and even Polly bobbed up and down on her perch. Toby kneeled by the combustion chamber, glaring through the grille, as if the heat of his gaze would make it burn hotter and faster.

The whine of turbines drilled into his ears, a drone that almost masked the clang of the closing hull. At least D'von and Oats had made sure that the *Phoenix* would not sink any lower in the water.

"How long?" Hiko fidgeted at his side, twisting his hands in his ragged shirt.

"Soon." Toby glanced at the delivery lines, which were beginning to shudder. With every minute that passed he imagined another pirate dying on the deck.

"Now." Toby leaped to his feet and pulled the lever that would throw the ship into reverse. Steam howled and the paddles began to turn, jerking the *Phoenix* like a fish on a line. Normally the process of undocking was slow and delicate, but this time Toby *wanted* to rip the pier out from under her. He threw all the power he could into the paddles and whooped as the *Phoenix* shuddered and a bone-deep grinding sound came through the hull.

"I'm going up there." He looked at Hiko. "Stay here and watch the boiler. Make sure the paddles don't stop working and keep feeding her fuel."

The boy nodded and ran to the fuel compressor.

He picked up Nix from where Toby had abandoned her. "Good luck." Hiko offered him the sword, pommel first.

Polly edged along the drum, half spreading her near-useless metal wings, as though to glide on to his shoulder again.

"You stay here, too, Polly." Toby threw off his goggles.

Toby wanted to see the *Phoenix* rip apart Tarifa's jetty. He was ready to fight.

The sun was low in the sky and the evening light bathed the deck with a baleful glow. Outside, the tenor of the sound had escalated – the *Phoenix* was screaming as she strained away from the dock.

Half of the soldiers were trying to get off the ship, running for their makeshift gangplanks, which were already tilting dangerously. The other half were fighting even harder, trying to prevent the *Phoenix* from leaving.

Officers on land couldn't decide whether to cut the ropes and save the jetty, or hope it would hold out and keep their prize trapped in place. So the lines stayed and the *Phoenix* shuddered as tension tightened her ropes. Metal groaned as the ship battled the dock.

Toby ducked as a soldier swiped for him. Already it was instinct for him to whip Nix from his shoulder in a strong

318

arc. He used one foot to push the Tarifan off the end of his sword and jumped over his falling body.

There he came face to face with Peel, panting and drenched with sweat. His shoulder remained bloody and a long gash now split his eyebrows. He had tied his sun gauze over the cut so that it didn't blind him, and the blood had soaked through, leaving the scarf crackling and brown at the edges.

Peel looked in surprise at the groaning soldier, then at the blood dripping from Toby's sword. "Well, then," he murmured. He reached down and finished the Tarifan off with his kitchen knife.

"Where's the captain?" Toby tightened his hold on Nix.

Peel gestured with his knife towards the prow where Toby could see the captain, bolstered by members of the *Phoenix*'s crew – and Ayla.

"Are we cutting the lines?" Toby gestured towards the ropes holding the *Phoenix* in place.

Peel shook his head. "Captain wants to take half of Tarifa with us. Crazy bastard."

"Too right." Toby ducked again as an arrow pierced the mast above his head. "Let the *Phoenix* tear them apart."

Peel stepped out of his way as Toby ran towards a break in the battle ahead, ready to fight his way to the prow.

Before the bridge, Uma and Marcus fought to protect

Big Pad and Dee. They had set up a car roof as a shield from arrows, and between them were pushing soldiers back. The fury and frustration on Big Pad's face was horrible to behold. Toby knew that Paddy was aching to move. Dee lay at Pad's feet, her eyes closed. Her hands were tucked across her chest, keeping them out of arrow range, but it gave her a terrifying semblance of death. Toby stumbled in shock, but then he realized that her chest was moving up and down.

"Toby," Uma cried. "You're alive." Her face lit up.

"Uma, pay attention," Big Pad yelled.

She turned and thumped a familiar pig-faced soldier across the shoulders with her club. He stumbled towards Marcus, whose eyes lit up. "You!"

Toby ran to help, but Marcus's blade came up and blocked his arm. Toby stared at him, incredulous.

"This one attacked Dee. He's mine," Marcus growled.

Toby backed away and took Marcus's place next to Uma.

The soldier licked his lips, nervously. One sleeve of his grey uniform was shredded and his left arm hung at his side.

"Remember her?" Marcus gestured towards Dee, forcing the soldier to turn towards the *Phoenix*'s second in command.

The soldier tossed his head and looked behind to call for backup.

"I don't think so." Uma raised her club.

The deck shuddered under Toby's bare feet as the *Phoenix* strained harder to escape the lines that held her to the dock. Several of the attacking force, unused to being on board a ship, staggered and fell.

"What's your name?" Marcus stepped towards the teetering soldier.

"Why, so you can tell your *puta* who put her down?" The soldier laughed, but his eyes darted, seeking the backup that was not appearing.

"What's your name?" Marcus roared.

"Why must you know?" The soldier wiped sweat from his face.

"So that when I rip your soul from your body, I can curse it." Despite his grief and exhaustion, Marcus was a whirlwind.

The soldier tried to lift his sword in time, but he was slow, perhaps still thinking of Marcus's threat and, between one breath and another, the soldier was staring down at the fishing spear buried deep in his chest.

He opened his mouth to speak, but blood bubbled out from it. He sunk to his knees and Marcus bent to his ear.

"What is your name?" Marcus whispered.

The soldier shook his head and dropped his sword from numb fingers.

Marcus picked it up. "This is for Dee." He grabbed the soldier by the shoulders and dragged him to Dee's side.

"She'll want to see that when she wakes up, too." Marcus's smile was a humourless grimace.

Toby ran forward into the battle. "I'm going to help the captain," he shouted.

A figure flanked him and he turned to see D'von with a Tarifan sword in one hand and a rusty bicycle chain wrapped around the other. The teen was stumbling against the movement of the ship, but just managing to keep his feet as he fought.

A lyrical whooping caught Toby's attention and he ducked just in time to see Ayla at the captain's side. The blade of her sword was crimson from pommel to tip and even though she held her broken arm close to her side, she moved with grace.

Toby altered his course and ran at a diagonal until he found himself next to them. Together he and Ayla engaged the nearest soldier.

Toby blocked a sword aimed for Ayla's head and stepped in front of her.

"What are you doing?" She spun around him and slashed at the pirate's legs. Toby blocked another slash of his sword. "I don't need you to protect me," she shrieked.

"I'm not." Toby ducked and Nix clanged against a railing as his arm was knocked aside by a vicious side sweep.

Ayla twisted in front of his torso, blocked and kicked. Toby pulled Nix back round and intercepted a slash aimed for her throat. She slid sideways, allowing him space to fight and aimed a sweep at the soldier's legs, pulling him off balance and on to the tip of the sword D'von had stolen from a fallen soldier.

D'von jabbed forward. "That's for my sister." Each time he struck, D'von said the same thing. Toby's heart clenched but he turned his focus as another fighter aimed for Ayla. He bounded in front of her, ending up shoulder to shoulder with his father.

"Toby." The captain acknowledged him and they thrust together, pinning the attacker, one on each arm.

Toby pulled Nix free just as he felt a kick to the back of his legs and staggered to one side.

"I told you to stop protecting me." Ayla lowered her foot and glared.

Ignoring her, Toby looked for the next threat just as the *Phoenix* quaked, shivered and, finally, something gave way.

For the length of a few heartbeats, everyone on board, soldier and pirate alike, stopped and stared as the jetty cracked. Pilings collapsed and bollards splashed into the surf. Timber snapped and rained into the sea but great hunks of the dock remained attached to the lines and these swung, clattering into the hull of the *Phoenix* like hammers. The soldiers on the pier screamed as the boards beneath them vanished and they fell, or were caught by sliding lines and dragged into the sea.

The *Phoenix* jerked and almost flew backwards, churning the pier into shards.

The soldiers remaining on board gaped for a moment, then the first one jumped. It was a long fall from the railing of the *Phoenix* into the sea; but it was that or be trapped on the ship as she left.

TWENTY-THREE

Toby leaned close to Ayla. "Mission accomplished," he murmured.

"Yes." Her voice was faint and Toby realized that she was swaying out of time with the rise and fall of the waves and the pressure of the wind. She was deathly pale.

"Ayla?" Toby reached for her, too slow. The girl collapsed as though someone had cut the last string holding her up and her head banged on to the deck.

"Uma!" Toby yelled, as he dropped to his knees. Ayla made no movement.

D'von put his hand on to her forehead. "She's hot."

"Uma!" Toby shouted again.

The ship's doctor knelt beside him, placing her cool hands on Ayla's head. "These burns need treating, this arm needs setting and plastering, there's some infection in there, and she's in severe shock. She might have concussion now, too." Her fingers moved swiftly, but gently, assessing each injury. "I can't believe she's kept on her feet so long, let alone fighting. Carry her to the mess hall, Theo." She tugged gently at the bag, but Ayla held it fast.

"Leave it with her," Toby said. "It's wrong to take it now."

Uma nodded. "Careful now, Theo." She spoke as the pirate lifted Ayla into his arms, almost snagging her broken arm.

"I'm coming, too." Toby hovered at her side.

Uma shrugged. "If you don't mind helping. I can always use a hand."

Ayla lay unconscious on the big central table with her face turned towards Toby. He held the fingers of one hand poised above her cheek, wanting to comfort her with his touch, but not knowing whether he should.

"She's pretty," Uma commented, giving him a shrewd look.

"She's brilliant," Toby said, without thinking. Then he flushed. Uma smiled into the big sink where she was washing her hands.

"First thing, we have to clean and treat these burns." She scrubbed between her fingers. "I'll have to get that disgusting shirt off her."

"Um." Toby reddened even further.

"I'll do that. Go and fetch me a sheet or a blanket."

Toby started towards the door.

"A clean one," Uma shouted.

Toby returned with the best blanket he could find. His own, he had been horrified to find, was covered in soot, but Rita's looked and smelled clean. He held it up and edged into the room, keeping his eyes firmly on the floor.

Uma took the blanket from him and he felt his ears growing hot. "Go and wash your hands while I get her ready," Uma said, her voice turning serious.

Toby edged towards the sink, keeping his back resolutely turned to the table. "You can look now." Uma threw the shirt towards the rubbish and Toby returned to the table.

Ayla lay beneath the blanket. Her good hand still clutched her bag, but her broken arm was twisted on top of the blanket and her sword lay on the floor beside the table.

"Sit down, Toby, before you fall down," Uma snapped. "You're almost as bad as she is, driving yourself to exhaustion. I'll take another look at you once I'm done."

Toby perched as close to the table as he could. Three buckets of water sat beside Uma, and two of them steamed gently. A pile of clean cloths lay to the side. "I've injected some morphine, so we can treat the burns." She gathered Ayla's hair and pushed it towards her good side. "Thank gods for that aeroplane you salvaged, Toby." Then she rested her fingers on Ayla's shoulder with a feather-light touch. "Some of these are third-degree burns." She shook her head. "She'll be suffering from dehydration on top of everything else. At least the nerve damage means they won't be hurting so much. The other burns will have been helped by immersion in the cold seawater. Now we need to soak the area in the cool water for ten minutes."

She handed some of the cloths to Toby. "Here, wet these in this bucket; then lay them on her arm and chest. Keep changing the cloths as they start to warm up or dry out."

"She's so hot." Toby flinched as the back of his hand came into contact with Ayla's throat.

"That's the infection." Uma chewed her cheek. "I've loaded her up with antibiotics and I'll have to give her some of my stock when she goes back to the *Banshee*."

Toby replaced the first cloth, which was already warm to the touch.

"You're doing great." Uma checked the cloths around Ayla's elbow. "A couple more minutes and we can start cleaning."

"Cleaning?" Toby swallowed. The skin beneath the cloths looked fragile – giant blisters threatened to pop with each press of material and singed skin curled around raw-looking wounds.

"It'll be all right." Uma peeled the cloths away and

dropped them into the bucket of cold water. Then she squirted some soap from a Médecins Sans Frontières bottle into the second bucket. As the water foamed she dampened two fresh cloths. "Here." She handed one to Toby. "Scrub the area *gently*. Be careful not to burst any blisters; they protect against infection. We're just trying to remove loose dead skin. Can you do that?"

Toby swallowed. "I can try." He dabbed at Ayla's skin gently with the cloth, holding his breath the whole time.

"A little harder, Toby. Like this." Uma showed him, moving in circles around the burns.

Toby pressed harder, terrified that he might burst a blister. He froze as Ayla groaned and twisted.

"Keep going." Uma didn't look up. "I want to get that arm reset and splinted before she wakes up."

Toby gritted his teeth and rubbed in wider circles. The cloth was soon blackened.

Eventually Uma smiled at him. "Done. Now we have to rinse off the excess soap with clean warm water." She dunked a cloth in the third bucket and washed Ayla's skin until the blanket covering her became damp at the edges. "I'm going to pat the area dry and you're going to cover it with this sterile gauze." She handed him a packet and he pulled it open. As Uma dried Ayla's skin, Toby lay piece after piece of gauze over the burns. Finally Uma wrapped a bandage around her arm and upper torso, holding the whole thing in place.

"Good job, Toby. If you like, you can hold her hand while I sort out this broken bone. When she wakes up, I'm going to need you to get her to drink as much as she can. In small sips. There's only one of me and I have to get back to Dee. She still needs help. And there are a lot of untreated injuries on deck, too."

Toby nodded. "And Rita and Harry."

"Rita and Harry? What? Where are they?" Uma faced him with a frown.

"They … they're in the wreck room. That's where we came in. They were too injured to come up on deck. Hasn't anyone said?"

Uma's brows came together, her face thunderous. "You just let me treat this sailor from the *Banshee*, when you knew that two of our own were too injured to *move*."

"I'm sorry, I-I didn't think." Toby choked. His hand twitched on Ayla's. Of course Uma was right – Rita and Harry should have come first. How could he have forgotten them?

"Toby, I get it." Uma was already gathering her medical kit and running for the door. "She's the first girl you've ever seen. But crew comes first – always." She disappeared down the corridor.

Toby sat next to Ayla, unable to move. He would never have believed for one moment that he could have put the *Phoenix*'s crew second to anyone or anything else. What did it mean that this girl had driven every other thought from his head?

"I'm a monster," Toby muttered. "This can't happen again." But one hand still covered hers.

Abruptly Toby was overcome with a wave of weariness and he laid his forearm on the table, dropped his head and slept.

Ayla twitched beneath him and Toby woke up. He opened gritty eyes and stretched. He ached in places he hadn't ever known he could ache. Even his thumb muscle hurt from gripping Nix. Toby rubbed his eyes and looked at Ayla.

She still slept. Her black lashes lay in stark contrast to her pale cheeks, but Toby realized that she had some colour now, and that her chest was rising and falling more calmly.

"She's looking better." The captain's hand landed on his shoulder and Toby jumped. Immediately he released Ayla's hand.

While he slept, the mess hall had become crowded. Lamps now lit the shadows and on a table to his right, Rita also slept, her torso tightly bandaged. Big Pad was back too, strapped to his table, his eyes firmly fixed on Dee, who remained unconscious. Marcus held her hand, his own injuries untreated. A queue of pirates with various minor cuts and bruises slumped against the far wall and to his left, Uma bent over Harry.

Toby's eyes widened as she stood up, and pulled Harry's scarf over his face.

"Is he…?"

"He didn't make it." Barnaby sank down on to the bench next to his son. "Uma did her best."

"If she'd have got to him sooner…?" Toby felt sick. His friend was dead.

A lamp flickered and Barnaby shook his head. "Uma was amazed he even made it back to the ship. He slipped away without ever waking up." Tears shone in his eyes. "I owe him my life. He and Rita, Carson and Dobbs took the brunt of the initial attack and gave me time to talk them into capturing rather than killing us."

"Which gave us time to come for you." Without thinking, Toby took Ayla's hand again and she settled into a more comfortable sleep, the frown lines on her face smoothing away.

"You saved us yesterday, Toby. I'll never forget it." Barnaby put his arm around his son's shoulder.

"Yesterday?" Toby blinked.

"It's after midnight." Barnaby rubbed his eyes. "We're anchoring in a smuggler's cove. Now … are you going to tell me why that girl from the *Banshee* was so keen to help me back to the ship?"

"Nell still wants the coordinates for the solar panels," Toby sighed. "That's why Ayla is here. She was sent to make sure you weren't captured by the Tarifans, so Nell could get the coordinates from you."

"Then the danger is as great as ever." Barnaby's lips twisted. "Ashes," he said quietly.

"Just protecting her investment, she said." Toby stroked Ayla's hand as he spoke.

"We need the solar panels ourselves," Barnaby whispered. "You understand that?"

"Of course. We can't get to the island without them." Toby was surprised that his father would even ask. "I just wish there was some way to pay her back." His fingers twitched. He lowered his voice, as if Ayla would hear him. "We can't even let her keep the map."

"Map?" Barnaby raised his eyebrows.

Toby glanced at the bag Ayla still clutched, even in sleep. "We found a map in the portmaster's office. I think it might actually show the way to the island."

Barnaby stared at his son. Then he dragged his fingers through his tangled beard. "You mean *the* island?"

Toby nodded.

"Such a thing can't possibly exist, we would have heard of it. No one knows for sure where the island is, therefore there can't be a map."

"The portmaster couldn't translate it." Toby's eyes remained on the bag. "He was obviously trying, but Hiko could read it. He said the title of the document was 'Volcano Island'."

"Volcano island," the captain repeated slowly. "That could be anything."

"But it could be *the* island. An unnamed isle, brought out of the sea by a volcano," Toby pressed. "The portmaster *really* wanted the map translated and it was locked up."

The captain sucked air in through his teeth. "And you say you have this map?"

"Not exactly." Toby looked at the bag again, just as Ayla opened her eyes.

As before, Ayla went from fast asleep to firing on all cylinders. The fog cleared from her eyes and Toby snatched his hand away from her as she shot into a sitting position, trapped the blanket edge to her chest with the bag, and alternated her glare between Toby and his father.

She didn't bother asking what had happened to her; instead she coolly assessed the dining-room-come-hospital and then looked at her arm, plastered to the elbow.

"Who did this?" She lifted her plastered fist.

"Uma is our doctor." The captain leaned forward. "How are you feeling?"

"Fine." Ayla tossed her head. No weakness showed in her posture or expression.

"You've just woken up, you must be feeling awful." Toby picked up the drink he had promised to make her sip. "Here. Uma said you needed this."

Ayla licked cracked lips, her tongue unconsciously tracing her scar, but Toby could see her mind racing. She was obviously thirsty, but to drink would mean either putting down the bag and blanket, or allowing Toby to hold the cup to her lips.

He waited patiently for her to work out what to do. In the end Ayla pressed the blanket to her with the cast, shifted the pack so that the back strap hung over her elbow and took the water with her good hand. She gulped the first cup and held it out for more. Toby took it to the sink for a refill. As he left he saw the captain shuffle along the bench, taking his place.

Hurriedly Toby filled the cup and sped back.

"It's mine," Ayla was saying. She was clutching the bag once more. "I risked my life to save it from the fire. I earned it."

"I'm only asking to *see* the map," the captain cajoled.

"I won't take it from you. I just want to know if it is what Toby suggests."

Ayla glowered at Toby. "It belongs to the *Banshee*," she growled.

Toby put the water down on the bench and she looked at it longingly, but let it stay. "We all found the map," Toby muttered. "And you wouldn't have got there at all without the *Phoenix*."

"The rescue mission depended on me," Ayla shot back. "You said so. Without me, you wouldn't have been in the castle. The *Phoenix* would have run."

Toby avoided his father's eyes, but a hand pressed his knee and he was forced to look up.

"If you had run, you would have done the right thing, Toby. That's what I ordered you to do." He turned to Ayla. "It can't do any harm to let me see the map, can it?"

"Nell would kill me." Ayla shivered involuntarily.

The captain inhaled sharply. "I know Nell – she would do no such thing."

"Maybe you knew her once." Ayla regarded him steadily. "*I* know Nell now."

"You knew Nell?" Toby stared. "When?"

"Before the *Phoenix*." Barnaby patted his shoulder. "It doesn't matter. What matters is this map. What if you keep hold of it, while I take a look? I might at least be able to verify its authenticity."

Ayla remained stony-faced and Toby leaned close. "You know, without Polly you'd still be buried in that dungeon. She saved your life. And I was the one who sent Polly after you."

"Are you saying that *I* owe *you*?"

"We owe each other." Toby tried to touch her hand, but she pulled away. "After all that's happened, can't we trust one another?"

Ayla glared. Her eyes were like flint, but as Toby's begged for her trust, they started to soften.

"Strangely, Toby, I do trust you," she said eventually. "I don't trust your captain." She sighed. "But if he can confirm that this map is really what we think it is, it'll be a more valuable prize for Nell."

She flipped the pack on to her knees and struggled awkwardly with the zip. "I keep hold of it at all times," she warned.

"Of course." The captain nodded.

"Let me help." Toby leaned forward and she tensed, but allowed him to open the bag. However, as soon as he reached inside, she batted him away and pulled the rolled-up papers free herself.

The top three were damp and the ink had run, rendering them unreadable.

"Damn it. They would have been useful." Toby threw them to one side. The two beneath showed planned trade routes between St George and Cadiz, including seasonal changes and notes on cargo. The captain's eyes lit up. "Now these *are* useful." He went to take them, but Ayla tightened her grip.

"No, you don't. I told you, these belong to the *Banshee*."

The captain dropped his hand. "What about this so-called Volcano Island map?"

Ayla and Toby held their breath as she unfurled the innermost map. Only a slight dampness at the edges showed what they had risked by swimming back to the *Phoenix*.

The captain looked at it in silence.

"What do you think?" Toby said, eventually.

"I don't recognize any of the land masses." The captain rubbed his beard. "Dee should be looking at this." He glanced at the unconscious body of his second in command and sighed deeply. "You say this means 'volcano island'?" He pointed at the script running along the top of the map and Toby nodded.

"What about all this text around the pictures?"

"I don't know. Hiko only translated the title."

The captain nodded. "It's an oriental script – Korean or Japanese maybe, I'm not sure. Arnav will know." The captain raised his voice. "Get over here, old man. Look at this map and tell me what it says."

Arnav weaved his way through the tables and sat beside Toby. He stared at the map for a long moment then pushed his false teeth in and out with a clacking sound. "What makes you think I can read this?" he said eventually.

"It's Japanese, isn't it?" Ayla said, narrowing her eyes.

"'Tain't no Japanese. Looks like it, but ain't."

"Korean?" The captain leaned closer.

"Nope."

"Then what is it?" The captain frowned.

"Don't know." Arnav shrugged. "Never seen it before."

The captain glowered at him. "Thought you'd seen everything, old man."

"Seen most things," Arnav nodded sagely. "Ain't seen that." He stood. "My turn to be stitched up, if you don't mind." He ambled off.

"And where's Hiko?" the captain asked.

"I left him in the boiler room with Polly." Toby rubbed his eyes. "I hope he's asleep."

The captain hummed. "Then we'll leave him for now." He traced one finger along a broken line of numbers that followed a swirl along one side of the map and Ayla twitched as if to pull the page away. "What are these? They don't look like coordinates."

"No idea." Toby shook his head and Ayla shrugged.

"Maybe a code of some kind, I need time to look at it with Polly." The captain leaned as if to take the map and Ayla pushed backwards, almost falling from the table in her retreat.

"Ayla!" Toby jumped to catch her as she teetered on the edge.

The captain held his hands up and Ayla shoved the map back inside the pack.

"There, you've seen it," she snapped. "Well, what do you think? Is it real?"

"I don't know." The captain shook his head. "It's strange enough to make me wonder. Look, you aren't going back to the *Banshee* just yet. Why not leave it with me till you go? I'll speak with Hiko and look at the numbers, then return it to you when you're ready to go."

"Sure you will," she sneered.

"Hey!" Toby sat up straighter. "If the captain says he'll return it, then he will."

"Right. And he's never been known to lie."

"The captain isn't a liar," Toby said fiercely. "And neither am I."

"Really? So those coordinates you tried to give us for the solar panels, they were correct?"

"That was different. You attacked us and kidnapped Hiko."

340

"And you've never just taken what you wanted? You're pirates, same as us." Ayla's eyes flashed and she swung her legs over the table as if to get to her feet.

"Ayla." The captain's voice was low, soothing. "We can just take the map from you. There are almost forty surviving pirates on the *Phoenix* and only one of you. I'm allowing you to keep control of the map out of respect. But I don't have to."

"Now you show your colours." Ayla jumped to the ground, holding the blanket with her cast, like a toga. She swung the pack on to her back and swept up her sword.

As soon as she raised her sword, Theo and Marcus rushed to their feet.

"Stop!" Toby yelled. "This is madness, Ayla. What did Nell send you for? She wants the location of the solar panels. Well, if you stick a sword through the captain, you'll never get it." Ayla swung her sword from Toby to Theo and Marcus, trying to keep them all at bay.

"The map wasn't your mission." Toby spread his hands.

"That's right." The captain spoke soothingly. "What will Nell say if you go back with a map no one can translate, instead of the coordinates she wants? Just put the sword down and we'll talk."

"Talk about me giving you the map, you mean," Ayla spat.

"All we want is to look at it. We could even redraw it, have a copy each – what do you think?"

"What do I get in return?" Ayla swayed. "The real location of the solar panels?"

"Sorry – no. The *Phoenix* needs those panels. That map might be something or nothing, but the solar panels are real. We're not giving up the *Phoenix*'s future for some magic beans."

Beside them, Toby narrowed his eyes. "Those solar panels – there should be enough for both ships, shouldn't there?"

"In theory." The captain rubbed his beard. "There was a whole shipment went down, so the old man said. But what we don't use, we'll sell. Solar panels that never got smashed in the riots, ready to work – we'll make a fortune."

"What if we *share* them with the *Banshee*?" Toby asked. "We lead the *Banshee* to the panels and split the salvage. In return, Ayla lets us copy the map."

The captain hesitated, considering.

"You could copy the map and then lead us nowhere." Ayla was trying to edge towards the door, but the pirates of the *Phoenix* had formed a loose circle around them. "I keep the map until we have the panels and then send you a copy."

"How do we know you'll copy it accurately?" The

captain shook his head. "How do we know Nell won't run off with both the panels and the map? That doesn't work for me."

"Well, your way doesn't work for *me*," she spat.

"You're bargaining with a bluff hand." The captain shrugged and turned his back on her. "At the moment, the map is a curiosity and nothing more. We don't even know what language it's written in." Ayla's cheeks reddened. "Right now, you're being offered a share in the solar panels your captain wants in return for a copy of a map that she knows nothing about and which might go nowhere. Think about it."

He gestured to his crew. "Let her past." He turned to Ayla once more. "Your clothes are in the sleeping quarters by Toby's bunk. Do you need help dressing yourself? I can send Nisha."

Nisha looked up and nodded.

"I can dress myself." Ayla backed out of the door.

"Do let us know what you decide." The captain bowed mockingly, and Ayla glared, embarrassed.

"You need antibiotics." Uma tossed a bottle towards her. Ayla didn't move, allowing them to fall at her feet. Finally she bent and, still holding her sword, picked them up. Then she turned and ran.

343

TWENTY-FOUR

"Now what?" Toby sagged.

"We wait for her decision." The captain sat back down. "She's an intelligent girl. She'll make the right choice."

"And if she doesn't?" Toby worried at his ragged shirt. "I don't want her hurt."

Uma snorted. "Careful, Toby. Remember – the crew of the *Phoenix* has to come first."

"I know." Toby hung his head, but his heart ached.

"I see." The captain's eyes met Uma's. "The *Banshee* will have fixed their steering by now, so if Nell's second is here and Nell has plans for me, the *Banshee* won't be far. I assume they're waiting in a safe anchorage nearby. Perhaps we can negotiate with Nell for the return of her daughter."

Toby looked up. "What if there's another solution? What if we were to offer Ayla a berth on the *Phoenix*?" He started to speak quickly. "If she's one of our own crew she has no reason to keep the map from us."

"She's Nell's daughter." The captain shook his head. "And she doesn't strike me as disloyal."

"But the *Banshee* is awful. She'd be happier on the *Phoenix*," Toby pressed. "It's worth making the offer."

"That'd be three new pirates you've brought on board. We should ask the rest of the crew." The captain raised his voice. "All in favour of offering the *Banshee*'s second in command a place on the *Phoenix*?"

"Aye." Those who had escaped the dungeons in Tarifa were first to speak.

Nisha looked at Rahul, then rose to her feet. "Without her, Rahul would be hanging from those ramparts. Aye." Her words drew a few more "ayes".

"The girl can fight." Peel nodded his agreement and shoved his brother.

"She's from the *Banshee*. Can she really be trusted?" Marcus twisted from his place next to Dee, but kept one hand on her as if to be reassured, at all times, that she still breathed. "This could have been her aim all the time. Become one of us, get our secrets and then return to the *Banshee*. I say 'no'."

Theo agreed with Marcus.

"Uma?" The captain turned to his doctor.

"She's brave and if she survives that infection, she'll be strong. She can fight. She can think. I believe she'd be an asset. But you'd need to watch your back all the time, waiting for treachery. I don't know if it would be worth it."

"Would the girl want to go from second in command on the *Banshee* to being babysat on the *Phoenix*?" Oats was groggy from morphine and the arm that now ended in a wrist was bandaged tightly to his chest. "If I were her, I'd say no."

Uma sighed. "I know you want her to stay, Toby, but—"

"Can't we let her decide?" Toby appealed to his father.

The captain exhaled, his breath shivering through his beard. "A show of hands – all in favour of making the offer?"

"Ayla?" Toby crept into the sleeping quarters. The space was dim, lit only by two lamps and the moonlight that glimmered through the portholes. He edged forwards with his eyes on the floor, feeling his way with his hands and feet.

"You can look." Ayla rolled her eyes as she straightened the leather of her Banshee uniform. She seemed older and more distant.

Abruptly nervous, Toby said, "Can we talk?"

"Is it about the map?" She sounded tired.

"Not exactly." Toby sat and waited for her.

With a sigh Ayla sank down next to him. Her sword was back on her thigh and it pressed against his leg, between them.

"I like you being here," Toby muttered, staring at his twitching hands.

When Ayla said nothing, he looked up. Her brows were raised and surprise etched her face. "I suppose without me you wouldn't have your captain back," she said eventually.

"It's not just that." Toby swallowed. "We worked well together."

Ayla shrugged. "It made a change to work with someone who didn't want to steal my command but, Toby, this wasn't some grand adventure. We almost died." She lifted her injured arm and let it droop. "It wasn't *fun*."

"I didn't mean that it was." Toby rubbed his hands over his bald head. "I just meant that we made a good team."

Ayla shook her head. "We're pirates – we obey our captain or die. Teamwork isn't important."

"Maybe on the *Banshee*." Toby dropped his hands. "On the *Phoenix* we're a family."

Ayla dismissed his words with an irritable wave, but Toby caught the flush that coloured her throat. He allowed his leg to fall closer to hers.

"Wouldn't you like to be on a ship where you don't have to be on your guard against your own crew?"

"Don't be ridiculous," Ayla snapped. But she fiddled with her sword.

"Do you have to be tough all the time?" Toby almost touched her, but let his fingers fall at the last second.

"I *am* tough, Toby. It's who I am. If you want some kind of simpering damsel in distress, you're looking in the wrong direction."

Toby lifted his hand on to his thigh, slipping his fingers close enough to brush the outside of hers. She blew her hair from her face and ignored his touch.

The lamplight glimmered in Ayla's green eyes and before he could think any further Toby lunged and pressed his lips against hers.

For a second Ayla froze, then she softened and her hand found his shoulder. She let the kiss go on, their breath mingling. Then, gently, she pushed him away. "What are you doing?" she whispered.

Toby moved back to her side, but instead of lowering his arm, he kept it around her shoulder. He expected her to shove him off, but she didn't. Instead her head came to rest on his collarbone. Her hair tickled his chin and Toby held himself still, terrified of disturbing her.

Finally he had to speak. "Do you want to go back to the *Banshee*?"

Ayla said nothing. Had she fallen asleep?

"Ayla?" Toby shook her gently.

"I heard you," she murmured. "It isn't like I have a choice."

Toby raised his chin from her head. "You do. You could join the *Phoenix*. You're welcome on board."

This time Ayla did shove him back. "Says who?"

"We had a vote. We want to offer you a berth," Toby persisted. "The captain agrees."

"He just wants the map," she sneered.

"No." Toby caught at her hand and she pulled away. "Well, that's part of it." She raised her head again. "But he's seen you fight, and you're brave and clever and strong – you'd be an asset to the *Phoenix*."

"You'd expect me to give you the *Banshee*'s secrets," Ayla retorted.

"The captain would never ask that." Toby shook his head. "We just want you to be part of our crew. Think about it," he pleaded. "You'd be happy on the *Phoenix*. And there's no future on the *Banshee* – without solar energy she'll be dead from lack of fuel soon enough."

Ayla bit her lip. "What position would I hold?"

"Does that matter?"

Toby felt her grow stiff beside him.

"I'm second in command on the *Banshee*. Something happens to Nell and I'm captain. Here, what would I be?

An old enemy no one can quite trust."

"It wouldn't be like that." Toby managed to catch her fingers and she let him hold her hand for a brief moment then pulled away.

"Yes," she said, "it would." She touched the plaster around her arm. "I'm not joining the *Phoenix*, Toby, just like you wouldn't join the *Banshee*. I'm not giving up the map and you won't give up the solar panels. Where does that leave us?"

"I-I don't know."

"I have to go back to the *Banshee*," Ayla said. "I'll take the map to Nell and ask her what she wants to do. If she decides to swap it for fifty per cent of the solar panels, then that's what'll happen."

"I'll come with you." Toby stood up. "We can speak to Nell together."

Ayla laughed. "You have a death wish?"

Toby hung his head. "If she says no, I'll never see you again."

Ayla sighed. "If she says no, you'll see us again all too quickly."

The sunrise woke Toby. He had fallen asleep with his head at the wrong end of his berth, so that the porthole above him angled the light directly into his eyes. He shifted awkwardly, expecting to find Polly at his shoulder and Ayla curled up next to him, but Polly was still in the boiler room where he had left her, and where Ayla had been, his side was cold, his bunk empty.

"Ayla?" He sat up, stretching. In the night he had thought of more arguments that he could use to persuade her to stay. The berths around him were full of soundly sleeping crew members so he rose quietly to his feet. At some point Hiko had crept into the sleeping quarters and now the younger boy was curled up on the floor in his little nest; tufts of his dark hair were all that showed beneath the blanket.

"Toby?" He raised his head and blinked, sleepily.

"Go back to sleep, Hiko." Toby stepped over him and tiptoed into the passageway and past the mess hall, where he saw Uma fast asleep with her head on a table, her medical kit spread around her and the worst of the injured lying on the floor.

Harry's body was no longer on a table; it must have been moved to the deck in preparation for his sea burial. Toby was relieved to see that Marcus still slept next to Dee and that Big Pad and Rita were also there.

He slipped past the galley, knowing that if Peel and Crocker were anywhere they would be sleeping inside. Then he climbed the ladder, opened the hatch and exited into the dawn light.

The day was already heating up, the sun a bright yellow. Automatically he turned to greet the watchman. But Arnav was lying on the deck, his arms splayed out, his eyes closed.

"Arnav?" Toby ran forward. The old pirate never, ever, slept on duty. He shook him, but there was no response. As his head lolled, Toby saw that there was blood on his scalp. "Arnav!" The old man's chest rose and fell and Toby sagged in relief, then he sprung to his feet, his head already knowing what his heart refused to accept. "Ayla," he shouted.

As he turned he realized that there was something missing from the deck of the ship – there was a space where *Birdie* should be. Ayla was gone.

Toby ran to the winches. *Birdie* was already floating on the salt but she was empty. Ayla must have winched her down, but where was she? Toby leaned over the gunwale.

A rope dangled from a chock and Ayla was abseiling down slowly, using her one good hand. The pack dangled from her back.

"Ayla," Toby yelled. "Come back!"

She looked up, face pale. "Your captain would never have let me leave with the map, Toby. I have to go."

"Not like this." Toby's knuckles whitened on the gunwale.

"What's going on?" Hiko stood at his side, rubbing gritty eyes.

Toby jumped. "It's Ayla, she's running." He punched the rail as she lowered herself closer to the salt.

"Why?" Hiko frowned.

"She's taking the map to Nell." Toby leaned over again. "Wait!" he called.

Hiko screwed up his face. "But it's no use to her without me. She can't read it."

"Gods, you're right." Toby stared at him. "Nell won't swap that map for solar panels. Once she has it, she'll attack the *Phoenix* and take both you and the captain. It's the only thing she can do."

"I'm not going back to the *Banshee*." Hiko retreated as if they were already coming for him.

"And I can't let Ayla take that map to Nell." Toby grabbed the winch and swung his legs overboard.

"What are you doing?" Hiko grabbed his arm.

"Stopping her." Toby abseiled backwards. Hiko flew to the railing and watched him drop.

"Polly's in the boiler room. I'll send her after you," he shouted.

Toby waved acknowledgement and sped down the

Phoenix's hull, the rope burning the palms of his hands.

Ayla looked up, realized that Toby was coming and started to slide faster.

They thudded into *Birdie* at almost exactly the same time, making the boat rock.

"Ayla, what are you doing?" Toby grabbed her arm.

She tossed her head in refusal. "This is the only way."

"No, it's not."

"Why can't you trust me, Toby? This is the best solution! I tell Nell about the map, she swaps a copy for a share of the solar panels. Then we can search for the island together."

"Nell won't make the deal you want, Ayla. She'll attack the *Phoenix* and you'll tell her exactly how weak we are, won't you?" His lips twisted.

"I wouldn't do that."

"Well, are you going to tell her that Hiko is the only one who can read the map?"

Ayla hesitated.

"Thought so." Toby made a grab for the bag and Ayla arced her body backwards.

"You haven't even asked about Arnav, the old man you hit."

Ayla winced. "Is he…?"

"He's alive, so you won't be in too much trouble. Come

354

back up." Toby closed his hand around the strap and pulled. "If you take the map to Nell, she'll come for Hiko." Ayla slid backwards and lost her balance, falling to the seat.

"Why couldn't you just give me the coordinates for the panels," she shouted. She wrenched herself round and kicked his arm, dislodging his hold.

Birdie rocked, dangerously and, as the *Phoenix* pulled ahead of them, Toby realized that they were in the open sea.

From the deck of the *Phoenix* even the largest junk didn't seem so big. Now, on either side of his head, mountains of rusting metal and pitted plastic tilted crazily in the oily waves, threatening to crush them at any moment.

"How did you row through this?" he breathed.

The junk creaked and rocked in the swell, leaning towards them and then away.

"Bloody idiot!" The squawk came from above his head and Toby looked up. Polly was gliding towards *Birdie*. Hiko waved from the deck.

Ayla took advantage of his distraction, rose to her feet and swung at his head. Her arm, solid plaster, connected with his forehead and he flew back. The last sound he heard was Polly's screech of rage, then his skull connected with the rowlock and everything went black.

TWENTY-FIVE

Toby groaned. His eyes seemed to be glued together. He rubbed them with his knuckles but, before he could prise them open, warm water washed over his face. He sputtered, rolled and rose on to his knees, confused and disoriented.

"Is that any better?" Ayla's voice.

Toby nodded but the light felt like metal spikes going through his eyes and into his brain. His eyes stung and his vision was blurry.

"My head!" He clutched at his temples. "Where's Polly?"

Ayla was silent for a moment. "Can you see yet?" she asked.

Toby forced his eyes open and looked around. Ayla squatted in a grey passageway. She wore a fresh uniform and new boots. Her hair had been cut so that the singed ends were no longer visible. In fact, one side of her hair was chin-length, the other reached her breast bone. Her braids were back, the beads once more brightening her face.

But she avoided his bloodshot eyes.

Toby tore his gaze from her face and stared instead at the bars that separated them. The mangy cat crouched at her feet, staring at him with yellow eyes.

"Where am I?" The accusation in his voice made Ayla wince.

"You're on the *Banshee*," she whispered.

"I figured that out for myself," Toby snarled. Automatically he felt for Nix, but his sword was gone.

"You're in the brig." Ayla fiddled with one thin braid and the cat purred.

"And where's Polly?" Toby fought to keep his voice even.

"Captain Nell has your parrot-thing."

"Ayla..." Toby struggled to keep himself under control. "Polly saved your life."

"I'm doing my best to get her back. Nell has the map. She's trying to translate it. She'll swap a copy for the solar panels, I know it."

"You hit me," Toby finally snapped. "This is the life you want, is it? Well, you're welcome to it. Let me out of here and I'll get Polly, take *Birdie* and go."

Ayla rose unsteadily to her feet, but made no move towards the cell door.

"Let me out, Ayla." Toby's voice dropped dangerously low.

Ayla shook her head. "I can't. Just wait. Nell will let you out when she decides to send a copy of the map to the *Phoenix*. You'll be sent back with the offer, you'll see." She retreated to the passageway wall. "She's just mad because I was burnt. When she saw my arm, she went insane. She'll calm down in a while. I have to go – I'm supposed to tell her when you wake up."

"You're a fool, Ayla." Toby grabbed the bars. "She'll never let me go. She holds all the cards now. Open the door, before it's too late."

Ayla shook her head, backing down the passageway. The cat followed her, tail raised and swishing. "If I let you go, I'll be the one who pays. Just hang on. Everything will be all right." She looked at him one more time. "You shouldn't have followed me, Toby." She and the cat disappeared leaving Toby in the cell, alone.

Despite the heat outside, the brig of the warship was cold. For Toby, who was used to the warmth of the *Phoenix*'s boiler room, it was worse than being on watch in the North Sea. At least when he was nestled in the crow's nest with his waxed hood pulled over his eyes he knew the day would end with one of Peel's soup cups warming his icy hands.

This cold was deceiving. It started out with a slight chill on whatever part of Toby touched the floor and it grew insidiously, until it was bone deep. There was no respite, only more cold.

As Toby wrapped his arms around his knees and shivered, he remembered that Hiko knew where he was. Maybe help was coming. Then he thought of the injured crew of the *Phoenix*.

It was selfish of Toby to hope for a rescue party, especially when he had betrayed them all. Why hadn't he called the alarm when he realized what Ayla was doing? If Theo and Simeon had gone after Ayla instead of Toby they would all be home right now. Once more he had put Ayla before his crew and now he was paying for it. He had no right to expect a rescue.

Although the cold seeped into his chest and slowed the beat of his heart, Toby's ears still pricked at the sound of Ayla's voice growing louder and a flare of heat burned in his belly at the thought of seeing her face again.

"Fool," he muttered to himself.

But it was not her face that was first around the corner. Ayla was backing towards the cells, waving her arms.

Toby sat up.

"You're not listening to me," Ayla was saying. "Toby saved my life! We could work together. The *Phoenix* isn't bad, not like you say."

"Stupid child," Nell sneered, striding ahead. "You're all of fifteen, what do you know?"

At Nell's reply, Ayla flinched. Then she straightened, searching for dignity. "I'm your second in command, you should listen to me," she said quietly.

Nell came to a stop outside Toby's cell and looked in, her eyes stony. The same as her daughter's, but without any of their warmth. Toby wondered, with a shiver, if Nell had ever laughed in her life.

"Captain." Ayla held out a hand. "Please."

"Begging now, Ayla? You know what that gets you on this ship." Nell stepped close to the cell, not taking her eyes from Toby. She pressed her hands against the bars. "You have no idea how long I have waited for this." She hawked and spat, forcing Ayla to step to one side. "Barnaby won't be long behind his son."

Toby shook his head and Nell cocked hers to one side.

"You disagree, boy? One thing about your father was never in doubt. He does love his son."

Ayla caught her mother's arm. "I-I don't think anyone knows where Toby is."

"Is that the truth?" Nell gave a shark-like grin. "Then, while Barnaby is distracted searching for his precious boy, let us ready the trebuchet. We take the *Phoenix*, the solar panels and anything else they have of value."

"No." Ayla gasped.

"Yes. We'll capture the other boy alive, but the rest we don't need. Go and give the orders. We'll fire as soon as we're in range."

"What about the solar panels?" Toby clutched at the bars between them. "You still need those, right? The captain is the only one who knows how to find them."

Nell threw back her head and made a sound that made Toby's knees quake. She was laughing at him. "You don't know?" She wiped her eyes. "Your father's not the only genius at sea, boy. Before I was on the *Banshee* I worked with him at a St George facility. I was in charge of the last working computers on the planet. And now I've got Polly – the most sophisticated AI ever made. If Barnaby Ford knows where the solar panels are, so does your AI. Everything she's seen is on her database. All I have to do is hack her." She smiled thinly. "So, you see, the only crew member on the *Phoenix* of any interest to me now is the boy. I will let your father live … long enough for him to see me cut his son into pieces. Then I'll strap him to the prow of my ship and let him starve. I need a new figurehead."

Toby would have fallen if he hadn't already been sitting down. "You worked with my father?"

"Your father and I were once very close."

Toby's head whirled. "He would have said." Then he

remembered his father's words; *I know Nell; she would do no such thing.*

"But if you were friends, then why?"

Nell just sneered.

Ayla caught her arm. "It isn't right." Her voice revealed a high-pitched desperation that Toby had never heard. "We can *each* have a copy of the map. We can find the solar panels *together*. We can all find the island – share the riches. There's no need for this."

"We're pirates. We don't *share*," Nell jeered.

"We could," Ayla pleaded. "Aren't you tired of living like this?"

For one shocking moment Nell's eyes seemed to soften. "I've been tired of living like this for a very long time," she whispered. Then she looked her daughter in the eyes. "Go and give the orders."

"Mother."

"Don't *mother* me."

Toby gasped as Nell raised her hand and backhanded her injured daughter across the passageway. "On this ship, what do you call me?"

Ayla stood upright, her cast by her side, her cheek reddening. "Sorry, Captain."

"Go and give the orders, Ayla." Nell's voice was savage.

To Toby's horror, Ayla nodded. Her mother's handprint

362

stood out on her white cheek as she turned, unable to look into the cell where Toby now stood, shaking with cold.

Nell stayed, examining Toby, tilting her head one way and another as she took him in.

"As soon as you're gone my daughter will get over her infatuation." She shook her head. "I'll hire a few younger crew members and let her take her pick. You may be the first boy, but you won't be the last." She turned on her heel and smiled back at him. "Think about that," she said, as she started to walk away.

The door to the passageway sprung open before she reached it. "Captain." A rangy crew member stood in the doorway. "We pulled these two out of a *Phoenix* lifeboat. They say they want to defect."

"What?" Toby leaned as close to the bars as possible and Nell looked back at him. Then she stepped to one side so that his view was uninterrupted.

"Little boy." Peel lifted one hand in a salute. "I bet they've got an operational oven or two on this big beauty." He rocked on his heels. "You must be Captain Nell." He smiled. "I realize that you might not be in the market for new crew but I'm an excellent cook and I have secrets to trade, oh yes, I do – the secrets of the *Phoenix*."

"You said two." Nell frowned.

Crocker stepped from behind Peel's bulk. "Aye, there are

two of us all right." He smiled. "Hello, Toby, you little shit. You look like hell. I hope I get to watch you die real soon."

"Peel!" Toby clutched the bars. "We should have known you'd do this. The captain should never have trusted you. You'll pay for this. Just you wait. I'll *make* you pay."

Nell watched the exchange with one hand resting on her long knife. "Well, well. I was wondering whether this was the rescue party … but it seems not." She stepped towards Peel and took his arm. "Come then, Peel, was it? I have time to interrogate you." As Peel's eyes widened she smiled sweetly. "Oh, sorry, did I say *interrogate*? Of course I meant *debrief* you."

And with a final glance at her prisoner, she escorted the defectors through the door and out of sight.

TWENTY-SIX

The great warship shuddered as she turned. Toby closed his eyes and pressed his fingers to the floor, feeling for the engines, wishing he could tell them to stop.

"Toby?" Ayla approached with the cat, Boudicca, once more at her feet. "You were right."

"That makes me feel better." Toby refused to look at her, keeping his eyes fixed instead on his fingers where he still tried to commune with the engine, pleading for it to just break down, run out of fuel, anything. "Peel give up anything good?" he asked in the end.

"Nell thinks so." Ayla touched the bars. "She's letting them out to fight."

"Great," Toby muttered.

"I-I don't know what to do," Ayla said suddenly. Toby's head jerked up. Her eyes and nose were red and her hair in disarray. Beads were missing from her braids and her mouth moved as if she tasted something nasty. "Nell's my mother and my captain. I don't even know *how* to disobey her."

"But…?" Toby rose carefully to his knees.

"This isn't right. We should be working together, like you said."

"I've been thinking about it." Toby edged towards her. "The traders wouldn't have stood a chance against both of us."

"We fought well together, you and I."

"Our ships could fight together, too." Toby leaned closer. "With those maps we stole no government could touch us. And imagine if we were first to find the island – to make the rules."

"I don't know what to do," Ayla said again. "If Nell destroys the *Phoenix* or kills you in front of Barnaby, it's over."

"So what will you do?" Toby was afraid to push her too far in case he lost his chance at getting out of the brig.

"Nell isn't thinking clearly. We can't go on like this. It isn't in the best interests of the *Banshee* to wipe out the *Phoenix*." She wiped her nose and Boudicca wove around her feet. "I'm second in command, I have to make the right decision. I'm going to let you out. Take *Birdie* back to the *Phoenix* and run."

As Ayla produced keys and opened his cell, Toby held

his breath, terrified that she might change her mind. When the door creaked open, she stepped aside and he ran out. Boudicca hissed and her hackles rose. Toby ignored her. "Polly?" he asked.

"Nell still has it." Ayla shook her head. "She'll know you're out if I take it. You'll have to leave it behind."

"*Her.* I'll have to leave *her* behind." Tears of frustration pricked Toby's eyes. "This was a mistake, I should never have followed you." He backed away. "I should never have…"

"Never have what?" Ayla swallowed.

"I should never have trusted you," Toby said quietly.

He ignored her outstretched hand, turned and ran down the passageway. At the end he stopped, not sure which way to turn.

"This way." Ayla strode to his side.

Toby nodded. Together they followed the maze of passageways towards the deck.

"What are you doing?" A tattooed crew member glared at Ayla with his hands on his hips.

"Out of the way, Harris, I'm taking the prisoner to the captain." Ayla shouldered him aside and, head held high, she grabbed Toby's elbow and guided him ahead of her. "Don't interfere with my business," she shot back over her shoulder.

Harris said nothing as Ayla dragged Toby to the final door.

"Ready?" Ayla whispered and Toby nodded. "Head port side and you'll find *Birdie*. Get in and I'll lower her as soon as I can." She shook his arm hard. "Don't get caught, or she'll make an example of us both."

She spun the lever, cracked the door and looked out. "The crew is readying the trebuchet and cannons so it's all clear. She's expecting me in the bridge, but I'll follow you as soon as possible. Go." She pushed him out and Toby turned. He thought she might say goodbye, but the door was already slamming in his face.

Toby sped along the deck, keeping close to the housing. Sure enough, *Birdie* had been winched into the same place she had occupied the last time he had been on the *Banshee*. *Wren*, the little lifeboat Peel and Crocker had arrived on, swung a few bollards further on.

He was running to the boat when movement on the other side of the bridge caught his eye. He froze as Crocker and Peel rounded the corner. Both had been newly shaved and their heads glistened with oil and flecks of blood.

Beside Toby, there were a pile of weighted lines, used to gauge sea depth. Before he knew what he was doing, he had swept up the shortest and was running, not towards *Birdie*, but towards Peel and Crocker.

A cry slipped from his lips, and the line whizzed above his head as he swung it round, faster and faster.

Peel turned and his eyes widened. Crocker staggered backwards, lifting one arm to protect his face. They were not alone. As Toby sprinted, too late to change his mind, Nell stepped out from behind the housing, thrusting a rolled-up map into her coat pocket.

"Now this is copied, I will be locking the original up below," she said.

"Toby, stop!" Crocker shouted and he ducked as Toby swung viciously at his head. The line smashed Peel in the shoulder and the monster staggered sideways.

"Take that, you traitors." Toby bared his teeth and pulled back the rope.

Three more *Banshee* crew saw what was happening and raced to join them. Nell held up a hand, making them watch the former *Phoenix* crew members fight.

"Toby, you fool. Stop!" Crocker yelled again, as Peel grabbed a knife out of the belt of the nearest *Banshee* pirate.

"Backstabbers!" Toby could barely see past a veil of red that had descended over his eyes. He burned with rage. Every muscle was tense, ready to fight. The anger of the last few days compressed to a diamond-hard point, aimed directly at Peel.

"I may be a dead man," Toby howled, "but you're coming with me."

"Stop it!" Crocker ducked again. "This isn't what was supposed to happen."

"Yeah, you thought you'd be living the high life on the *Banshee*, while the *Phoenix* dies. Well, guess what, I'm here to make sure that before we go, you do, too."

Toby's rope weight was racing in a figure of eight now. Peel was dancing on his rubber soles, passing the knife from hand to hand, searching for an opening. Crocker awkwardly threw himself backwards and the weight whistled past his head.

"You don't understand." Crocker held his hand up again, but pulled it back as the rope skimmed skin from his wrist. "We're here to help you!" he cried eventually.

"Shut up!" Peel spat.

"Is that so?" Nell's head snapped up and in one movement she drew her knife and stabbed.

"Peel!" Crocker's cry was torn from his heart and, as Peel dropped to the deck, clutching at the knife in his belly, so did Crocker.

"What do you mean, you're here to help?" Toby's rope slowed and he paled.

Crocker ignored him; instead he pressed his hands to the blood seeping from his brother, trying to stem the flow.

Toby got between Nell and the two *Phoenix* crew members.

"Tell me!" he yelled, swinging the rope as fast as he could.

"Everyone knows how you an' us are," Crocker sobbed. "The captain thought it'd be most convincin' if we came over. If you didn't believe we was here to rescue you, then Nell wouldn't either. We were meant to distract her, while you were released from the brig."

"You mean there's someone else on my ship?" Nell shrieked. She turned to her crew. "Find them and bring their body to me."

Toby swallowed, his mouth suddenly dry, the adrenaline starting to ebb, leaving him shaky once more. "Who is it?"

Peel shook his head urgently and Crocker fell silent.

Nell stalked closer to Toby, her eyes on the swinging rope. "I wanted to kill you in front of your father, boy, but you can die now, as you seem to prefer it that way."

She drew a second knife and the blade flashed in the sun as she traced a pattern. He was hopelessly outclassed. Nell was going to kill him.

He tried to step back, but Peel and Crocker were in his way. Frantically he kept swinging his rope, seeking some way out. There was a flash of movement from Nell and the rope flew sideways to smash into the deck housing. Toby stared at the cord fraying in his hands. Nell had sliced it in two. Now she advanced and Toby was defenceless.

Although he knew it was futile, he threw the rope at her and dropped into the basic fighting stance he had seen Ayla use – one fist protecting his sternum, the other his face.

"Toby," Peel rasped. Toby spared a swift glance to see Peel pulling Nell's knife from his belly. He shoved it into Toby's unresisting hand. "A fairer fight," he gasped.

Toby lifted the knife in front of him and turned back to Nell, who was sneering with cold humour. "It only prolongs the inevitable."

Toby stepped over Peel's outstretched legs as Nell prowled closer. His eyes flicked from the knife in her hand to the map curled in her pocket. He was going to die, and yet his mind was racing, trying to come up with ways to take back the most valuable thing he had ever heard of.

"Toby, what are you doing?" Ayla ran along the deck, her coat flying, her face a picture of panic. "Captain, don't hurt him."

The watching crew of the *Banshee* laughed and a burly woman sneered, "Looks like Ayla's got a fancy boy."

Nell glared at her daughter and Toby took the opportunity to leap over Crocker and give himself some space. Nell saw him move and followed. But as she stepped over Peel, he caught her legs, dragging her off her feet.

After the briefest hesitation, Crocker caught her arms and Peel met Toby's eyes over her struggling form. "Run, stupid!"

Already the *Banshee* crew were pulling Crocker off their captain. But Toby couldn't leave; his eyes were glued on the map. While Crocker held Nell's knife hand, Toby dived forwards, grabbed the map and scooted back.

"What are you doing?" Peel cried as he tried to roll Nell over, but she kicked at his legs and he groaned in pain, more blood running from his stomach wound.

"You're no longer of use," she screamed, as Harris and the red-faced pirate finally pulled Crocker away. "Keelhaul him," she howled.

Toby clutched the map, backing through the closing gap towards the boat.

Nell stalked towards Toby once more.

"Don't!" Ayla hurdled Peel and threw her arms around her mother from behind.

Toby glanced at the gap behind him. Then he growled with frustration, threw himself at the injured Peel and started trying to drag him along the deck, but Toby could barely shift him.

"Get off me." Peel tried to push him off, but Toby dug his fingers into his shoulders and pulled harder.

"I'm not leaving you, so you might as well help me."

Peel cycled his legs to get purchase on the deck, but he was too heavy and too badly injured to move quickly. He shoved Toby as hard as he could and Toby lost his grip, slipping on the bloody deck and falling backwards.

"Get out of here, Toby," Peel groaned.

Nell opened both her arms, while simultaneously slamming her head backwards. Ayla saw the move coming and tilted her own head, but still caught a blow on the chin. Her arms loosened and Nell spun free. She clutched the knife in one hand and with the other she knocked her daughter across the deck. Ayla spun in mid-air and Toby winced as he saw her land on her cast. The colour fled from her face and she cried out in sharp pain.

Nell stopped in her tracks. She turned.

Ayla was lying on the ground, cradling her broken arm, shaking with agony. She stared up at her mother, ignoring the rest of the crew. Boudicca wound herself around her mistress, eyes narrowed, hissing wildly.

"It doesn't have to be this way," Ayla pleaded. "We should be working with the *Phoenix*. We can share the solar panels and look for the island together. Why destroy everything?" Tears were running freely now and she rolled on to her knees. "We could start a fleet. Think, Captain, the traders wouldn't stand a chance. And imagine if we could surprise the Greymen for a change. Take them on and win. We could do that with two ships."

The crew murmured as she spoke and all eyes pinned on Nell.

"She's right. We could work together."

Toby gasped as Captain Barnaby pushed his way to Toby's side. "I see you're no longer in the brig." He nodded at his son. "Sorry it took me so long to find you. It's a maze down there. Where's Polly?"

"She has her." Toby nodded at Nell and Barnaby clasped his son on the shoulder as he passed, taking a position between his son and his rival.

"We'll need to get her back," he said, lowering his voice. Then he spread his hands, showing that he had no weapon. "Your daughter and my son are right, Nell. Why not work together? We could be great – the *Banshee* and the *Phoenix*, rulers of the waves."

Nell snorted, but Barnaby pressed on. "We were friends once, Nell. We worked well together. Why can't we do so again?"

Ayla lurched to her feet, wiping her eyes. She sidled past Crocker, where he struggled against the rope wrapped around his waist, and came to a stop next to Barnaby.

"Captain." She held out her hand to her mother. "We can change our future."

"Change our future?" Nell was shaking and Toby realized

with sudden horror that her laughter was sharp-edged with hysteria. "The only way to change our future is to change our past. You think you can change the past, Barnaby?"

Barnaby shook his head. "I don't know what you mean."

"Don't you?" she spat, suddenly serious. "The only satisfaction I'll have out of today is carving your son into pieces and making you watch."

"At least tell us why," Ayla cried. "Why do you hate them so much?"

Nell stopped, her head on one side. Her jaw tightened and she pursed her lips. Then she shucked off her coat, lifted her knife and held it to her own throat.

As Ayla opened her mouth to scream, Nell pulled her collar up, dug the knife into the thick, waxed material and, with a ripping of cloth, sliced her tunic from throat to stomach. As it fell open Toby gaped and Barnaby's own gasp cut across the sudden silence.

Nell stood still, her chest bared.

Ayla stepped closer to her mother. "I-I didn't know. I've never seen—" She raised a hand and let it fall. "Does it hurt?"

"Of course it hurts." Nell turned slowly, giving the crew a clear look at the hideous scarring that covered her whole left side, from just below her ear to the top of her trousers. The burn still looked agonising, as if it had barely healed.

"Some of you may be thinking that my second in command is right." She spread her arms, showing herself. "Some of you might be asking yourselves if it would be good to have a *fleet*." She spat the word. "To work with the *Phoenix*, who, after all, was once strong enough to fight us to a standstill. Well, do you really think it is a good idea to trust the man who did this to a woman he called *friend*?"

TWENTY-SEVEN

"Liar." Toby jumped from behind Barnaby. "My father never touched you."

Barnaby nodded. "The boy's right." He put a heavy hand on Toby's shoulder, holding him back. "I never did that."

Nell started to shudder and when she turned back to them Toby flinched at the expression on her face – she looked like a goddess, burning with fury.

"Years I've waited for you to see what you did to me, for you to feel my pain." She talked only to Barnaby. "And now you deny it." She raised her knife and stabbed it into the air, as though she was stabbing him in the eye. "You say you did nothing? You did this to me as surely as if you set the fire yourself."

She turned back to her audience. "You know that I worked for St George. You know that I worked with this monster." She pointed at Barnaby. "You know that he called me *friend*," she sneered.

"We *were* friends." Barnaby strode forward, but Harris dropped Crocker and moved to block him.

"We were never friends." Nell shook her head and spoke to her crew. "Barnaby argued with the Greymen. They wanted him to use his genius to make weapons for St George, but he wouldn't. I was working late and I overheard them when they decided to take his son and hold him hostage to force Barnaby to do as they asked."

"That never happened." Toby shook his head.

"You wouldn't remember, Toby," Barnaby whispered.

Toby stared at his father, eyes wide.

"I told Barnaby their intention and he made a plan to escape," Nell continued. "He was going to collect Toby from school and run with him to the *Phoenix*. I was to find his wife, take her to the shipyard and get her on board. He wanted me to join them, too, but I loved my job." She shook her head incredulously. "I didn't want to go on the run. So I planned to return to my own family afterwards and pretend I knew nothing."

Ayla swallowed, never taking her eyes from her mother's lips. "Family?" she murmured, but Nell ignored her.

"His *bitch* wife worked security for the facility. I found her but had to wait for her to leave her post before I could take her to the meeting point. Once there we found that

Barnaby had already left in the *Phoenix* with his son. He didn't wait."

"I had no choice." Barnaby choked. "They were on to us. I tried to go back for her. For you. But sailing back into St George would have meant giving ourselves up. Once we were safe I tried to contact her, but I had no way of knowing if my messages were getting through. We never heard from her again."

Nell ignored him. "When I realized he had abandoned her, I hid Judy in my own home. I thought Barnaby might get a message to me. I still thought to reunite him with his wife. Ben wasn't happy. He said I was putting him and the girls in danger, but I disagreed." Now Nell laughed, bitterly. "I said there was no way the Greymen knew I was involved." She shook her head. "And it was true – they didn't know I was involved. Not until Judy told them."

Barnaby staggered backwards as if he'd been punched. "She didn't."

Nell sneered. "Judy decided that she didn't fancy a life on the run any more than I did. She wanted you caught and your son returned to her. So she waited until we were asleep, went back to the facility and gave us up. The soldiers came at dawn. Ben was already dead and the house on fire when I woke. Freya burned in her bed." Her voice was shaking now, barely comprehensible. Toby leaned closer, unable to stop listening, but nauseated with horror.

"Astrid was on the top bunk, Ayla on the bottom. Astrid was already unconscious. I couldn't carry both twins and with one of them unconscious and the fire already at the door. I had to choose. So I grabbed Ayla. I hid her in a bush outside the kitchen window. Then I went back for Astrid … but the flames." She indicated her own body. "I had to let my family burn." She swallowed. "I heard the soldiers laughing, but they hadn't spotted us. A neighbour helped us escape. I knew where the *Banshee* was berthed so I boarded, worked my way up the ranks and here we are." She pulled her shirt closed. "You still want to work with the man who abandoned his wife?" She looked at Ayla. "Who killed your sisters and your father?"

Toby tore his gaze from Nell to stare at Ayla. Her face looked as though it had caved in.

"Astrid," she breathed. "I thought she was an imaginary friend. I didn't remember."

"You blocked it all out." Nell lifted her coat and put it back on, closing it over her chest like armour. "You understand now why I hate him? Why I want him to suffer, as we have suffered, and why I will never, *ever* work with the *Phoenix*?"

Ayla nodded. Her eyes flickered past Toby's and down.

"How could you blame me for this? I knew nothing

of it." The deck rang as Barnaby strode forward. "Be reasonable, Nell."

This time Ayla spun in front of Nell, her sword lifting. "Get off our ship, Captain Ford, while you have the chance."

Toby touched his mouth with a trembling finger. "It's over, then," he murmured.

"How can it be anything else?" Ayla's back was straight, but her voice was pricked with pain. "After what your family has done to mine."

Toby shook his head but said nothing. He kneeled by Peel and Barnaby helped him lift the cook.

"Crocker," Barnaby snapped. The *Banshee* crew, with no further instructions, allowed Peel's brother to join his crewmates.

Nell growled. "What are you doing? I never said to let them go!"

Ayla held a hand to her mother's arm. "Release them, Captain. This time."

Nell glanced at the bridge and nodded, slowly, exhausted. "This time, Barnaby. But never again."

"Download complete." Polly's squawk rent the air and Toby's eyes widened.

"Polly!" He looked towards Nell, who was suddenly grinning and rubbing her hands.

"Bring it here." She nodded to Harris, who entered the bridge and exited with Polly dangling from one hand. If it was possible for a metal bird to look bedraggled, Polly did.

"You gave it a personality, Barnaby, so it's no use to me." Nell took Polly from Harris and shook her. Her wings rattled and Boudicca went wild.

"You think you're the only one to keep your old skills?" Nell continued bitterly. "I've hacked the AI's system and downloaded everything it knows." Nell grinned and tossed Polly overboard. "I guess it's a race to those solar panels after all, Barnaby."

Toby was already running to the gunwale, straining to see if Polly had managed to get herself into a glide.

"Now get the hell off my ship," Nell screamed.

Toby looked back. Ayla was watching him, her face unreadable. He raised a single hand in goodbye and she dropped her chin in a tiny nod. Then Crocker boosted him into *Birdie*. The captain dragged Peel in.

"We need to winch 'er," Crocker shouted as he leaped after them. "Quick before the bitch changes 'er mind."

"Everyone hold on!" the captain roared. Then he drew his sword, cut through the rope and Toby screamed as *Birdie* dropped through the air.

TWENTY-EIGHT

A few hours later, Toby sat in the crow's nest with Hiko at his feet. His eyes were covered by a light sun-gauze, but instead of watching the horizon, his eyes kept returning to *Birdie*. She had barely managed to get them back to the *Phoenix*. Her metal casing had been cracked during their brutal smash into the sea and Toby had been forced to bail frantically, his hands peeling from the acid salt, as Crocker and the captain rowed them home.

From habit, he reached a bandaged hand up to locate Polly's soft feathers. When his fingertips met sun-warmed metal Toby hesitated, then stroked her anyway. She wobbled on his shoulder.

Toby strained to see the *Banshee*; she was a vanishing dot in the distance, but at least the *Phoenix* was able to sail in her wake. The lack of junk in the way meant the paddles could move them a little faster. But not fast enough – the *Banshee* was winning the race to the solar panels.

"They don't have enough fuel to get them all the way." Toby stroked her again. "You just wait and see. The *Banshee* will have to slow down to conserve energy and then we'll pass her."

Polly bobbed up and down, wildly anxious. "She set up a program to bypass my firewalls on that piece of trash she called a computer. Where did she even get the batteries? That's what I want to know." Polly rubbed her head on Toby's cheek. "She immobilized me, Toby, or I would have escaped. Honestly."

"No one blames you, Polly." Toby stroked her and stared after the *Banshee*. His eyes supplied the outline of her shape, but he knew that he was seeing what he wanted to see. Although all the sails on the *Phoenix* were open and the paddles were working at full speed, she couldn't compete with the engines of a warship.

Toby clenched his fists. Nell was almost out of fuel, running on fumes. He repeated the phrase like a mantra. Soon the *Banshee* would be dead in the water. She had to be, because if she got the solar panels fitted and found someone to translate the map, she would find the island first.

Hiko laid his head on Toby's leg, quietly comforting him. Toby forced a smile. "I never said thanks, Hiko."

"For what?" Hiko looked up.

"For telling the captain where I was. You were right

about Ayla all along. She was Banshee through and through."

"She let you out, you said so." Hiko fidgeted. "Maybe you'll see her again."

Toby nodded. "Probably. As an enemy." He looked down at the deck again to find Simeon showing D'von how to coil rope. The former dock rat was laughing and his shoulders were relaxed. How quickly he had come to believe that the *Phoenix* was a safe haven. Simeon whooped and a cheer rose from all around the boat.

Toby grabbed the comms tube. "What is it?" He held the earpiece close to his ear and grinned as the garbled message reached him.

"What's happening?" Hiko squirmed to his knees. His knuckles were white on the railing, but he looked down nevertheless.

"Dee woke up." Toby felt like dancing, but instead sat down carefully. "Dee's going to be all right." He smiled. "I'm even happy that Peel won't die on us." His eyes tracked the celebration below. "Why don't you go and join them?" he said to Hiko. "You've seen me abseil down. You can do it."

"I-I don't know." Hiko looked down again. "Do you really think I can?"

"I know you can." Toby handed him the rope. "I'll hold

it from the top. If you freeze I'll just lower you. You're light enough."

"All right," Hiko stammered. He allowed Toby to wrap the rope around his legs and tighten the old leather hand protector that Nisha had found for him. One of Toby's first, it fitted Hiko perfectly.

"Look at me, not at the deck," Toby instructed.

Hiko nodded. His teeth were clenched and his hands trembled on the rope. His wide eyes fixed on Toby's.

"Hold on tight and climb over the railing. You can do it."

Hiko took a deep breath. Then, in a swift movement, he swung one leg over the crow's nest, perching on the rail, his hands tight on the rope.

"Now the other one," Toby said gently. "You'll be fine. I won't let you fall."

Hiko looked down then he swung outwards. Toby held his breath as the younger boy planted his feet perfectly on the main mast. He started to walk down and Toby fed the rope through his hands.

"Halfway there," Toby shouted. "Keep going, Hiko. You're a natural."

At the bottom D'von helped a shaking Hiko from the rope.

"I did it." Hiko's triumphant cry was almost whipped away by the wind, but it reached Toby and he smiled.

But he felt empty. "Ayla," he whispered. Then he settled back in the crow's nest to watch the horizon.

"Who's a pretty Polly?" Polly nudged his face and Toby looked up, realizing that his attention had drifted. He tightened his gauze and stared. There was definitely a ship in sight – it was not a trick of his eyes.

"It's the *Banshee*," he cried. "I told Hiko we'd catch up. I said, didn't I?" He grabbed the comms tube. "It's the *Banshee*. We're catching them."

As his message made its way from the bridge to the crew, renewed activity transformed the deck. Her sails were adjusted and, if anything, the *Phoenix* flew faster towards their rival.

The Jolly Roger snapped above his head.

"You're right, Bones, we're going to make it." Toby fixed his eyes on the ship. Somewhere ahead Ayla was working with Nell, helping her try and steal the solar panels out from under the *Phoenix*.

His memory flashed an image of Nell's scarring. No wonder she had been so angry when Ayla had returned with burns. Toby swallowed. His parents had done that to her; had made her the way she was. Ayla had sisters once – a twin. There had been no need for her to grow up alone. That was the fault of his parents, too. Maybe the *Phoenix* didn't deserve the solar panels, or the map to the island.

Guilt squirmed in his belly, sickening him. How could Ayla even begin to forgive? He tore his eyes from the *Banshee*'s deck. There was no hope for the two of them.

Only then did Toby realize that the *Banshee* was not alone.

"Polly, do you see that?" Toby leaned as far out of the crow's nest as he could. "Is the *Banshee* under attack?"

Polly perched on the rail and her glowing eye grew bigger as the lens focused.

"It's a St George ship. It must have been on its way to Tarifa to pick up the captain."

Toby's breath caught. "They're fighting our battle."

"The *Banshee* is a pirate ship." Polly cocked her head. "They're fighting their own battle. You think St George isn't as keen on capturing Nell as they are Barnaby?"

As the *Phoenix* chugged closer, the sounds of fighting floated over the sea. Toby's ears rang with shouts and screams, the boom of cannon, the smash of the *Banshee*'s trebuchet, and the clash of metal on metal.

"They've already been boarded! We have to help them." Toby grabbed the speaking tube. "The *Banshee* is under attack from St George," he screamed.

Below, the cheering intensified.

"We have to help them." Toby swung from the crow's

nest and raced down the pylon. "What are you doing?" he yelled, dropping to the deck. "We have to help them. They're losing."

"Good." Crocker spat a gob of phlegm on to the gangway. "Hope they all die."

"No." Toby ran to the gunwale and gripped it hard. "We can team up and take the St George by surprise. They're fighting the *Banshee* so they might not have seen us."

A large hand dropped on to his shoulder. He looked up into his father's eyes.

"We have to help them, don't we?" Toby strained, as if he could reach the *Banshee* himself. They were close enough now to see pirates on deck and his eye was drawn to two black-coated figures, standing back to back, fighting like whirlwinds.

Captain Barnaby held him still and pinned him with a steady gaze. "Toby, do you really want to put our own crew in danger to help a captain who has promised to kill us the next time we meet? They don't want our aid."

"That doesn't mean we shouldn't help them," Toby pleaded.

The captain shook his head. "That's exactly what it means." He turned back to the crew. "Set a course to bypass the battle. Now we can get those panels."

"It's wrong." But already the *Phoenix* was turning.

Miserably, Toby began to climb back up the pylon, automatically finding old hand- and foot-holds.

He watched from the crow's nest until the two warring ships blurred into one and vanished over the horizon. Soon the only thing left to see behind the *Phoenix* was the junk clogging in their wake.

Ahead, waves were breaking in a pattern that showed Toby something large had sunk just below the surface of the ocean.

"What are our coordinates, Polly?" he asked.

"We should be almost there." Her glowing eye pulled at him. "Have you spotted something?"

Toby nodded and reached for the speaking tube. "Salvage mission!"

He acknowledged the excited reply and replaced the tube on its hook, but he made no movement as the paddles slowed. Instead he rubbed his stubbled head. He should be running to get to the boiler room, but first he wanted one last look back.

"We haven't seen the last of the *Banshee*, Polly, I'm sure of that."

Toby helped Polly into his shirt, grabbed the rope and jumped. When he was a body length above the crew's heads, Toby swung outwards. A whoop burst from his chest.

"Let's get those panels!"

They were alive and free and with the solar panels they would rule the seas.

It was the turn of the *Phoenix* to rise.

ACKNOWLEDGEMENTS

Although it can be lonely in my study, no book is truly written in a vacuum, and it is certainly true that *Phoenix Rising* would not exist without the wonderful team at Stripes, led by my fantastic editor, Ruth Bennett. It is she who brought Toby and his crew to life. My grateful thanks to Ruth, Emily, Jessie and the team.

Thanks also to my readers, especially those who have bought or borrowed my books then gone on to write reviews or even to contact me with kind words about how my work has affected them. I write for you.

I must also mention my family, who have unlimited patience (although perhaps this cannot be said for the five-year-old), are endlessly supportive and without whom I would probably not be writing for a living. So my thanks and love to Andy, Maisie and Riley – who I thought of most while giving Toby, Ayla and Hiko their personalities.

Thanks also to my friends, who keep me smiling through difficult times and bring the fun in easier ones.

Despite my love for Toby and his crew, 2014 was a hard year, blighted by the death of my mother on July 4th, so final thanks is due to the doctors and nurses of the NHS who fought to keep her with us a little longer. I just wish she had been able to see the book dedicated to her.

Mum, I will think of you always.

Do YA
Read Me?

Do YA Read Me? is the place to go for the latest buzz in YA books. From author insights to jacket reveals, book reviews to sneak peeks – we've got it covered.

Whether you're into romance or horror, dystopia or geekery, this is the site for you.

doYAreadme.tumblr.com

Follow us on Twitter @doYAreadme

THE ADVENTURE
CONTINUES...

PHOENIX
BURNING

OUT MARCH 2016

More YA books from **stripes**!

Also available as ebooks

Also available as ebooks

ABOUT THE AUTHOR

Bryony Pearce has always loved to write. She studied English Literature at Cambridge University and after working in London for a few years she dedicated her time to writing. Her debut novel *Angel's Fury* was longlisted for the Branford Boase Award and won both the Leeds Book Award and the Cheshire Schools Book Award.

Bryony now lives in a village at the edge of the Peak District with her husband, Andy, and two children, Maisie and Riley. She can usually be found reading, writing, ferrying children from place to place and avoiding housework.

For more information about Bryony and her work, visit www.bryonypearce.co.uk or follow her on Twitter @BryonyPearce.